Pickles lives in London.

PICKLES

———

QUEENS

PENGUIN BOOKS

PENGUIN BOOKS

Published by the Penguin Group
Penguin Books Ltd, 27 Wrights Lane, London W8 5TZ, England
Penguin Books USA Inc., 375 Hudson Street, New York, New York 10014, USA
Penguin Books Australia Ltd, Ringwood, Victoria, Australia
Penguin Books Canada Ltd, 10 Alcorn Avenue, Toronto, Ontario, Canada M4V 3B2
Penguin Books (NZ) Ltd, 182–190 Wairau Road, Auckland 10, New Zealand

Penguin Books Ltd, Registered Offices: Harmondsworth, Middlesex, England

First published by Quartet Books Ltd 1984
Published in Penguin Books 1995
1 3 5 7 9 10 8 6 4 2

Printed in England by Clays Ltd, St Ives plc

For Nic and Hol,
and in memory of
N.A.C.

CONTENTS

Most of what happens in the following pages begins on any Thursday evening. The place is London. A motley band of fictional queens are drinking in a pub. Some stay; others go elsewhere; several go to Heaven. Most of them are looking for sex, and some are luckier than others. Whatever their success, it is largely brief and insufficient. Still – tomorrow is always another day. Pages from a queen's diary are interspersed throughout. They tell of a similar search. For all these queens, there are countless more who might have flaunted themselves or sulked during the following hours. Although unmentioned, most of them are there.

Yet, despite obstacles and disappointments, the great queen continues to inhabit a fantasy or dream-world, however sordid and unglamorous the real one may be. Through sheer self-possession, she can transform a privy into a palace. She adorns a bus-queue with all the charismatic presence of an empress travelling incognito. Her dramatic instinct and flair bring to the most tedious commercial transaction a ceremony and grandeur rarely witnessed, save on state occasions. Were it not for the queen's presence, there would be no colourful and sensational challenge to drab, day-to-day life.

Pickles

PREFACE TO A NEW EDITION

It is not surprising when a book such as this excites adverse criticism as well as praise. I was disturbed by the earnest and self-righteous tone of some, and amused by the facile post-Freudian analysis of others. The gay scene is not a sacred cow, nor is gladness a compulsory state of mind – one need only look around to realize that. Much has changed since the writing of this book; friends have died and others are struggling to live. These pages satirize a world largely unmindful of its terminal decadence, and understandably so. In many respects, therefore, *Queens* is about the past.

Pickles 1986

THE QUEENS

THE SCREAMING QUEEN

The boy with a turkey-red face has just come from the solarium, which is his second home when he's not mincing around this place, his favourite pub and hunting-ground. He speaks 'dead common', and has been around for years: although young, he started young. He is a statistic, one of countless runaways who began life hanging around Playland, or drinking Coke outside the kiosk café near the Gents' loo in Piccadilly Underground. He calls his friends by various girls' names, and most of them have the characteristics of a Doris or Mavis. They call him Gloria, and he seems to be the queen bee of his squalid little coterie. Whenever he tries to pick someone up, his friends are always on the sidelines shrieking encouragement like 'Don't be shy, Gloria!' His technique, such as it is, involves getting abusively drunk on Pils, and luring his victim – ideally (though infrequently) a big butch man – into sitting with this hysterical gaggle. There then follows a communal seduction scene, involving filthy jokes, malicious remarks about nearby queens and last night's screw. Then, having impressed the easily impressed fool, they stagger down to Heaven, screaming and cavorting on the street, Gloria firmly in possession of the victim – tool of her trade. Gloria might have been a rent boy, but avoided it. She had her pride, and did not like old men. Feeling effortlessly superior, she always scowls at anyone in the bar on the game, dismissing them with a confidential remark to Doris: 'Rent, dear!' Having arrived at the pub, the first thing Gloria does is look for her backing group. Once found, they all rush down to the loo where Gloria has a pee, while the others fill her in on the trade upstairs, or lack of it. After a certain amount of titivation they re-emerge, ready for action. It is never long before Gloria descends again, closely

3

followed by Doris or Mavis, or the entire group once more. They have almost no topic of conversation beyond sex and bitchery, and sex is discussed in forensic detail. But sometimes they fall silent as they lean in the archways, eyeing up the newcomers or trying to attract the attention of a winsome tourist, who cannot help smiling a broad, charming smile — a smile he lives to regret. Gloria likes to look butch, and has a smart new black leather bike jacket, as well as sportif training shoes, especially useful for all that running up and down the loo stairs. A gold earring and recently cultivated moustache are two exquisite details which Gloria considers sexy highlights, finishing touches to her 'look': the butch, suntanned superstar. She has heard about cancer and the solarium, but always maintains she is more likely to get clap at the sauna — something she knows from experience.

THE STRAIGHT-ACTING QUEEN

The boy standing near the arch loathes queens, and particularly the queen in himself. He does not like to think of himself as queeny – at least, not in the same way that others are. He is an art student and knows the trendy set, from long-haired models to minor rock-stars. He is quite quick with words, particularly when someone he does not like tries to cruise him. The odd thing about him is that he always wears that fixed critical expression, as if he hates everyone in sight, although he often comes here. He is offensive and aggressive by nature, and even snarls and growls when he is peeing, just to keep the willy-watchers under control. He loves his dark good looks, and especially his eyes, which he likes to think look sinister. He is often the most interesting-looking boy around, but hardly anyone dares to speak to him, apart from middle-aged queens, whom he always gives the brush-off. A queen once sent him a pint of beer from the other end of the bar, but he would not drink it. He sent another, and another – three pints lined up in a row, completely ignored. The queen came round, overweight, with a chubby face; the sort that never gets anything. But the trendy boy simply ordered another beer, never looking at his desperate benefactor. When the fat queen had plucked up courage to refer to the three beers, the reply came: 'I never talk to, or take drinks from, a stranger.' He thinks that sort of thing is straight and cool, when it is no more than a rude queen's patter. And this is his problem: the harder he tries not to be, the more a queen he appears. He makes his voice go deeper than is natural when ordering a beer, and keeps his head and limbs as still as possible, forgetting that poised repose can be just as queeny as wild gesticulation. His friends come in later on, usually intelligent, but trendy and superior with it. He is also rude to them, but they seem used to it, even finding it funny. He is very vain, and always has to stand where he can see a mirror, so he can fiddle with his fringe, which is never how he wants it. He is not very tall, so prefers to stand. If his friends wish to sit, he refuses to leave his place, and they go their separate ways. Stationary cruising is his forte. When he does speak to someone he fancies (any of several types), the extent of his cynical pose becomes clear. He relaxes, making himself approachable and a privilege to be with. He is very unpopular with the regular queens, whom he dislikes and patronizes with occasional acknowledgement. Guys like him because he is not a queen — at least, not like other queens. Or so he likes to think.

THE STRAIGHT QUEEN

He is straight but he is a queen. Although he sleeps with his wife and loves his children, he is tormented by the memory of a wicked fling in Cambridge with a lay-clerk. And his tastes are too twee. He likes Waugh and High Church paraphernalia, especially the vestments. The Passion interests him most, and purple is his favourite colour. From his thick tweed suit it is clear he is rather old-fashioned, and his expression is poised between shock and titillated delight — not unlike a schoolmaster discovering a pupil with his flies undone. He has a sharp and brittle wit, which gives him instant credibility in the queens' environment, where the damning throw-away remark is admired and applauded. Shabbier queens like film-stars, but this chap's pin-up is the Virgin Mary. He loves women (which would shock those queens who think of them as fish), and She is the ideal in whose image his perfect woman would be. Like many religious types, he is secretly thrilled by the idea of wickedness, and the lash holds more fascination for him than he would admit. Even so, he is never to be found at an S & M party. He is more likely to have strange ideas about the Roman Centurion at the Crucifixion than the average Christian would. Socially he is capable of delightful charm, but it is difficult to gauge his sincerity since his manners are so accomplished. His most closeted preoccupation is with sex, about which he fantasizes like someone anxious to lose his virginity. Dirty talk and semi-detailed accounts of sordid encounters and sexual excesses interest him almost more than doing the deed itself. It is this which lends him a slightly seedy air, as if he were a defrocked priest with a wide repertoire of choirboy limericks. He is rather snobbish, which is not out of place in this pretentious gathering, although he is more a coy spectator of low life than most of these genuine participants. Being here is a naughty treat, and he savours the moral dilemma of terrible guilt mingling with sordid pleasure. His dandified appearance does homage to the arty and literary queens of former times, and he enjoys toying with superficial effects, relishing the idea that he need not be a practising sodomite to look and behave like one. He has come here to tweak his bisexuality into life for an hour or so, then go away and pray for forgiveness.

THE NORTHERN QUEEN

The boy leaning against the pillar, looking round occasionally when there is laughter, is a Northern queen. He is trying to look like a regular, but he asked the guy next to him where the toilet was, which means he is a stranger. His clothes are very sub-Carnaby Street, probably bought in a Manchester shopping precinct, which is not a sin, except that he wears them like somebody who thinks London is the youth capital of the world, and looking really trendy is a 'must' when you come here. He also looks like a nice guy, which is quite unusual in here and almost indisputable evidence that he comes from somewhere friendly like the North. Maybe he is down on a gay away-weekend, doing the clubs. Provincial queens see themselves as poor country cousins, and always have that desperate desire to do every bar and disco before traipsing to King's Cross on Monday morning, sleepless and, if lucky, fucked. London! How they love it! Dragging around Soho, thinking it is the most immoral place they will ever see. Always wanting to go to Piccadilly; living off Wimpys and chocolate, like runaway schoolchildren; trying to have fun against the clock. The classic provincial trendy is credulous and usually considered to be an easy lay. You can pretend you are a peer of the realm or close friend of Mick Jagger's and he will probably believe you. The younger ones are often looking for somewhere to stay, and carry a pack around which always seems to contain a bottle of after-shave and a copy of *Capital Gay*. The tedious thing about the easy lay is that although he agrees early on, he still wants to go to Heaven and Spats and Bangs and the Copacobana, and all you want to do is have a few drinks and drag him home. But if you give him the address and tell him to come on after, you both know he will meet someone else. He is usually over-polite, which can sometimes mean he will not let you down, and so turns up at three in the morning when you are with someone else, or the last thing you can face is rolling around, especially since you got very drunk after he left. Sometimes they come to London in pairs, and if you want one you have to take both. The other is invariably a scruffy camp little sister, who smokes all your cigarettes and drinks one gin and tonic after another. The cute one asks if his friend can come too, he is all right really, and will not mind sleeping on the floor. The scruffy little queen tries to look winsome but begins to resemble an embryonic 'Dilly boy. You deliberate, and lust triumphs over your paranoia that they might get rough. Two will almost always give up the club routine, lucky to have found a bed and a floor for the night, so at least you avoid the greater expense of showing them the bright lights. But one Northern queen is enough. He may be polite, but seems to have a chronic inability to understand anything you say. Or he smiles like an idiot and nods a lot, completely gaga about everything you do, thrilled to be in London and talking to someone as famous as you have said you are. It can be very wearing, being treated like a celebrity, a queen on the London scene. And the endless questions about how good this place is, or have you ever been to the Subway, drain your energy and increase the desire to take him home where perhaps he will be silent and passive.

THE INSIDIOUS QUEEN

He is called Chicken Biryani, because it is served in Indian restaurants and he is Indian. He also likes what used to be called chickens – young good-looking boys with fresh appearances. He is to this place what the locust plague was to Ancient Egypt – a pest. Whenever he sees any solitary youth his eyes gleam, insatiable appetite sensing food, and he attacks with natural ease. It all seems very civilized, as if the only thing in the boy's mind is a desire to be eaten alive. There are smiles and manners, Biryani using charm as a lubricant. Often he fondles the stranger – an Eastern massage melded with straightforward Western grope. He appears to talk about others in the bar, gesturing in this direction or that, denigrating anything the boy may have found attractive. The boy looks around, hoping for some immediate rescue, or at least a sympathetic glance from anyone. Unfortunately, the other queens are busy trying to achieve what the insidious queen has done so swiftly. There may be one hope – another attractive young queen who had been plucking up courage to speak to Biryani's victim before being beaten to it. He may become so incensed that before long he interrupts the unlikely couple and manages to pick up the boy, or at least supplant the oily charms of his rival. The insidious queen is always very gracious when this happens, and tries for them both with renewed enthusiasm. But once it is clear that they have found each other and not him, he merely looks around with penetrating and rather desperate eyes, seeking out another. If there is no rescuer the youth has to fend for himself, which he may or may not be able to do, however much he wants to escape. Doubtless all manner of exotic promise is made, and occasionally the victim succumbs out of misplaced politeness and weary resignation. Perhaps some are even willing, although given his repulsive looks and execrable taste in clothes, it is surprising that more do not tell him to fuck off. He is certainly no elegant prince, or jewel in the crown. But a solitary young queen often enjoys a little flattery, and finds it difficult to treat fawning charm with abuse. This is a pity, and frequently her undoing. Any reciprocation on the young queen's part, however politely superficial, is taken for encouragement by the insidious queen, and justifies the attack. The longer he has with a victim, the more confident and ingenious he becomes. Locusts should never be allowed to alight on crops, nor Black Widow Spiders given the opportunity of amorous contact. If they are, the result is certain death.

THE RENT BOY

Rent boys capitalize on the frustration, closetry and despair of others. They are also a fortunate and logical conclusion to the 'scene', giving the not unreasonable pleasure of sex to those queens too old to cruise successfully. Whilst some of them are curvy made-up androgynes, the majority appear to be hard-faced working-class lads, just out of the army, or unemployed runaways, anxious for cash. They stick together, know each other's game, afraid of almost nothing. They fulfil a dream many queens have of screwing straights, and the best of them display a careless brutish manner made acceptable by their sarcastic good looks. If they try to conceal their motives, they fail. Patter is a rent boy's charm, but it is never sentimental, just as sales talk could never be interpreted as heartfelt. On the game the object is to sell, and eyes always give the game away. Some are dulled by the routine of emotionally irrelevant encounters where the spirit is dead and the flesh is willing. Others gleam like rats' eyes, conniving and parasitic. Impossible to possess, the rent boy is often kept by a pimp who might venture out with him to organize more business. Together they are able to create an atmosphere of threat which, though unpleasant, fascinates and disturbs. The successful pimp is often dressed in tasteless Sixties finery: a wide-lapelled suit, still wider garish tie, and flared trousers with wide bottoms flapping over grey leather shoes. This smooth and slippery type is usually weighed down by a gold identity bracelet and sovereigns dangling round his neck and set in his several ostentatious rings. The rent boy will look like a regular suburban guy without his girlfriend, out for a fuck. This one wears a Fred Perry T-shirt — lemon — and always sports white socks and cheap Italian slip-on shoes. His slacks are grey, his

V-necked sweater maroon. He has one gold rope chain round his neck, a trapping of success. He epitomizes the joyless and logical reduction of much gay experience to little more than wanting sex, whatever the cost, although to want is more redeeming than to sell. And so the rent boy is sexy, and watching him is like fingering a porn magazine, and you want to do it there and then, no talk — just silent business. He will not like you because you are a punter and only want to jerk off over his mean face. He will let you because it is money, and he might enjoy it because he likes coming more than anything else.

THE CITY QUEEN

Do pinstripe suits always turn their wearers into fascist pigs? And blue-and-white-striped shirts? And executive briefcases? You might think so, looking at the City queen standing in the middle of the bar, the one who looks like Oswald Mosley at a Party rally. He is one of the most detestable people ever to come in this place. And he comes almost every evening, six-thirty, without fail. He has all the style of a bachelor sauntering up the Burlington Arcade, but he could be married with two sons at Eton and a stupid daughter struggling to be a secretary. Perhaps he is not a banker; a barrister maybe, a bent barrister good at getting queens off indecent exposure charges. He leers too much, especially at the bulging crotch or tight round buttocks. He is like a gentleman farmer looking for a prize bull or young filly. In another it would be easier to ignore, but his curiosity is somehow insidious. He probably thinks of animals when he is having sex — clean-cut middle-aged pervert! That gold signet ring on his little finger — they always wear one — is a seal. You can see it if you ask him. Rent boys always ask him and he always gets into a boring speech about his family and the Normans, and his motto — probably 'Nil Desperandum' considering the silly smile stretched across his fat pink face. Any queen with an overblown silk paisley handkerchief blossoming out of his top pocket should be regarded with suspicion. This one drinks Scotch after Scotch after Scotch. In an hour or so he will be pretty drunk — he is probably an alcoholic — and start staggering around the place, talking in a loud snooty voice to any likely lad standing on his own. He will offer each of them a drink; one after another, just moving on when he has got the brush-off, and offering someone else a love potion, or elixir, or whatever affected nonsense he shouts when he is well on the way. Once, he bought drinks for a whole gang of rent boys — five or six of them, pretending they had friends down the loo and ending up with perhaps ten pints of lager and assorted Pils and rum and Cokes. He always takes his wallet out like that, very prominently, like a black prayer-book, feeling for money slowly, as if the very touch of it gives him some sordid pleasure: a sense of power. Even the notes are clean-cut, unfolded, cash-dispensed. It is the smile constantly playing on his face that tells you his mind is filled with filth and degradation. City queens are fastidiously clean because their sexual habits are usually dirty, something which gold-digging nances find sexy and debonair. When this one is not wearing a pinstripe suit, they say he wears a scarlet satin corset trimmed with black lace, and likes smacking. It's unlikely he has told his mama any of that, though.

THE CLONE

The clone standing at the bar probably has a date with another clone, and has arranged to meet here because it is not a clone bar, and therefore an easier place in which to spot a particular clone. For a clone, it is very hard keeping a date with another clone anywhere, and especially in a clone bar. It is impossible to overestimate the number of clones in the world, and they are multiplying all the time. They are very difficult to distinguish one from another, unless they are anorexic, or still struggle with a mangy attempt at a moustache. Otherwise, baldness may be a clue to identity, and might narrow down the field except that so many are balding. Size is quite hard because they tend to be a standardized large, with the odd medium and small thrown in. To complicate matters, what interests them most is the size of parts, far more than the whole. Expression tells you nothing, beyond whether growly or sweetness and light – some frown like men, others shower everyone with smiles. There may be a speech impediment, uncommon distinguishing feature, but many clones favour monosyllables, grunts or nods, so it would be hard to catch in a crowded bar. There is a strong chance he might be a touch effeminate, but only like the average housewife, and not in too hysterical a way. Perhaps the best hope is his nickname, which will be something like 'Divine Stella', or 'Angela Jockstrap' – memorable and often very appropriate. Otherwise a date with a clone is frequently blind. The date, however, will have the same problem on arrival. If he has the classic psychology of his kind, he will probably have chatted up someone who is virtually his double. So in the last resort each can go to the loo to remind himself of the meagre characteristics distinguishing him from others, then go looking for them. If there are mirrors in the bar the task will be severely multiplied. Almost everyone is familiar with the lumberjack look: checked shirt, well-worn 501 Levis, especially faded round the crotch, cream wool socks and heavy boots . . . The final touch is the moustache, which is worn to define the mouth as a sex organ, resembling in a Dada manner the female genitalia. The clone thus enjoys the best of both worlds, and by best he usually thinks of something as fabulous as he is, coming from all directions. The simplicity of his kind is demonstrated by the handkerchief code, whereby the choice of colour and back pocket signifies sexual preference and intention. This is a charming allusion to Nature's habit of using colour and plumage as a mating aid. The shame is that these creatures are so blatantly unnatural. Nature relies on appearances to organize instinct, and so avoid bizarre couplings and hybrid offspring. For obvious reasons queens need no such safeguard, and the clone's codified signs and responses are merely a symptom of dullness, complacency and lack of adventure. Even the keys dangling from his belt have some tremendous significance. It is as if the silent cruising in gay bars had necessitated inventing a sign-language to help the dumb find appropriate partners. Unfortunately, the sexiness of silence is far removed from the queeny neatness of the clone's articulate apparel.

THE OPERA QUEEN

The supercilious queen over there, next to the pinstriped suit, is passionate about opera. That is why he is carrying a book on great prima donnas. They are the classic obsession, because the opera queen is usually a frustrated diva longing to wear a big glittering frock and powdered wig. His interest in opera is yoked to his fetid vicarious imagination, and to his inability to control or check its obsession with heightened fictional passions and their tragic consequences. He loves music because it speaks directly to the senses, and in the case of Wagner, Mahler and Strauss, his sensitivity is anal and receptive. This is a shame, because music also speaks to the intellect. The opera queen is rarely well endowed in that heady sphere, however, apart from a copious knowledge of repertoire, casts, conductors and dates. None of this means much to him beyond a damning reference or affected historical preference. He is very piss-elegant, his manner frequently snobbish and unnecessarily superior, particularly during intervals, when he peers down his nose and looks disappointed in a fashion intended to suggest that only he is sensitive enough to know how dreadful (or moving) the performance is. His touchstone will be coloratura, and his conversation filled with references to either Joan (by whom he means Sutherland) or Callas (by whom he means a tragic international superstar). This queen is never without a programme, or some biography or book on opera. As now, these are always sported so that the title is prominent, functioning like the clone's handkerchief as announcing some leitmotiv for the guidance of initiates and confusion or contempt of others. He always wears a tight-fitting suit, and probably works in an office or department store. The very exclusiveness and cost of opera represent for him a sort of aesthetic microcosm of his ideal world. He is always a Tory, and as a sensitive cultured chap is very popular with middle-aged Tory women, who enjoy his compliments on their new blue rinse. His emotions are likely to be unstable, and he will be able to offer strict guarantees of tears during this aria or that duet. When not snivelling, he is probably upstaging the maestro in his lap, cueing Siegfried's horn motif, or hushing the *divisi celli* in some exquisitely moving passage. Another of his passions will be gramophone records, particularly rare off-the-air albums which are difficult to find and prestigious to possess. He is also wild about applause, always yelling '*Brava*' whilst all about him bellow their ignorance of gender. Standing ovations are his forte, and he loves leaping to his feet in moist-eyed adoration – especially when he is the first to stand.

THE LEATHER QUEEN

The ebonized bodywork parked provocatively near the stairs probably spent hours rubbing saddle-soap into his Lewis Leathers ensemble. He seems unrelaxed, perhaps because looking the part is one thing, but playing it quite another. And although very butch, the mystique of black leather is closely related to the old debutante's adage that every girl needs one black frock — it looks good, and when the entire wardrobe lies on the floor, rejected, it saves the day. For the leather queen it is the only frock. In an Indian summer and drought the leather queen sweats for her image; in the rank equatorial atmosphere of a back room she creaks and squeaks from partner to partner. It looks sexy and it is too expensive and desirable to leave at a coat-check. The more it stinks of sweat the less it smells like new, and the newer it is the tackier the effect. Like dishonest advertising it can proclaim a dark cruel man, of huge masculinity, but peeled off reveal a puny drip with a sweet tooth and a cuddly old mum. Of all costumes it is the hardest to live up to, and ought to be the easiest to interpret. But there are so many pretenders dressed for the fast lane that the wild ones are more difficult to spot. A bike helmet seems a good sign that he did not travel by bus or taxi, but some fetishists stop at nothing, and even if it is used there are still a depressing number of L-plates outside the Coleherne. Of all images it is the most explicit, since it implies a wide range of accessories. Sailor suits are fair-weather friends, soft, cute and useless, but a studded leather belt and steel toe-capped boots can serve a purpose more sinister than merely clothing or high fashion. The leather queen may be a harmless fantasizer with a Brando poster on his bedsit wall. He may also be a scatological monster with his own pit and pendulum and no bathroom. If he is greying at the sides and talks posh, then he is likely to be a barrister or banker by day, in which case he will put the bike jacket on a coat-hanger, Mozart on the turntable, and mix a cocktail before showing you some of his toys. He may be rough but it will still have something of theatrical illusion about it: chains rattling off-stage, and blood capsules to chew on. Contraptions and paraphernalia are expensive sex-aids for men starved of imagination. They are rarely evidence of a sophisticated sexual taste but substitutes for one, a sort of glamorous pretence. Unable to rid themselves of some prehistoric guilt, such queens forever associate sex with fear and danger. However black and silver the shining armour, it often conceals a shameful little heart.

THE YMCA QUEEN

The guy with wet tousled hair and pink day-pack slung over his pink Lacoste T-shirt is wildly in love with his body and his blond good looks. High cheekbones and chiselled features suggest a *Wunderkind* of the master-race, or cute Californian, but he comes from Parson's Green, so keeps his mouth shut most of the time, unless he is drinking his orange-juice, or taking another stick of gum. He is a model. You can see him wandering about during the day, wearing an expensive fussy leather blouson, carrying his black portfolio and walking rather like a ballet dancer with diarrhoea. Everybody fancies him but nobody talks, which he cannot understand. He has just come from the YMCA, where he has seen enough well-toned bodies to feed his imagination for the short time he will spend in this wilderness of monkeys. He is heavily cruised by the weights-queens, who grunt and wink at him during aerobics. Physical jerks stimulate his sex-drive, and his nipples harden at the slightest sense of strain, which gives the others a turn-on. Their imaginations are generally tactile, rather than specifically genital. He does not want to be big and pumping iron, so while the tits-and-biceps queens shove and groan he lounges by the pool, stripped to the waist, breaking hearts. One thing he likes is flexing before the mirror, slowly and deliberately, just every now and then. He likes everything to be as perfect as possible, and is saving for the final detail – capped teeth, at the expense of a second holiday in Mykonos. He stands, legs apart, shifting his weight self-consciously because he likes to accentuate their shape. So he wears tighter jeans than many YMCA queens, and always tennis shorts in summer. Though he likes his legs best, his entire physical appearance stands as a reproach to these assorted misshapen

23

queens, who swill beer in miserable envy of his self-regarding
composure. Although he looks arrogant he is easy-going, full of
bland charm and winning manner. A classic YMCA queen, he is
poised between simple college-boyishness and cosmetic contri-
vance. The accommodating, characterless trendiness of such
queens makes them popular objects of fantasy, and this nice guy
is no exception. Moreover, like his admirers, he believes his own
propaganda. He is the ideal, the image in the minds of wankers,
the boy next door, bringer of wet dreams, midnight surfer and
day-dream lover, elegant like a well-dressed woman, stunning in
black and white, like a film-star at a gala performance. He is
always the colour of honey, his tan lines the merest triangle. It is
hard to decide whether he looks better on or off the glossy *GQ*
page. He can never make up his mind. But most of the queens
here are after the real thing, their minds already filled with heavy
breathing and sculptural embraces. And he looks almost shy, so
capable of fulfilling all their impossible hopes and wildest
dreams: the gigolo from Parson's Green.

THE OLD QUEEN

There is an old queen who usually stands at that end of the bar, with a profile like a parrot. His face is lined with a lifetime's disdain. The sides of his mouth turn down in permanent disgust, whilst his eyebrows arch upwards as if he were Lady Bracknell or some other snobbish great lady. His skin is shiny and fine, and there are tiny pink veins patterned like frost on his cheekbones. He does not have much need to shave any more, and his hair is fine and wispy, like a gingery grey veil folded back from his forehead. He is extremely polite to the bar-staff, and has been coming here for centuries. He never smiles, and huffs and puffs if anyone is standing in his place when he arrives. He always carries a shoulder-bag and the *Daily Telegraph*, which he glances at occasionally as he sips his half of lager. He may chat with a barman about something topical of which he does not approve. But usually he looks around with an air of confusion mingled with *hauteur*. His clothes date from a time when men's fashion was firmly the preserve of Dunn & Co: brown tweed sports jacket, pinkish beige slacks, rather curiously brogued shoes, slip-on and tan. His shirt and tie, however, show that he threw a little caution to the winds somewhere in the mid-Sixties. The shirt is purple, with a spaniel collar; the tie what used to be called kipper, its pattern a swirly psychedelic doodle in primary colours. Occasionally he fidgets with his shirt cuffs, making sure the tiger's-eye cuff-links show, and maybe smooths his hand lightly over his slightly bouffant hair. Otherwise his habit is to drink the half of lager; then go to the loo, where he leans far forward, peeping beyond the gap in the trough's formica partitions; and another half of lager when he returns. Sometimes he gets very worried about his shoulder-bag, a wrinkled tan leatherette creation. Having checked that it is safe, he takes a few moments to relax, then continues to sip his lager.

He has a friend, gaberdined like a retired fifties CID officer, but more likely an unpromoted clerk in one of London's smaller and undistinguished accountancy offices. Or perhaps he is kept on by a whizz-kid firm, slightly snobbish about old-fashioned reliability, and anyway embarrassed to fire him until his time is up. He may be sixty or seventy. He has a strong but colourless appearance, masculine and quite distinguished in a commonplace way, like an Eastern European politician seen in black-and-white newsreels. He has a profile more like a hawk, and small glassy eyes, just as the regular old queen's are quick and beady. His manner is thorough and deliberate, particularly evident in the strange precision with which he takes up his pint glass − he drinks a pint of bitter in a straight glass. He takes it up, pauses for a moment to finish his remark, the glass held as if a social gesture, then drinks a long pleasant drink, after which the glass is held aloft another moment, before he places it in exactly the same place on the bar and resumes the conversation. Together they smile, very occasionally, which has an air of absolute privacy about it. If his friend does not arrive, the old queen leaves after his second lager. He usually fusses with his shoulder-bag and general appearance, then leaves after glancing at the bar crowd. There is no sense in which it is certain that he has arranged to meet the taller old queen in the gaberdine (or suit in the summer, with gaberdine hung over his arm). It is not a date or assignation. It is always treated by each of them as a pleasant accident, a meeting in this place. Each has rarely addressed a remark to anyone but the other. It is something which they do not do. Their lives are the refinement of habit, their expressions the same. The regular old queen, the one with the shoulder-bag, is called Leslie. He usually stands at that end of the bar, with a profile like a parrot . . .

Ben's Diary

¶ MONDAY: I went to Bangs for the first time in ages and had a fabulous time. Ricky was there in a new turquoise outfit — all baggy cotton and blotches — it looked really good, though, and everybody looked at us on the dance floor. I wore my grey baggy trousers, with a big black leather belt, and collarless white shirt — like a labouring boy out of *Tess* or something. Very simple and sexy! There was no one there worth looking at, though. Just a boy on the tube as I went into town, who kept staring at my reflection in the window. Do people pick each other up on trains? I never have. Sometimes they are very cruisy — in the rush hour, when something incredible gets on, and you can press against him because there's no room.

Ben's Diary

¶ TUESDAY: Bought a navy sweater from the Army Stores —
very chunky and butch. The guy behind the counter was
something else — faded Levis and a torn white cotton
T-shirt, wonderful body — quite muscular, but not too
much. Just firm from hard work. Really ordinary, with a
good smile and bright eyes. Ah well! Maybe he'll go to
Heaven sometime! Some hope! Stayed in and started a book
by Yukio Mishima, which Robert had recommended as
escape and fantasy. Suicide queen! Still, it's exactly what I
need.

THE PUB

IN THE PUB

All subcultures have their rituals, and queens are no exception. It is a measure of their discretion and taste that they frequent only those places where their own kind are to be found. This may appear rather old-fashioned in these days of relaxed social and sexual mores. But queens are no ordinary class of people; they have remained essentially aloof from the humdrum existence to which most of us are born. Though kings may speak with beggars, queens are rather more particular. Quite apart from the problems of etiquette presented by mixed meetings, one can experience great difficulty in understanding the queen's English. Male and female pronouns are quixotically confused, and the vocabulary contains many peculiar words whose meaning and very pronunciation are hard to fathom. Reginality, like Free-masonry, demands a communication system sophisticated and complex enough to remain a hidden secret for all but the initiated. This private language, with its symbols and funny sounds, plays a central part in the ritual which queens perform in their chosen bars. It strengthens their subculture, alienates and excludes the uninvited spectator, and explains very simply why queens prefer speaking to other queens: only they can understand each other. It is therefore rather surprising that they often complain of being a misunderstood minority.

A significant part of the queens' ritual is standing around, alone. There may be a pride of queens, a gaggle or den of them, but for each little gossiping group there are as many solitary ones. And these are the ones who usually stand around. Now the solitary queen is very skilled at looking mysteriously miserable. Indeed, it is remarkable how many miserable-looking queens can be seen standing around at any one time. Some sit if rather tired, eyes searching earnestly for companionship. Tall bar-stools are popular vantage points with meat-rack queens, who treat them like stalls on which to display their goods. Some loll in doorways, others float about in casual desperation, anxious in case they are missing some demi-god newly arrived in another bar. When they come to rest it is often near the entrance to a lavatory, or similar place where there is a lot of coming and going. A few have their favourite places, strategic points from which each new arrival can be vetted immediately. All of them present a curiously lifeless dumb-show, like actors responding to stage directions when they have no lines. Their movements are regular as clockwork, from the simple repetitive actions of drinking and smoking to the occasional variety of looking at a watch or the clock. All these gestures reveal is that the queen is looking for a pick-up and pretending to wait for a date. Some time-watchers have dates, but most are con-artists. After all, it is difficult not to look bored and lonely after an hour or two, and these little actions keep the blood flowing and seem to justify being in the place when little else does. While standing around, queens also pay a certain amount of attention to their appearance. Those who seem to be staring into space are probably gazing into a conveniently placed mirror. They make minor adjustments to hairstyles, flicking fringe or tweaking moustache, fancying that attention to detail will better their chances. It is astonishing that a loosened shirt or fly-button can arouse in an instant what a fastened one could not in a night. Keeping up appearances is particularly important in those situations where the spoken word is hard to hear, so the mirror in any pub's lavatory is never without attention. Young queens have a special affection for these visits, using the loo as a convenient meeting place where they can lisp and giggle while helping their friends with cosmetic advice. It is also the centre of operations for many queens, a place to review tactics and commiserate over failures. In the queen's world the lavatory is no mere convenience: it is almost a shrine.

Of course some of the queens who stand around are very shy. They may stare at a man for an hour or more, longing to speak and lacking the courage. This is very sad. It can also be extremely frustrating. But conversation is rather old-fashioned. Depending on the intellect, it is usually far less exciting than staring at some Latin god who cannot speak English. Nevertheless, it can clear up misapprehensions and stimulate sexual attraction where there was none in silence. The principal fault with chatting up is that the last to speak is always convinced that it is just another way of saying 'Come to bed'. The subject may be Matisse or a new bar in Earl's Court, but the subtext is sex. So where is the point of it? The point is that it ought to be interesting; but queens are divided on this. The onus, after all, is always on the first to speak. The other can favour monosyllables or silence, but the chatter-up has to perform and amuse, part with information, express entertaining opinions, try to hit on subjects in common. And he can fail, as so many do. Queens have become so used to standing around that the shock of a verbal approach finds them with only one idea they can articulate — sex. Queens who want to talk have something wrong with them, and it is probably that they are attempting to give casual sex a little more significance. The impatient queen who finds being chatted up a nuisance is usually a peevish and un-ironic creature, and ought to spend her time in back rooms, day and night. There is a time for silence, and a time for words. The pity is that words have fallen from the queen's grace and favour. This may be out of ignorance, shyness, boredom or merely habit, but words are usually unspoken.

For the first half-hour, however, silence can be a source of great pleasure and is a part of the ritual which most queens perform. After noticing a possible conquest at the far end of a bar, the queen will pay a swift visit to the shrine to check that everything is in place, carefully exposing her better points and hoping that the worse are outshone. Then after the customary gesture of fancying herself (so why shouldn't he?) she returns. It is not unusual for the desired object to have moved, so a few minutes have to be spent floating about again, this time with a clearer sense of purpose. But there are difficulties even at this early stage. If the object is deeply desirable, he will not have escaped the attention of other queens. Although flattering to the queen's taste, it is very trying to discover the man of her dreams surrounded by several competitors. Some may have better bottoms, or Mediterranean tans and even teeth, but undaunted by invidious comparisons, the true queen draws strength from the competition and begins the struggle for supremacy.

But the struggle can be immense. Perhaps the commonest threat to success is the arrival of friends or former fucks. If friends are sensitive they will smile or nod, then go off and leave the cruiser to his cruise. Yet some friends lack all discretion and barge in, hugging and kissing, leaving the poor queen very ruffled and obliged to say 'Piss off!' Meanwhile, the victim has moved on or despises the queen's taste in little playmates. These interruptions often happen just as she has found the courage to step across and ask for a light, or whatever. It is hard not to excommunicate even the closest friend for such appalling bad timing. Another common occurrence is the victim thinking the friend is the lover, and losing interest completely. That has always been one of the perils of cruising in pairs, and explains why so many queens say 'I want to be alone' when rejoined by a friend just as eye-contact has been made with a dream-boy. Some friends are treacherous evil queens, and talk to a friend with the express intention of spoiling everything and cruising the pretty victim themselves. Friendship is irrelevant when cruising, and comes into its own only when the queen needs reassurance and comfort after some particularly painful humiliation, like the brush-off.

The problem of old flames is a world in itself. For many promiscuous queens it is hard enough recalling the name, and for several the fuck has been completely forgotten: face, name, and who did what to whom. It is not unusual for a queen to start cruising someone who has already been had. The consequent shame of being reminded is just another cross the promiscuous have to bear. It is almost worse when it is someone who turned them down the last time, and does it again. Experiences like these are intended to firm the queen's resolve, make her start a new life and find a boyfriend. They rarely do. Many queens simply ignore old one-night stands, cutting them as they pass and hoping nothing will be said. The strain is sometimes too great, however, and the queen decides to relent and speak, only to be cut herself by the slighted screw — poetic justice! And all of this has to be endured in the hope that someone will give a nod as good as a wink, and end the struggle.

Patience! So much is required. Silent cruising may be mysterious, full of pleasurable uncertainty and devious ploys which prolong the hunt and heighten the taste of success — if it comes. It may also drain the initial enthusiasm and spontaneity, giving the queen too long to rehearse a bad opening line, which consequently falls very flat. And by this time something better may have appeared, introducing the dilemma of one bird in the hand or two in the bush. There is also the time spent trying to interpret the fancied victim's expression. He may frown at someone close by, but the queen is instantly paranoid and desolate, certain it was intended for her, sure of his rejection. If he talks to a friend the queen instantly fears criticism, and convinces herself that all is lost, that they are damning her legs or mocking her taste. Even the most attractive are prone to this loss of confidence and let it destroy what, with more patience, might have been success. All that this waiting to speak does is give the queen more time in which to fuck up everything.

Silence has its perils, as does the chat-up. One of the first decisions to be taken is whether to get as physically close as possible or keep some distance until an impression has been made. Closeness makes it easier to be the first to speak, offer a light or, if close enough, gently press against his body. Its disadvantage is its obviousness: few things are more irritating than moving nearer to someone only to see him turn up his nose and move to the other end of the bar. Distance allows the queen the opportunity of posing to advantage and a better opportunity for eye-contact, perhaps with his reflection in a conveniently placed mirror. It also enables her to assess the wily tactics of competitors, who often bitch about her loudly enough for the pretty boy to hear, as well as herself. A quick thrust towards cigarette machine or computer game can thwart a rival's sudden attempt to pop the question. A tackier tack is interposing at the bar just as conversation has begun. A queen who suddenly drinks a glass of Pils in one is not a quick drinker but a fast mover, poised to interrupt the most optimistic preamble –

'Excuse me! Can I get to the bar?'

– all shove and groinward glance, when there are acres of space elsewhere; and once there, impossible to move. The first to speak takes an advantage which the queen cannot afford to lose. However handsome the Californian beachboy and flat-bottomed the squat rival, once they are twittering together about American lifestyle and English pubs, the pitch has been queered.

If the rival chat-up starts, the queen begins a waiting game. A favourite ploy is trying to exchange a look of sympathetic boredom with the suffering surfer. When the dwarfish rival descends to the loo, the queen takes immediate advantage and starts a counter-chat-up:

'You look pretty bored.'

'What?'

'I said you must be bored.'

Silence.

'How long are you here for?'

'What?'

'I said do you want a cigarette?'

'Don't smoke.'

'I know – I should stop. It's terrible, isn't it?'

'Yeah!'

Nervous pause.

'Are you waiting for somebody?'

'What?'

'You keep looking at the time. I thought you were waiting for somebody – that's all.'

'No!'

'Oh!'

('Well, that's all right then!')

Hard to know what to say next. Deep breath.

'You're not very talkative, are you?'

'What?'

'I said I only came over here to talk, and you're not very talkative.'

'What do you want to talk about – the weather?'

Difficult moment – to persevere or not.

('Arrogant prick! . . . am I getting anywhere?')

'You're very brown. I suppose there's a lot of sun where you come from.'

'Yeah!'

'It must be nice. I have to use a sunbed at the sauna before I go on holiday. The English are so white, aren't they? I'd be ashamed to go on the beach if I hadn't used the sunbed. They're marvellous really.'

Pause. The surfer sighs.

'Still – it's not as good as the real thing. My name's Tony, by the way. What's yours?'

'What?'

'Your name – don't tell me – let me guess. It's Scott, I bet.'

An old trick – lip-reading earlier. Getting the name right is usually a winning ploy.

'You look like a Scott'.

'Pretty good. It's Scott.'

Success looms large. The queen glows with confidence, relishing the embittered stares of envious rivals. A quick glance in the mirror . . .

'(Is my hair all right? I wish I'd washed it now. I look quite good though, really.) Would you like a drink, Scott?'

'No thanks. I'm just off. See you around, maybe.'

Facial muscles tighten.

'(Shit!) Yeah! Maybe! Nice meeting you.'

Weak smile.

'Ciao!'

'Ciao!'

After this Italianate parting a terrible sense of bitterness and

37

loss begins to poison the queen's outlook, as she begins the search for someone else.

Yet a failed chat-up is sometimes better than a successful one: a queen may take a sudden dislike to her pick-up. The problem then is how to drop him. Some find it easy; others impossible. So they make their way home, she rather moody, and he rather pleased. The bore is always whether it's her place or his. If it is hers, she can pretend a lover is returning and kick him out after sex, if sex is still on. But if it is his, she is trapped for the night, unless a faked migraine means she has to leave. And then there is the cab fare, and he is certain to live in Streatham. It is all very difficult. At times like this, most queens wish that pubs had back rooms, so that the nitty-gritty could have happened without chat, and purely on the basis of silent attraction. And even if things are still fine on the Underground, there is always the possibility that he might not be into the same thing as her — bitch meets bitch, and that sort of problem. Maybe it would have been better to discuss sexual preferences rather than Torvill and Dean. Promiscuity and queenery have constantly changing moods, and even one-night stands can be marred by a smelly groin or pet budgerigar. Perhaps cross-examination should be substituted for the chat-up.

Not all gay bars are the same. Some are like private clubs, and some very mixed. Some are run by queens, who cruise the customers and gossip like fish-wives. There will be a continuous soundtrack of gay disco music, which gets even the most sedentary type tapping his foot. The more liberated and energetic ones dance minimally on the spot, trying to look cool and part of the 'scene'. Other bars have no music at all, just hubbub, a mixture of serious and catty conversations, the latter punctuated with peals of inane hysterical laughter. Although the commonest sight in these places is men without men, some queens stand with weird or beautiful-looking women. YMCA queens might have a *Vogue* model in tow, reinforcing their gigolo credibility as well as trendy social mobility. Otherwise, it is rockabillies who drag around some shaggy fashion student, hoping to set themselves apart from the boring 'scene', basking in their lack of conformity and spectating at arm's length. Most regular queens have no time for this unnecessary flirtation with the opposite sex, and believe that fag-hags should be left at home. Invariably there are ordinary hag-fags around, however, using their women as girl-guides, and sending them out on reconnaissance missions to discover where the pretty queens are.

Though there is more variety in some bars than others, just after opening time, there will be dressed-up office workers in all of them. These tired drones wear cheap suits and ties, and are usually having an early drink before retiring home to slip into leather and denim – the cruising kit – and then reappearing in the guise of so many others. Some never make it home, having seen something too good to miss which, alas, they often do miss. By eight-thirty they are already quite drunk and, if they stay for the evening, frequently knock something over or fall over. Those who return look like boutique manikins, especially when their hair has been blow-dried and their leather jackets are maroon. They are neat and tidy, and tend to touch themselves, brushing away dandruff or making sure they are thoroughly clean-shaven. Like all queens who are seen in suits at six-thirty and casual clothes at nine o'clock, they feel rather nervous about the change. Clones cope best, because even in suits their uniformity is apparent. When suit attracts suit, it is largely with the instinct that at home there will doubtless be a pair of faded Levis.

The early evening might even offer some beauty, but it always seems to disappear in time for dinner, or the cinema, or some other cultural time-filler. Even so, some queens are lucky enough to pick up someone early on, and either disappear for an evening at home or ditch him after the fuck and return for second helpings. Others are less fortunate, and may spend the entire night dragging from pub to club to Soho dive-bar, only to find that, when they fall into bed with someone whose name they cannot recall, nothing can happen except drunken sleep. The sensible queen has one drink after work, then goes home for the dead hour or so, experienced enough to know that hardly anything happens between eight and nine.

When the action begins again, the types converge almost simultaneously. There are the young Oriental queens, wide-eyed simperers and willing prey for any snotty City queen who has heard of Hong Kong. If it is a lucky night, there may be a visitation from a pair of chic male models. They are not to be missed. Nor can they be, since they make a grand entrance on arrival, followed by a disdainful pause whilst they survey the unfortunate ugly, then swiftly down a fruit-juice before disappearing into the night in search of other superficial attractions. There may be solitary tourists struggling with maps, asking for Heaven and finding themselves picked up by a genial map-reader all too grateful for so convenient a question. Inevitably there will be a new face, someone attractive who stands alone and becomes the centre of attention for the regulars, giving them new hope. If he is unlucky, one of the squat predators will approach him with a smile and buy him a drink. Since such novelties are often over-polite, the predator may be in with a chance, but if he senses the new boy's attention wandering he will probably introduce him to another of his young acquaintances, deriving some vicarious pimping pleasure from the deed and hoping for a threesome. Within a week or two, this fresh face will have learnt to exploit its novelty value until the circuit has been done. Then it is just another familiar face. There will be solitary queens who have obviously been stood up, and others who sit alone, pretending to do crosswords or read novels — ridiculous pastimes in a gay bar, and invariably mocked, as are the readers. There may be the strange sight of a pretty boy standing alone, watching everything as if for the first time and behaving neurotically. He speaks to hardly anyone and rejects all comers: the mysterious regular. And of course, there will always be the unfortunate queen who is sadly and utterly ignored by everyone.

Sometimes bars are strangely empty and dead, and on evenings when there is nothing doing, queens get rather drunk! If, however, some shy Adonis wanders into such a desolate atmosphere, all eyes dart till he retires from the scene, like St

Sebastian with invisible wounds. Or worse – he has arranged to meet someone. This is never so bad if the lover is equally attractive – it gives the ugly something to look at and fantasize about. If, however, his date is another of those squat clones with drooping moustache and modish brown leather blouson, then tempers fray and everyone muses on the unimaginable fact of their being together. The pretty boy will usually look around, apparently uneasy about the riveting contrast between his partner's looks and his own. It is probable that he is a nice person who cannot say no to every chatty little pariah who launches attack. Or he may be one of those rare and unusual beauties who have a sophisticated taste for the grotesque. Good-looking queens are the most wounded by and uncomprehending of these unnatural unions. They preen and strut, moving seats and changing bar positions, desperately trying to seduce Adonis away from Quasimodo. A long stare, the deliberate licking of lips, a flicked-back fringe – these, and many more little gestures, are employed with great concentration. They hardly ever succeed. Adonis may give an encouraging glance, but it is tinged with desperation, since he knows the impossibility of escape. As the couple leave, Quasimodo is the epitome of puffed-up pride, and makes a point of looking round with a smug and faintly damning expression before boasting his trophy to the night. A beauty queen can get very drunk indeed after such disappointing encounters, and usually wants to, especially on a dead night.

Whatever the night, the ugly amuse themselves in a different way. Like experienced voyeurs, they gawp at couples groping in corners. Or they bitch with each other about how naff and stuck-up the solitary scornful beauties are. Knowing themselves at heart to be physically unacceptable, they prefer carping and destruction. They watch every move a beauty may make when cruising another of his privileged kind, hoping to sour the cruising and embarrass the cruisers. These appalling queens are seen in every bar, wantonly molesting the sexual ambitions of their physical superiors. Some of them are violent in manner as well as mouth, especially when drunk, as they frequently are.

41

The more effeminate and grotesque of them play a part of being everybody's friend, buying endless expensive rounds in the hope of leaving with something for the night. They watch the lavatory door like hawks, praising or damning each entrant, and lurching after the best. They are always too drunk to achieve, however, and usually exit with a foul expression, keeling like inebriated duchesses. Pubs are their palaces, but their court is very base.

And then there are the strangers: the married couples who open the door, and flee when once they have perceived the nature of the place. Some are amused; others definitely disapprove. The resident queens are always amused by these little forays and nod confidentially to each other, as if some victory has been won. There are also strangers to the scene, who enter nervously and struggle to get served, glancing about to see if what they've read or heard is true. Often they are middle-aged middle-class gentlemen, wearing Viyella shirts and Harris Tweed jackets, forsaking their wives or mothers for a night of exploration and discovery. And there are the old queens, saddest of all. Tottering in with plastic bags and trilby hats, the stereotypes park at the bar and dart their tired lashless eyes at anything at all. Whatever their expectations, nothing ever happens to them, and almost no one speaks to them. Polite and without hope, they trespass on a scene which effortlessly ignores their existence. A few scraggy bits of mutton dress up as lamb, courageously wearing their 'young-looking' gear to the amusement of all. And one or two speak like retired sergeant-majors, gruffly offering dinner without sex to any young queen around, groping him like a blind man fumbling.

On an exciting night the new number of *Capital Gay* arrives, giving the solitary something to help pass the time, and strangers an opportunity to discover where they should go next, or ought to have gone first. Someone may receive a Tarzanogram, which can brighten the evening, but the Tarzan is usually more like Jane or Cheetah. There may be a sweet lady collecting for charity, or that most thrilling experience of half the Everton football supporters finding themselves in a poof's paradise. Such evenings

42

can be very noisy, full of song and send-up, the atmosphere threatening violence and frustrated prejudice. But a true queen queens on, and hoists her colours with the flamboyance of an armada. After all, football supporters are real men, and some of them might be a little bit curious. Certainly when one of them returns from the lavatory there is always laughter and derision about how some pansy tried to look at his cock while he was peeing. There usually follows an energetic mime in which they simulate buggery and flop wrists to demonstrate their contempt, but not, perhaps, their ignorance.

After the bell there is a lot of pushing and shoving as the last desperate attempt is made to secure a partner for Heaven or home. Some have already found each other. Others visit the loo like incontinent yo-yos, hoping for any victim to descend. Many are left with untouched pints bought in the last minute to make hanging around look more justifiable. And the pavement outside sets the final scene, before going to a club or reeling home. Loitering can be very thrilling if the longed-for victim is still about. It involves some bizarre choreography, casually propping up a lamp-post, or pretending to look in shop windows, wandering aimlessly up and down as if waiting for a chauffeur! Eventually someone swallows and tries the queen's gambit, which either succeeds or fails dismally. By this time, however, so many are so desperate for sex, that some very bizarre couplings may be seen. What began as the usual evening's search for the ideal usually ends in the spirit of drunken compromise, or a taxi home, alone.

THURSDAY. A PUB. EARLY EVENING

THREE SCREAMING QUEENS:
MAVIS, DORIS, AND GLORIA

MAVIS. That's nice, over there, in the faded denims.

DORIS. I saw it first, dear. Ages ago.

MAVIS. No you didn't. It's only just come in, so there!

DORIS. It was on my tube, dear, cruising me something rotten.

MAVIS. It never! You're a liar, Doris Richardson.

DORIS. Anyway, you're not his type.

MAVIS. Oh no! And I suppose you are, dear. Don't tell me. He's crazy about short-arsed Marys.

DORIS. Bitch!

MAVIS. You started it!

DORIS. I never!

MAVIS. Yes you did. Every time I see somebody you spoil it. It's not fair, Doris.

Gloria arrives from the loo.

GLORIA. Hello, again!

DORIS. Hello, love.

GLORIA. You're in a bad mood, dear. Been turned down *again*!

MAVIS. It's Doris's fault. Every time I . . .

GLORIA. That's a bit of all right. Over there in the faded denim. I wouldn't mind throwing my lips round that. Give us a smile, stranger!

DORIS. It's Mavis's latest.

GLORIA. You what!?

MAVIS. I saw it first, whatever Doris says.

DORIS. You saw its *cock* first. That's what you mean. Well, you didn't. *I* did.

GLORIA. Well, I don't know who's right or wrong, love, but

47

you'd have to be blind to miss *that* one.

MAVIS. You're just size queens, you two, and the bigger the better.

GLORIA. Fuckin' Ada! Listen dear, since when did you start collecting winkles! Size queens! Don't pretend you're not into whoppers, Mavis. They're all you ever think about.

DORIS. Exactly! You should write to the *Him* doctor, dear. The problem page: 'Dearest Doc, I like big cock, whatever shall I do? I've tried them small, and none at all, but nothing else will do!'

GLORIA. That was fabulous, Doris. You should be a songwriter, dear. Make a fortune! Try one about that queen with only one ball – the one who wrote asking where it had gone! Go on!

DORIS. I can't, Gloria. I'm not in the mood. Anyway, Mavis is sulking.

MAVIS. I am not! I just think you're both being cowish, when I saw it first.

DORIS. Well go and get it then! You're always the same, you. 'That's nice. That's nice!' Like a bloody parrot. *Do* something.

MAVIS. If you give me a chance, dear, instead of spoiling it. You make me look a real queen, you do.

DORIS. Ooh! Get her! Want to be left alone, love?

GLORIA. It's looking at me, anyway. So you might as well give up.

MAVIS. Hark at her. The competition's killing me!!

GLORIA. Have you got a 10p?

DORIS. Who are you phoning, Gloria?

MAVIS. I bet it's that Brian!

GLORIA. Well, what if it is? He gave me his number, didn't he!

DORIS. You and a thousand others!

GLORIA. Nobody gives *you* phone numbers. You're just jealous.

DORIS. I am not. He won't remember you, anyway.

GLORIA. After the night I gave him, dear, he'll be scarred for life!

MAVIS. Did you beat him up, Gloria?

GLORIA. Stupid! I gave him the works, didn't I.

DORIS. Not the *works*, Gloria! (He probably went to sleep on her!)

GLORIA. Bitch!

MAVIS. Oh shut up, Doris, and let her phone if she wants to.

DORIS. It will all end in tears, dear. They always do!

GLORIA. Hello . . . Hello . . . bloody money won't go in properly . . . Hello. (Shit!)

MAVIS. Fate!

GLORIA. You what?

MAVIS. It's fate. He obviously doesn't want you to phone him!

GLORIA. Fuck off, Mavis, and give us another 10p! And get us a Pils, will you?

MAVIS. I suppose so. I don't know why it's always me that gets the drink.

DORIS. Because you're rich, dear, that's why. Some poor queens are on the dole, dear.

MAVIS. Well, I can't help having a job, can I?

GLORIA. Oh shut up, misery face, and get us a drink!

GLORIA. Hello . . . Hello . . . (get in will you!) . . . Hello . . . can I speak to Brian please? . . . What? (It's somebody else . . . he wants to know my name . . . I can't say Gloria, can I? It's all he knows me as: Gloria!) Hello . . . it's a friend of his . . . from last night, tell him . . . ta! . . . (What if it's his boyfriend, Doris . . . he said he didn't have one, lying queen! . . . maybe it's a flatmate, though) . . . Hello . . . Hello . . . Brian? . . . hello . . . What? . . . Last night, you remember? . . . Gloria . . . yes, Gloria . . . that's right . . . remember now? . . . no, *Gloria*! . . . Last night, down Heaven . . . well, you were *quite* pissed. I just thought I'd ring, that's all . . . it's all right . . . you did give me your number, after all. I wondered what you were doing, actually. . . . Nothing really; just in the pub with Doris and Mavis. Why don't you come? . . . Telly what? . . . Oh, *telly*! . . . Well, what about when it's finished? I could meet you somewhere else if you like . . . well, what are you going to do then? . . . Dinner? . . . Well, I haven't got much money, actually . . . oh, *there*! I thought you meant going out to dinner . . . you're cooking it? . . . Your *boyfriend* is? . . . Oh! . . . I see . . . that's all right

49

. . . no, you didn't tell me! . . . Well why give me a phone number then? . . . I did *not* ask for it . . . Well, what did you give it for if you don't like people phoning? I was good enough last night when you were pissed and randy . . . Nasty! Me? Whatever gave you that idea? . . . Well, fuck off then, and choke on it. Bastard!

MAVIS. What's the matter? There's your Pils.

DORIS. I told you they never mean it. When they give you phone numbers. It's just something to throw away, that's all.

MAVIS. What did he say, Gloria?

DORIS. Never you mind, dear. Auntie Doris's here. Cry on my shoulder! 'It's my party, and I'll cry if I want to.'

GLORIA. Fuck off, Doris!

MAVIS. What happened, Gloria? Is he coming?

DORIS. Mavis! Leave Gloria alone. She's upset.

MAVIS. You can have the one in the denim, if you want, Gloria. I don't like it any more. It's got funny legs.

GLORIA. Thanks a bundle, dear! I'm going downstairs. And then I'm off. I'm sick of this hole!

MAVIS. But it's only quarter to nine, Gloria.

DORIS. Wait a minute . . . she's upset, poor cow! . . . I'm coming too . . . Come on Mavis. Lift your skirts up, dear.

Ben's Diary

¶ WEDNESDAY: Called into the pub to get a free ticket to Heaven. Hideous people, mostly really raddled-looking clones, and Chinese boys with mad staring eyes and silly smiles. Jon was there, sitting alone and looking down. Jeremy – the boy he met at Kitty's opening – has stopped seeing him. He's found a work-out freak, with muscles. Trust Jeremy. Felt sorry for Jon, though. They seemed to be going quite strong. Anyway, Jon's talking about joining the Y, and building himself up. What a waste of time! There's no point, once it's all over. Competing doesn't solve things. I'm sure it would be really good to have a boyfriend, but how do you get one? And how long does it last? Heaven was good, though. We danced a lot, and I rolled around a bit with a Canadian under the stairs. Almost anything goes in that place. Ricky's got a fabulous new boy he found looking in a shop window in South Ken . . . It's all right for some!! I think he fancied me more than Ricky, but when he talked it was all a bit too queeny for my taste. Lovely blond hair, though. And smooth, healthy skin. Pity he was so girly. Maybe it was all an act for Ricky, maybe!

THE STRAIGHT-ACTING QUEEN
SOLILOQUIZES

Another bad mood! Why didn't I stay in, or go somewhere else?
It was exactly the same last night, and the night before. To think
I've actually fucked that queen in the corner! I must have been
really pissed. I hope he doesn't come over; I can't even remember
his name. There's been nothing worth having in here since the
French boy who sat in the back room in a black leather jacket
looking broody and bored. He was really good. I can't remember
what he looked like now, except when I try I always get a picture
of that other French boy, the one with bad breath but incredible
cheekbones. He was something else! I can remember lending him
a toothbrush, and sneaking a glance at *Everyday French* in case his
English dried up altogether . . . It didn't, but mine did. It's
really difficult using basic vocabulary. The weather and how
beautiful London is, in riveting monosyllables. Then me ringing
him in Paris, trying to say I missed him in French and saying I'd
forgotten him by mistake. Anticipating the inevitable! I suppose
they forget too. Not that it matters after you've forgotten. It's
just irritating, being aware of the process and trying desperately
to remember, like a little test, until only the clothes remain and
the face is gone for ever. The one with the hair on his back I'll
never forget. Disgusting! So good in his clothes, so disappointing
without them. And what about the one who was near-perfect,
and then spoiled it by having a hairy bum? He was good though,
really good apart from that. I see the little Indian's on the prowl.
Probably after the young queen at the bar looking new and lost.
He looks good from behind, but the face is a disaster. Still, he's
just another boring English tart and only good for one thing. He
obviously fancies the subhuman gnome playing with his prick.

Some people will stoop pretty low for a basic commodity. Get on with it. See if I care. He'll probably go for a pee in a minute so you can follow and have a good look. That's probably as big as it gets anyway!

I should have worn the bike jacket. Cruising never works in here when I'm in a shirt and tie, apart from pulling fascist punters, like that toad in the pinstripe. Try smiling at me again, sweetheart, and I'll bite your head off its stiff-collared neck! That's better . . . try the rent boy. He'll flirt for a few Scotch and Cokes, before deciding whether you're rich enough to roll. He's got a nice bum – the rent boy. I suppose I could go and stand over there. Hate moving though. It always looks so wilful and planned. Besides, I can see more from here – if anything worth seeing turns up. When I see myself in the mirror from a distance – like now – I'm amazed more guys don't try it on. I would! Perhaps I should smile, except I hate my mouth when it's smiling. It looks odd, somehow, as if I'm a nurd. Anyway, what is there to smile about? Maybe a half-smile, just to let them know I'm human. No! Doesn't work. I look as though I'm drunk. Back to the frown, Alex. It's less queeny and more charismatic. Besides, it helps to concentrate the mind. Ah! So he finally had the courage to speak to the dwarf. 'Didn't I see you in Heaven last night? I thought so. You dance really well. I could have watched you all night. Are you going tonight?' Him and another five hundred look-alikes. Finding him should take an hour. I don't know why they don't market inflatables – more hygienic and about as characterful.

'I like the Hippodrome because people make an effort. Nice clothes, nice hair, and really nice boys – some of them unbelievably beautiful. I just dance and dance, and the boys are so beautiful, especially the blond ones. You've never been?! You don't know what you're missing. This Monday is Come as Your Favourite Hollywood Star night. They have themes like that quite often. This one's for AIDS research. Usually it's charity or just for the sake of it. But everybody tries. Well, nearly everybody. There's always some boring queen who doesn't bother. They just look stupid with everybody else all glammed up. It must take some of them hours. Especially the Marilyns and Joan Crawfords. There's always lots of them. And Tarzans of course. It's fabulous; really nice!'

I can just see this one at the Hippodrome nancing around with a gang of girly hairdressers from Streatham: a huddle of pear-shaped bottoms poured into stretch denims, wiggling and giggling. Trash! They're not even witty. Camp is like Variety: when it's good it's OK, and when it's bad it's fucking awful! This queen loves her audience, but stays unloved because her act's all over the place. So unlovely too. If she were dumb it would be a step in the right direction. There you go. Off to the loo for a quick lick of the mascara stick. Pathetic! I suppose I could go and change. It wouldn't take long. Quite who for I don't know, but at least I'll feel better and look good. Maybe there'll be something later. Yes, sweetheart, I'm leaving you boring fuckers, so break your heart. But I'll be back. Try smiling at me then!

Ben's Diary

¶ THURSDAY: Depressed! The streets seemed to be full of really good-looking boys. It was like a conspiracy. Two Italians walked into the Chinese bookshop, one of them in white cotton baggy trousers, and black preppy shoes, with white socks. His hair was jet-black, with a sort of tousled fringe across his forehead. As I passed he saw me, turned away, then looked again with a smile. Ah!!! Then gone for ever. There was a vision in the butcher's, buying a pie! Quite tall, with blond streaks, and a Wimpey construction worker's donkey-jacket, dusty jeans and muddy boots. It's always the hands of those boys. So big and scarred. And after that a courier, in full black leather gear, just sitting astride his bike. As I passed he was taking off his helmet. His hair was quite long, blond and straight. He shook it carelessly, and I caught his eye. Full of contempt. Why don't any of these go to Heaven, or the pub?! They're all such flirts, knowing how good they look. One day I'm just going to go up and proposition one. Like hell! I felt ugly the rest of the day, and went to the Asylum in a vile mood. And of course there was no one there even remotely as good as the bike-boy. Still, the music was OK, and Ricky's friend was there alone, which was quite strange. I didn't ask about Ricky, and he didn't mention him, so maybe that's all over. As usual! He's more intelligent than I thought, which makes a change. He wants to be an actor, and we talked about *Hamlet*, which he'd played at school. A bit pseud, I suppose. But at least it was conversation, and he's not as queeny as I thought. Just quite young. He seems to like me, but left early. Probably just as well. Drama-school queens can be a real pain. Always quoting plays in fake voices, as if Hamlet lived down the King's Road and liked a line of coke!

55

THE INSIDIOUS QUEEN
TRIES HER LUCK

INSIDIOUS QUEEN. You look very lonely!

NORTHERN QUEEN. Beg pardon?

INSIDIOUS QUEEN. Lonely. You look very lonely boy. Very lovely
boy, also.

NORTHERN QUEEN. Thank you very much, I'm sure!

INSIDIOUS QUEEN. Would lovely lonely boy like a drink?

NORTHERN QUEEN. I've only just got one, thank you . . .

INSIDIOUS QUEEN. You are very silent boy. You are thinking
about the boyfriend?

NORTHERN QUEEN. I wasn't, actually, if it's any of your business!

INSIDIOUS QUEEN. It's not my business. Oh no! Not my business,
sir. You are very right. Not my business.

NORTHERN QUEEN. Well, why don't you find somebody else to
talk to?

INSIDIOUS QUEEN. But I like talking to you, lovely boy.

NORTHERN QUEEN. I wish you'd stop calling me stupid things.
Can't you take a hint?

INSIDIOUS QUEEN. You are looking for fun tonight, yes?

NORTHERN QUEEN. I'm not looking for you, that's for sure.

INSIDIOUS QUEEN. Oh, the boy is very funny. Very funny, yes!
What is the funny boy's name?

NORTHERN QUEEN. You don't think I'd tell you, do you?

INSIDIOUS QUEEN. Funny boy is even more lovely when his eyes
are flashing. Like a tiger.

NORTHERN QUEEN. Like a tiger! You do talk rubbish, you do! Do
you talk to everybody like that? It's a wonder you don't get
kicked in!

INSIDIOUS QUEEN. Everyone likes Mr Ali. All the young boys.

They are all my friends, the young pretty boys . . . They can, as you say, have a bit of a laugh with me. I make them laugh, you see.

NORTHERN QUEEN. I'll bet you do. You certainly make me laugh. I'll split me sides if I'm not careful. Laugh?! You must be jokin'.

INSIDIOUS QUEEN. A Pils for this young man, Mr John, if you would be so kind.

NORTHERN QUEEN. I told you, I don't want a drink. How many more times do I 'ave to tell you?

INSIDIOUS QUEEN. Never mind him Mr John. Bring him a Pils lager beer. He is just being difficult as you say.

NORTHERN QUEEN. I won't drink it. Don't think I'm drinking it, 'cos I'm not!

INSIDIOUS QUEEN. Would the lovely young boy like to come home with Mr Ali tonight? Eh?

NORTHERN QUEEN. You what?

INSIDIOUS QUEEN. Coming back to my place, as you say.

NORTHERN QUEEN. I wouldn't go if you paid me. What do you think I am? I'm not common, you know. You've only been talkin' to me two minutes together, and you're already askin' me back! I've got me pride, you know.

INSIDIOUS QUEEN. Mr Ali likes proud young boys.

NORTHERN QUEEN. I'll bet he does. I wouldn't like to think what he does to 'em, either. I wouldn't let you touch me with a bargepole.

INSIDIOUS QUEEN. You are very lovely boy. You know that? Very lovely boy indeed to be sure!

NORTHERN QUEEN. Give over will you. You make me fed up, people like you. 'Aven't you got the message yet? I don't want your bloody drink, so fuck off!

INSIDIOUS QUEEN. Mr Ali likes to fuck the lovely boy very much.

NORTHERN QUEEN. You'll get more than a fuck in a minute! Piss off, will you!

INSIDIOUS QUEEN. Before Mr Ali go, will the boy tell his secret name? No hard feelings and all that!

NORTHERN QUEEN. Me name's Kevin if you must know. Now sod off!

INSIDIOUS QUEEN. Kevin! It is a very nice English name. Soft, like the touch of a young boy.

NORTHERN QUEEN. Fuck off, before I gob you one. Go on! Find some other fuckin' tiger lily, you filthy little creep!

INSIDIOUS QUEEN. It has been very pleasant talking with you, Mr Kevin. A great pleasure to be sure, as you say. We are both friends, yes?

NORTHERN QUEEN. Bog off!

Ben's Diary

¶ FRIDAY: After seeing all those boys yesterday, I woke feeling really pissed off, and couldn't get them out of my mind. Especially the Italian in white trousers. It's just the thought that all last night he was fucking some pretty little girl, while I lay sleeping — and dreaming about it! I don't mind the girl at all. But sometimes it's a real pain, knowing that there are all these guys you'll never be able to have. And they're always the pretty, straight ones. I made a resolution never to go to the Asylum again, and when Ricky rang to see if I was going to Heaven, I said I was ill, and couldn't. In fact I felt incredibly randy, and wanted to fuck all night. But after lying in bed half the afternoon, fantasizing about the Italian, I couldn't be bothered going out, even though I was wide awake at ten o'clock. About half-past ten I suddenly decided I'd go to the pub, and see if there was something worth dragging back. But after dithering about what to wear, it was already quarter-to, so there was no point. Instead, I dug out my dog-eared porn mag, blew off the dust, and wanked like a schoolboy.

THE STRAIGHT QUEEN TALKS TO
THE NORTHERN QUEEN

STRAIGHT QUEEN. Cheer up!

NORTHERN QUEEN. Beg your pardon?

STRAIGHT QUEEN. You look miserable. I said 'Cheer up'. He's gone, now. See! You can smile if you try. Want a drink?

NORTHERN QUEEN. Beg your pardon?

STRAIGHT QUEEN. A drink. What would you like? My name's Christopher, by the way.

NORTHERN QUEEN. Oh! A Pils please. Thank you. Mine's Kevin.

STRAIGHT QUEEN. Pleased to meet you, Kevin. Have you been here before?

NORTHERN QUEEN. No! It's me first time here.

STRAIGHT QUEEN. Well, we've something in common then. It's mine too.

NORTHERN QUEEN. What do you think? Do you like it?

STRAIGHT QUEEN. It's a pub, I suppose. What does one expect?

NORTHERN QUEEN. They're all the same, at the end of the day!

STRAIGHT QUEEN. You're not from London are you?

NORTHERN QUEEN. Oh no!

STRAIGHT QUEEN. Where then?

NORTHERN QUEEN. Beg pardon?

STRAIGHT QUEEN. Where do you come from?

NORTHERN QUEEN. Leeds.

STRAIGHT QUEEN. Oh!

NORTHERN QUEEN. It's really boring. Not like London.

STRAIGHT QUEEN. I don't know. Never been. Passed through once on the way to York. Now *there's* a lovely city.

NORTHERN QUEEN. Leeds is really ugly. Just flats and things.

STRAIGHT QUEEN. What are you doing then? On holiday?

NORTHERN QUEEN. I'm trying to find a job.

STRAIGHT QUEEN. Difficult!

NORTHERN QUEEN. Yeah! Me boyfriend came down about six months ago, and . . . well, I decided to come down too. About three weeks ago. There's no jobs up there, so nothing to lose. Me mam didn't want me to, but I came anyway . . .

STRAIGHT QUEEN. How do you like it?

NORTHERN QUEEN. It's all right. Better than Leeds, but that wouldn't take much doing. I don't like the people though. I'm not much of a talker but nobody talks down 'ere, unless they fancy you. Like that Indian. I don't really mind though. At least it's better than Leeds. It's dear though. Me mam said it would be an' it is. It's all right for Eric — that's me boyfriend — 'cos he's got a job.

STRAIGHT QUEEN. Oh really! Where?

NORTHERN QUEEN. In a pizza place. It's long hours though and dead boring. But the pay's OK, so it's worth it for a bit. He wants to be a photographer. Last birthday I bought him a camera — second-hand, but really good quality; you know what I mean: really good. Anyway, he's really into it. His mam calls him Lord Snowdon.

STRAIGHT QUEEN. I see. I see.

NORTHERN QUEEN. London's really dear though. 50p it costs to go to Oscar's — that's the club in Leeds. 50p. We used to go every night. When it opened, I mean. Heaven's three quid! I make a lager last all night. You have to.

STRAIGHT QUEEN. Would you like another drink?

NORTHERN QUEEN. Oh, I didn't mean it like that!

STRAIGHT QUEEN. That's all right. Would you?

NORTHERN QUEEN. Well, if you're offerin'. I want to be a model, you know. It's really hard though, and everybody says it's impossible. But anyway I want to. I met this fella last night who said he knew some agent or something. Anyway I don't have a phone yet so I gave him me address and keep me fingers crossed. He said I looked like James Dean. Imagine! Me! Anyway, Eric's taken some photos of me. We greased me hair,

61

then scruffed it about a bit, and I wore a red leather jacket with black and white striped jeans we bought in Carnaby Street. No shirt, just open at the front. A bit of a laugh really, but anyway we did it — 'cos you need photos of yourself to take around. I've got some here actually. Do you want to look? That's a bit embarrassing, that one. Eric wanted one stripped to the waist, no top or anything. Anyway that was just a joke, but that's the sort of thing. And this one. You've got to look moody, you know. It's the way they all look. As if you're in a bad mood. What do you think?

STRAIGHT QUEEN. Very good. Quite sexy, actually.

NORTHERN QUEEN. Me mam would die if she saw them!

STRAIGHT QUEEN. Does she know that you're gay?

NORTHERN QUEEN. 'Course she does! She knew before I did. She caught me with this fella in our back yard. I were only thirteen, but she didn't 'it me. She just cried. She's really camp, me mam. She loves ornaments. You know what I mean. Anyway Denise — that's me sister — I told her when I was twelve. She just laughed. I miss 'em a bit. They're great. But not Leeds. Never!

STRAIGHT QUEEN. Apart from the cheapness.

NORTHERN QUEEN. Beg pardon?

STRAIGHT QUEEN. Only 50p to get in the clubs.

NORTHERN QUEEN. *The* club. There's only one really. It's good enough. There's acts and things. Not groups, but comedians and drag. You know what I mean? Much smaller than Heaven, but I like that. At least you can see who you fancy. I always lose 'em in Heaven. And all me mates went too. From school and all. There were three of us in our class: me, Dennis, and Garry. They're still there, but Garry says he's coming to London. She's a scream. We call her Camp Sheila. She really is terrible. She used to wear suspenders and nylons under her jeans. Her boyfriend's a butcher and beats her up. Sometimes she has a black eye. So she makes the other up and puts lots of mauve silver eye-shadow on. Camp! There's nobody like that down 'ere. She'd 'ave a ball bein' the only one. Exhibitionist.

That's what they call it isn't it? She thinks she's a real star, and she is in Leeds, especially at Oscar's.

STRAIGHT QUEEN. She sounds extraordinary.

NORTHERN QUEEN. Incredible. She's done everything. Everything! Eric can't stand her though. He says she's too obvious. And she does a lot of cottageing. I don't mind. Anyway, that's 'ow she met the butcher. Love in a cottage!

STRAIGHT QUEEN. Hasn't she been caught?

NORTHERN QUEEN. Course she 'as. There was this fella standing there – the one in the park. So she starts fiddlin' around a bit, then goes into the lock-up. There's no lock on the door, just a hole. Anyway he went in and found her – well, you know what I mean – and he was a copper. She said he'd raped her, but nobody believed it. Anyway she was in the nylons so it was all a bit obvious. But she's not ashamed or anything like that. Eric says she probably raped the copper anyway. I wouldn't put it past her. And I wouldn't put it past some of the coppers in Leeds, either!

STRAIGHT QUEEN. It all sounds very different from London.

NORTHERN QUEEN. Oh, it's a different world. Cottages are all there is until you look old enough to get into pubs. It's all right though; I mean until you find a fella or meet somebody or something. I talk a lot don't I? Anyway, I've got to go now.

STRAIGHT QUEEN. What a pity! I was enjoying our conversation.

NORTHERN QUEEN. Well, folk never talk down 'ere. In Leeds we talk all the time! See you sometime, then. Ta for the drink.

STRAIGHT QUEEN. Goodnight!

Ben's Diary

¶ SUNDAY: Felt really restless and couldn't stay in all day. I wandered around the National Gallery, gazing at paintings I hate whenever some cute French or Italian boys were hanging around in the Rubens room. A hunky American looking at Rembrandt, though. Almost unbelievably clean. They have such odd-shaped bums, Americans. It must have been the Wild West, and all that horse-riding. He knew my game — which can't have been difficult — and looked at me a lot. I followed him, and flicked through a few postcards in the shop, until he left. When I came out he was standing on the balcony, looking into Trafalgar Square. So I stood nearby, doing the same. Why not?! Just as I was about to speak, after dithering for so long and having a cigarette, he turned and asked me the way to Soho. Soho! I said I was going that way, and off we went. He's on a six-week Fine Art course at Sotheby's, and incredibly 'preppy'. He boasted that all the girls on the course were madly in love with him. Well done! I made some obvious remark about the all-American male, and suddenly he asks me if I want to fuck. So that was the afternoon taken care of. He was a bit heavy, though — kilos as well as boring!! Art history does things to people. Anyway, he left after tea, and his body was magnificent. I felt like a toy rake and half-apologized, but he said he'd had enough Californian beefcake to fill an abattoir. Well, I haven't, and Sunday sex made a pleasant change to newspapers. Sam rang (Ricky's friend), and wanted to go to the Bell. Everybody was there, and we got really drunk with two of Sam's friends from drama school who'd never been there before. Jimmy the skin was falling about, wittering about young boys and how many he'd had — rubbish! — and all of us letting him hold court, as usual. He told us about some gay copper who kept

64

following him around, trying to get him on the
thing. And one night he caught Jimmy stealing a Be
beacon shade, and said he'd do him unless Jim screwed
him. So they fucked on some waste land down Commercial
Road, and Jimmy's still got the shade. Trust him! And the
poor copper's been transferred to Maida Vale! I was amazed
he didn't do all the fucking. You imagine coppers liking the
humiliation scene; S & M, and all that jazz. Apparently he
knocked Jim about a bit, but Jimmy can take that kind of
thing better than most. He says the guy's really into nances
and drag queens, so none of it made any sense to me. Thank
God I've never slept with someone into the mental
put-down scene! Anyway Jimmy liked Sam (he looks so
young), and kept asking him to do a strip. Poor Sam said he
was an actor, not a stripper, but Jimmy said they were the
same thing, and so it went on. Then somebody ripped off
Sam's full pint, and Jimmy declared war on the nearest
suspect, and I had to calm them all down, and Kitty arrived
with a shocking-pink beehive, maybe two feet high! Jon
was wandering around looking for a screw and a smoke. He
soon latched on to one of Sam's friends, and they went off
together in a blaze of achievement. Quite good in there,
where nobody gets anything together, or already has done,
or doesn't believe in that sort of thing any more. A guy
walked in just before we left, really dark with piercing eyes
– wonderful – and moved through the bar (packed solid)
like a demon heart-throb. Almost!! I hung around to see
where he'd gone, but it was too crowded, and the
dance-floor seemed miles away. He was wearing one of
those black PVC coats – I must get one! – and was the best
thing I've ever seen. Ever! So home alone, making myself
remember his face as I sat in the taxi. God! I hope he's there
next Sunday. Maybe he'll go to the Asylum. I must know
someone who knows him – Ricky, or somebody. He's
probably into film or dance. Whatever he is, I want him.
Please, please let it happen!

65

HE STRAIGHT QUEEN
AND THE VICAR

CHRISTOPHER. (Such a pity that Northern boy left. Still, I ought to be going, too, I think. Bad enough missing the exhibition, without being late for dinner. It's awfully hard, though – like leaving the theatre before the play's ended: what's going to happen next? The pathetic little Indian, for example. He's scurrying about, trying to find a solitary victim, smiling too much, and looking rather desperate. In fact, they all look rather desperate. And just looking at each other, as if they can't speak. Apart from the little cliques! There's almost no one who doesn't look like a fully-paid-up-homosexual. Apart from me! There was that studenty-looking boy, earlier. He looked so bored and superior. Not surprisingly! I wonder what Forster would have made of it all – or Firbank? It's a far remove from that arty and intellectual world of upper-middle-class queenery. These are just suburban sodomites, locked in a hopeless routine of bars and lavatories, looking for sex. I don't think I've heard anyone speak about anything other than sex all evening. I suppose that male prostitute is the most interesting person here. A shrewd operator – making a living out of other people's miserable desperation. And probably not homosexual, either! It's as if all these people were plugged into the most elementary kind of intelligence, not much more than animal instinct – a few unsophisticated gestures of courtship, with a great deal of time spent on plumage and ruffling! For what? A life of sensations, brief encounters and, as time passes, ∩ ┌qualid, desolate future! And all the time, searching for some kind of security, dimly aware that life can be richer than this. When one considers that homosexuals are often insisting on

66

some kind of superior emotional sensitivity, it's surprising how emotionally stunted most of them appear. That little gaggle of giggling pansies was a perfect example of how queens can be outwardly animated, and inwardly lifeless. Quite what brought me here, I don't know. Watching it all gives one the same feeling as leafing through a pornographic magazine — as if it needs some great effort of imagination to participate. The feeling that all of them are engaged in some form of sexual activity, like being aroused when watching a dirty film, but ultimately excluded and alone. The pathetic thing is that even when someone does reveal some kind of depth, it's mostly an irrelevance to the more serious business of having sex. So what do I want here? What is it about this dismal world which intrigues and fascinates — the wandering up the street, and round the block, and up the street again, before coming back and lingering by the door, wondering. Then coming in, like a guilty thing, nervous and ashamed in some way.)

THOMAS. Good evening!

CHRISTOPHER. Hello!

THOMAS. May I join you? You look rather alone, and out of place here.

CHRISTOPHER. I was just finishing my drink. I wouldn't say *you* had a great deal in common with the clientele. It's not exactly a synod, is it?

THOMAS. Ah! Now there you'd be correct. You're obviously an educated sort of man. A teacher? Or perhaps a journalist, I'd say!

CHRISTOPHER. Quite close, really. And yourself?

THOMAS. The church!

CHRISTOPHER. Really?

THOMAS. You sound surprised. I suppose it is rather odd, meeting a cleric in here, but I duck in occasionally for a G and T.

CHRISTOPHER. You've been here before, then?

THOMAS. Heavens, yes! It's one of my little haunts, after choir

67

practice, you see!

CHRISTOPHER. I see!

THOMAS. Do you sing? You look very musical, I don't know why – but you do.

CHRISTOPHER. At university I did.

THOMAS. Ah! A choral scholar, eh? Cambridge, or Oxford? I'd say Cam!

CHRISTOPHER. Right.

THOMAS. And King's, was it? The school for spies!

CHRISTOPHER. I'm afraid so. Although it's quite some time ago now.

THOMAS. Well, well! You are in a different world, here. I know it's naughty, but I can't help thinking you're a happily married man. Am I right?

CHRISTOPHER. Well – yes, as a matter of fact I am.

THOMAS. I get a little forward after two of these, I'm afraid. So you'll have to forgive me. I wonder what brings you here, then. Eh?

CHRISTOPHER. I already told you – I was having a drink before dinner.

THOMAS. Ah, yes! So am I. But we both know what sort of person comes here, don't we? I mean, the sort of person you are perhaps struggling against becoming. Forgive my being so presumptuous, dear chap.

CHRISTOPHER. I'm not sure it's any of your business, actually.

THOMAS. Come, come. We can be friends, can't we? I went to Durham, actually. I suppose that's a touch redbrick for you, but if you count the Venerable Bede, I think we go quite far back. One doesn't often find someone in here one can make conversation with. Have the boys left, do you know?

CHRISTOPHER. The boys?

THOMAS. Oh, you won't have missed them if they were here. And they always are. Rather an effeminate lot, and always talking dirty and swearing too much. But actually they're quite amusing. They call me Mother Teresa!

CHRISTOPHER. I see. Well, actually, some young men answering to that description have just left.

THOMAS. What a pity! Never mind, though. *You're* here. My name's Thomas. And yours?

CHRISTOPHER. Christopher.

THOMAS. Like the saint! A charming name. I can just see you wading through water! That's a very elegant tweed suit, Christopher. Rather posh for this place. What do you make of the gay boys, then? Very sweet, some of them, don't you think?

CHRISTOPHER. I think they're rather a miserable lot. I was just thinking what a profound waste of time, actually.

THOMAS. And I came and rescued you from disillusionment. The good Samaritan!

CHRISTOPHER. I wouldn't say it was an act of rescue.

THOMAS. Well, pity perhaps. I know how hard it is, you see. When you're not on the scene, I mean. This is what they call the 'scene', you know.

CHRISTOPHER. I didn't.

THOMAS. Well, it is, Christopher. This is a way of life for most of the people here. Every night, most of them. It's a little overwhelming the first time, isn't it? I remember how I felt — lonely and out of place. Then someone came up and spoke, and it was like unlocking a grand piano — Chekhov, you know. And now I'm speaking to you.

CHRISTOPHER. Actually, I don't feel at all like a grand piano — locked or otherwise. I feel mildly sick, if you really want to know.

THOMAS. Understandable. I understand, Christopher. You mustn't worry about it, dear chap. It must be very hard, leading a secret life. Do you suffer from feelings of guilt and anguish? That's very common among people of our kind, you know. It takes such courage to break out, doesn't it. To find the places to go, and dare to walk through the awesome portals, in search of unnatural love. Oh, I know what it's like, Christopher!

CHRISTOPHER. I'm not sure that you do. I mean, you appear to be

69

quite a celebrity here — Mother Teresa, and all that! You're not exactly an outsider, are you? I think it's rather disgusting, considering what you do! It's just the sort of seedy involvement I couldn't bear.

THOMAS. Dear, dear! We are in a prickly mood, aren't we? You're just struggling to find your real voice, Christopher. I've seen it all before. You're happy with your family, but you want something more — something forbidden. And I can help you. Make no mistake, dear chap — what you need is help!

CHRISTOPHER. Can you stop talking to me as if I were some kind of patient! I find it utterly ridiculous. We've only just met, and you're engaging in some ludicrous in-depth analysis. I was perfectly happy standing on my own, thank you.

THOMAS. But you weren't, now were you? What you must do is give up struggling and start to live! Let things happen, if they're going to. Don't resist, or you'll be unfulfilled for the rest of your life.

CHRISTOPHER. I can't believe it!! Do you talk to everyone in this extraordinary way? Have you tried listening to yourself? It's appalling!

THOMAS. I've listened to my heart, Christopher. And I've taken my questions to God. And He answered. And now I am hearing what your heart is trying to tell you. And I'm trying to give some help.

CHRISTOPHER. But you're wrong. I'm not like that — like these people. Like you! I'm just curious, that's all. Just curious!

THOMAS. And have you wondered why, Christopher? You're alone, like most of these people! All, all alone. And I am extending the hand of friendship. Are you going to brush it away — you, a choral scholar with an unsung song? I want you to sing, Christopher. I want us to sing together!

CHRISTOPHER. Look! — Oh, what's the use! Perhaps you'd like a drink?

THOMAS. Another G and T would be awfully nice! And then we can talk about the organ stops at King's. Ah! That glorious Great Swell! What majesty! We have so much in common, you

70

and I, Christopher. We have so much to talk about. Who would have thought it possible that we might meet here, in this den of iniquity?

CHRISTOPHER. Who indeed? It's a pity I have to dash, but otherwise I'll be late for dinner. Still, I'll get your G and T.

THOMAS. It really doesn't matter, thank you. Not if you're going.

CHRISTOPHER. Oh, I am. I must!

THE RENT BOY LOOKS FOR
PUNTERS

Christ, there's not much in 'ere tonight, Eddy! Like a bleedin' funeral. Be better off down the Golden Lion: least they got a juke-box. Mighta run into Big Mickey and 'ilda. They're always good for a larf. Jesus, wotta borin' bleedin' 'ole. Even the fuckin' beer's disgustin'. Nice bit of arse on that: 'All right?' Stuck-up little cunt! Nice little arse, though. Be a bit of all right, that would. 'Ave a few pints, knock it about a bit. Give it a quick one down the lock-up, if I weren't on a bit of business. Wot's that, I wonder. Looks like one of 'er Majesty's civil servants. Either that or a fuckin' lawyer or somefin'. Nice bit of cloth, that is. Might even be an MP! That's it. Now 'ilda wouldn't mind a bit of that. Fancy car; big posh flat: I bet he's got the lot! Rich cunt! State of that handkerchief! It's like a bleedin' serviette floppin' about. Wot's he want that stuck in 'is top pocket for? Know wot? I think we've nailed a big fat rich poofta! Eyes off, sonny! This one's Eddy's. All right! That's it, nancy-boy. You go play with the girls like a good boy. Eddy'll take care of this one, won't you Eddy? 'Course you will! Always fancied myself in a pinstripe, double-breasted, fly-away lapels. He'll 'ave a few grand, I bet. Not short of a few bob for our Eddy! Now if I go and play a nice little computer game, he can get a good look at my arse, which should get 'im goin' a bit. Usually does, a bit of bendin'. That's right, pal, you're gettin' the message all right. Just keep smilin'. Not goin', are we? 'Ave another Scotch. One for the road, eh? A 'large one', is it? I think you might be a little bit interested in wot Eddy's got to offer, guvnor. Isn't that right? 'Course it is. Wot could be more natural than you an' me gettin' together for a bit of fun?! Fancy a spot of water-sport, do we? I'll bet we fuckin' do. Filthy bastard!

Ben's Diary

¶ MONDAY: Really pissed-off. Just couldn't think about anything except him. Went to Bangs. Not there. Even Ricky wasn't. Stood around and got drunk, then staggered out and devoured a Kentucky! It was raining. Why doesn't the summer come? Just rain and darkness!

THE CITY QUEEN'S PROPOSAL

CITY QUEEN. Looks very complicated!

RENT BOY. Piece of cake!

CITY QUEEN. You're obviously very good at it.

RENT BOY. Had a lot of practice, 'aven't I?!

CITY QUEEN. Practice makes perfect.

RENT BOY. So they say, guv, so they say. I wouldn't say I was perfect, myself. Nearly perfect, maybe.

CITY QUEEN. If you don't mind my saying so, I think you're a very charming, handsome young man.

RENT BOY. Say wot you like, mate. It's a free country.

CITY QUEEN. Damned right it is! Very handsome indeed!

RENT BOY. Come on, guvnor! Cool it down a bit, yeah? Handsome young man! Gettin' a bit fruity, aren't we?!

CITY QUEEN. I do apologize. I was merely expressing my . . .

RENT BOY. I know wot you was sayin', guv. Now wot about that little drink you was goin' to get me, eh?

CITY QUEEN. I'm so frightfully sorry! What can I get you?

RENT BOY. Rum and Coke for me, pal, if that won't break the bank!

CITY QUEEN. I think we can afford to get you a rum and Coke, dear fellow!

RENT BOY. (I'll bet we bloody can. Who the fuck's 'we' anyway? Like the bleedin' Queen! 'Andin' out the compliments, left right an' centre! Piss-artist!)

CITY QUEEN. One rum and Coke!

RENT BOY. Cheers, mate!

CITY QUEEN. Charles! Call me Charles, do.

RENT BOY. Pleased to meet ya, Charles. Eddy's the name!

CITY QUEEN. Eddy!

RENT BOY. Short for Edward! Only my ol' man was so pissed when I was christened, see — he couldn't spit it out, so all he said was Eddy! Fuckin' typical!

CITY QUEEN. I see.

RENT BOY. And wot's your line of business, then, Charles? A banker I bet. Or somefin' down the City way.

CITY QUEEN. Quite close, but not a banker. I'm a barrister, actually.

RENT BOY. You into wigs, then?

CITY QUEEN. Very funny, dear boy! There's a good deal more to it than dressing up.

RENT BOY. Come on, mate. You've got to be kinky about all that dressin' up!

CITY QUEEN. Not in the least. It's only a uniform.

RENT BOY. Like to see Eddy in a uniform, would you?

CITY QUEEN. I beg your pardon?

RENT BOY. Used to be in the army, didn't I?

CITY QUEEN. I guessed as much.

RENT BOY. 'Ow come you could tell, then? The crew-cut, is it?

CITY QUEEN. You just look rather tough. Quite violent, I imagine.

RENT BOY. Like that, do you? A bit of violence?

CITY QUEEN. Not especially. I was in the army myself, actually.

RENT BOY. I bet you was a stuck-up officer. Gettin' up everybody's nose, I bet. Boer War, was it?!

CITY QUEEN. Good Lord, I don't look that old, do I?

RENT BOY. Just pullin' your leg, that's all. You don't look a day over thirty-five, all right!?!

CITY QUEEN. Very flattering, I'm sure!

RENT BOY. 'Onest, mate. You're a well-preserved geezer! Must be all the Scotch.

CITY QUEEN. Thank you for those few kind words. Is it one of your hobbies, insulting strangers, because if it is I'm afraid I don't find it very funny?

RENT BOY. Now come on, Charlie. Give us a break, will you. I was only 'avin' a little joke, all right? Here's you gettin' all 'ot under that stiff white collar of yours. You want to watch it, Charlie. One of these days, you'll get an 'eart attack if you ain't careful. Man of your age needs to relax, all right? That's why Eddy's 'ere, see?! It's all part of the service. Know wot I mean?

CITY QUEEN. Well, if you promise to behave yourself, like a good boy, I'll overlook your remarks. If we're going to be friends, I'd also prefer a little less of the 'Charlie'. Is that possible, do you suppose?

RENT BOY. If you're callin' the tune, guvnor, that's all right by me, so long as we understand each other. Know wot I mean? I mean it's got to be worth my while, this little friendship of ours.

CITY QUEEN. I'm sure we can come to some satisfactory arrangement — Eddy — as long as it's within reason.

RENT BOY. Well then! 'Ows about another drink, Charles?

CITY QUEEN. Of course, dear boy. Rum and Coke?

RENT BOY. Ah! You remembered, Charles. You remembered!

THE CLONE IN CRISIS

Hate this shirt! It's just not butch enough. The colours are all wrong, and the checks are too small! Not that Philip will notice. I don't know why I bought it. Quite like the pockets, though. Makes the pecs stand out a bit more! Every little helps, when a girl's trying to look butch, except I'm just not in the mood tonight. Oh, Philip! What are you doing now? Screwing some waiter from Joe Allen's, I know! Jesus! What am I doing here? Hate the place!! Hate the people! Hate the bar-staff! Hate myself for coming! There's bound to be somebody here who knows Philip. When he's not at the Y, he's always here if he's not with me. I know he is. He always says he's been with Sandra, but I can tell where he's been. It's like his thing of coming home and going straight to the bathroom. OK, so he wants a piss! He also wants to wash his dick so I can't tell what he's been up to! I don't even care . . . if he told me it would make some difference. What's he trying to prove – that he can still pull a trick! Cunt! *I* can't do it, but he does it all the time, the randy faggot. That's what he is – just a faggot. Why did I ever get mixed up with someone so anybody's? He is! Anybody's. Christ! I've seen him, without him knowing I was even in the place! Rubbing his dick up, like a fucking 'dilly boy! It's like *Zipper*! OK, so *I* like it too. But why the fuck does he always look at it before we go to bed? Sometimes I really think he's fucking some bloody photo! And the personal ads in *Time Out*! He reads them like a closet queen! Every last one. Even asks me what I think about 'Hirsute; big; needs playmate'. If I put an ad in, I'm sure he'd reply. The classic Philip playmate: 'Rich big boy. Young. YMCA fan. Into dance, Divine, *Querelle*, Virginia Woolf, Colt 45, saunas, cacti, winter sunbreaks and Mrs T. Wants intelligent, sensitive, masculine guy with no inhibitions. Preferably your place!' He'd send that photo I took in Malaga, with his briefs round his ankles, and a smile like cheesecake! Oh, Philip, Philip!! Why can't you see I love you in the way you really want?? Why has it become Mr and Mrs, with all the boring rows about washing-up and putting the cat out? Why can't you look at me properly when I talk to you, without fiddling around with the hi-fi, or wanting to go to the loo? Why can't you just say, if it's all over between us? Then I can start to be myself again, and stop playing second fiddle to somebody who doesn't even notice what colour shirt I'm wearing, let alone whether I'm pissed-off or blueberry pie! So I came to this fucking dump, in case there's something for a quick frig! And I feel guilty about it! While he fucks up hill and down dale, as if I didn't exist! I suggest a dinner party for his birthday, and he arranges a fucking orgy! I spend hours trolling round Covent Garden finding a sweater he'll love, and he asks every Tom, Dick and fucking Harry to come to an orgy because it's his thirtieth birthday. And what am I supposed to do? Cook Spotted Dick, and drape a few rubber sheets around the flat, so the carpets won't get tacky! My beautiful new Axminster, defiled! Not to mention the sofa's new velour covers. I won't go, that's all. And I won't cook. They can all go for a Wendyburger as far as I'm concerned. I bet Trevor will come to his rescue. Florence-bloody-Nightingale! He thinks I don't know a cuckoo when I see one. Big butch Trevor, with his Burt Reynolds body and black wet-look briefs. He's nothing but a glorified travel agent. Adonis Travel! A tacky fortnight in tacky Mykonos, the gay paradise of the Aegean. I suppose the leather queen's not too bad. Looks a bit posy in those chaps. Still, it gives the place a touch of New York. Maybe I'll give it a whirl. Nothing else to do. It'll probably turn out to know Philip very well from some fuck-party in Vauxhall. Wouldn't surprise me! Still, it's worth another Pils. Just in case! Anything's better than this culture queen. Look at her! C & A suit, and a spot of Aramis behind the ears, thinking she's the bee's knees. Look all you like, Mary; it's not for you! There's that Y queen again! Philip's type, if ever there was. So bloody posy, the way he took his jersey off, showing off his arms, and tan, and pink T-shirt! They're all the same, those model types. Bending from the waist to put his bag down, just so he could stick out his bum and let everybody know how athletic he is. Nice bum, though. In fact, he's quite nice altogether, except she looks so up herself. The leather queen's probably a better bet. Philip would love the pink boy, though. He's probably had him, for all I know!

Ben's Diary

¶ TUESDAY: Sam rang, wanting to go to the new Bond movie, but I said no. Instead I stayed in, trying to finish *Orlando*. Hopeless. I washed my hair, which was filthy, but then it dried all wrong, so I had to gell it, which slightly pissed me off. Went to the pub, and saw Jon with his new actor friend. They kept snuggling and cooing, which made me feel really good! I promised myself two pints, then home. But in the end I had maybe five, and felt as if I was going to fall over. Believe it or not, a royal gardener started to chat me up. He was about twenty with longish, straw-coloured hair. Nice! But I was too far gone, and after a double vodka I began to see double. So the inevitable stagger home, miserable and quite out of it.

OPERATIC DUET

OPERA QUEEN. That's a nice shirt. Lovely colours.

CLONE. What?

OPERA QUEEN. I was just remarking on your shirt. It's really nice.

CLONE. Oh!

OPERA QUEEN. Where did you get it? If you don't mind my asking.

CLONE. LA.

OPERA QUEEN. Los Angeles? Really? I've always wanted to go. Well, San Francisco, actually. They have a fabulous opera house there. Did you go? To the opera, I mean.

CLONE. No!

OPERA QUEEN. What a shame. You'd love it, I'm sure. If you like opera, that is.

CLONE. I don't.

OPERA QUEEN. Well, I'm sure you could. You just need somebody to take you to the right thing. That's all. *La Bohème*'s a good one to start with. You'd like the tunes. Puccini's very accessible. I wouldn't take you to Wagner the first time. Too heavy for a first-timer.

CLONE. Wagner's all right!

OPERA QUEEN. You like Wagner! What a surprise. I thought you'd prefer disco music, actually. From your appearance, that is. Appearances can be very deceiving though, can't they? Have you seen *The Ring*?

CLONE. The what?

OPERA QUEEN. *The Ring*! It's the longest opera ever written. Well, it's three operas really, with an introduction. You must have heard the 'Ride of the Valkyries' — well that comes from *The Ring*.

CLONE. Yeah?

OPERA QUEEN. What draws you to Wagner's music-drama? Is it the epic conflict between gods and men, between good and evil — the age-old struggle?

CLONE. What?

OPERA QUEEN. Or is it something more romantic? You like to be overwhelmed by the passion of it all, don't you? I can tell from your eyes that you're basically a very emotional person, although you try to hide it from others.

CLONE. Getting a bit carried away, aren't you? You don't know me from Adam, dear. Now why don't you let me get on with my drink and find someone up your own street?

OPERA QUEEN. I'm very sorry. I hadn't realized I was interrupting. I was only trying to be friendly.

CLONE. Well, you've tried.

OPERA QUEEN. If you ask me, I think far too many people stand around in here, never talking. It's like a disease. And when you do talk, you're wrong.

CLONE. Some guys just like to stand and drink, dear. If I need to talk to somebody, I'll get a psychiatrist. OK?

OPERA QUEEN. I can't see why you're so unfriendly, that's all.

CLONE. I don't like poncy intellectual queens, dear. Not my type! Maybe if you wore jeans and a T-shirt. I like men. Know what I mean?

OPERA QUEEN. Of course I know what you mean. Just because I'm wearing a suit and going to the opera, doesn't mean to say I'm not a man. You're a bit of an inverted snob, if you ask me. At least I've got interests, and don't just spend my time hanging around bars and Heaven.

CLONE. Look, Julie Andrews! Nobody's asking you anything! If you want to wank over fucking Caruso, that's your business. I just don't want to know about it, that's all. I'm sure you'll make somebody a very nice interesting friend, with your clever-arsed talk and stuck-up taste. Why don't you try somebody else? The guy in the pinstripe suit looks the sort that likes classical. Give him a whirl, dear. He's probably

82

going to the same thing tonight. You can share a box!

OPERA QUEEN. Well I must say, for somebody who looked friendly you're certainly a disappointment.

CLONE. Run along, dear. You might miss the start. Don't want that, do we?

Ben's Diary

¶ WEDNESDAY: I have never felt as lonely as last night. Sick in the corridor as I got back, then slept like a log. Today I felt ugly and ill. Ricky came round, and I told him I was in love with the nameless beauty from the Bell. It's incredibly hard to talk about someone you've never even met as if he was the most important thing in existence. And Ricky said it was just sex, which put me in a bad temper. Wanted to go to Heaven in case the guy was there, but after a couple of pints in the pub I felt really pissed again, and came home.

THE LEATHER QUEEN GETS HOT

It's so hot in here, I may have to go and take my cock-ring off.
Apart from anything else, it's killing me. I knew I should have
tried it on when I bought it. They're always the same when you
get a hard-on, like a collar on a mad dog. The Americans have
got it sussed, just letting it all hang out. That way there's no
pinching round the balls, unless it's someone you know. Trouble
is, it looks so good. Turns me on, anyway! It's these chaps — I
always feel a bit of a nance whenever I wear them. It takes me
about half-an-hour, wandering up and down the flat, looking in
the mirror, making sure they look OK. Then halfway down the
tube escalator I begin to feel like Tony Curtis in *Some Like It Hot*.
And on the train I could earn a fortune charging the spectators.
It's so exhausting, being looked at all the way from Notting Hill
to Leicester Square. And then here, surrounded by dull,
miserable-looking queens. I should have gone to the Coleherne.
I'll give it another half-hour, then maybe take a cab. Don't think
I could face any more public transport tonight. The clone's all
right, I suppose. Could live without the queen he's with. They
can't be together! The clone looks bored out of his box. Some
queens always want a little conversation; coming out to meet
people. Who wants to talk? It's a bad sign. Makes guys think
you're lonely. Better to grab than gab, as Kurt used to say. Good
big bum! Knows it, though. The way he stands, like a
construction worker at ballet class! When the queen's gone,
maybe I'll move in. He looks available, unless he's waiting for
somebody. Still, he hasn't been clock-watching, so maybe it's my
lucky night. If I take the shades off, very slowly, it will look sexy
and I'll be able to see a bit better. That's it. Not bad! In fact,
really quite good for this dump. OK, guy. You're coming back

to my place, whether you like it or not! And if you want to fight about it, that's all right with me. We'll soon have you strapped up, or tied down. If you really want, you can choose the weapons. A touch of the belt perhaps, or maybe a little whipping. If he asks where the bike is, I'll say it's at the garage, or I had a bad smash-up! Trouble is, there may be something better at the Coleherne. It's a risk, if I pass this one up. He's not looking at the goods like he should be. Roll on summer nights cruising the Heath. Ah, fuck it! Down the Coleherne; then the cellar. It's more fun and more fuck. I'll be here all night waiting for this one to make up his mind. If he's not into the gear screw him. What he needs is a good beating. Maybe next time.

Ben's Diary

¶ THURSDAY: Ricky rang saying he'd seen him last night. The first time I don't go to Heaven on Wednesday in months – and he's there! It might not have been him. After all, Ricky has never seen the guy. But the description was right. I asked if he was on his own; apparently he was with two or three friends. What were they like? He said they were attractive, rich-looking trendies, blond-tipped fringes, and cute angular faces!! So I'll have to suck my cheeks in, and wear highlights! Maybe he works in Flip. I'll try there tomorrow, and see what they've got – probably black PVC coats!

NARCISSUS AFTER THE SHOWER

Why am I always the only beautiful guy in this place? It's incredible. All they do is stare, trying to work out how to get closer, or have the nerve to offer a drink. They might even be nice guys, some of them. Not many though! It's hard talking to ugly queens when you're not used to looking at them. They're so grubby, too. Not like Americans. Just hopeless miseries, out on the scene, night after night. If they disciplined their bodies, it would be a start. Beer guts or pigeon chests – who would want to go to bed with that? What's the point of being gay if you're ugly? Just pubs and frustration. They might as well stay in the closet. God, it's so depressing! And so fucking English! What I need is a holiday. California! Sun, sand, randy guys! Or lying by a pool: a long cool drink: and some cutie swimming around, like *A Bigger Splash*. Fantasy time! And why not? It's the only thing to do in this place. Drab London queens. The guy at the Y was great, though. Really cool, borrowing someone's room to fuck in. I wonder who else he's dragged up there. Better than going back to Streatham or wherever. Maybe it will happen again. That would be good: Thursday evenings for adultery. David would go crazy if he knew. Maybe they know each other. Problem is, if I casually ask about the big guy with dark cropped hair, he'll get suspicious. But what if they get talking, and I'm mentioned? It could just come out. I should have said I've got a boyfriend who trains there as well. Then he'd know to keep quiet. Still, there's no reason why he should talk about me. Except he did say I was the best fuck he's ever had – so he won't forget that, at least. Unless it was bullshit, which I can't believe! I wonder what David would do. He always says he's faithful – and I'm sure he is. But he's obsessed with this idea that everyone wants to screw me.

I suppose they do. It's not surprising! But does he actually think I let them? He'd go mad if he knew. It's not worth it — guilt, and all that shit. Why should it matter, though? Most guys do it, even when they're together. It's only sex, not love or anything. They always go back after a fling. It gets boring, sleeping with the same guy. That's what was so good about this one in the gym. I've seen him in the showers, so I know what he looks like. And I've imagined making it with him. But having him was better. It was the best! David thinks I'm beautiful, and I like that. But when you hear it from a stranger, it's sexier somehow. And you get sick of just cruising, especially at the Y. Sometimes, it's impossible not to do it. Anyway, I wanted it. It's all this feeling bad about it afterwards. That's the pain. It's just like being married, which is ridiculous.

Ben's Diary

¶ FRIDAY: There's no doubt that half the boys in London are gay, or like to behave that way. Last night at the Asylum there seemed to be everyone I've ever met or seen or slept with (nearly empty!) And thousands more. I wandered around, which got harder as more came, but couldn't see him anywhere. Saw a few contenders for his sort of friends, and there were more model types than usual. One tall slim blond, hair short at the sides with a quiff, wearing pale blue and white — stunning! Nice legs, and a sharp straight nose which made his expression very aristo-ideal. He was with a similar type. They were probably just friends, but I couldn't be bothered finding out. Once you've seen something as good as him, the others look like dummies. I wouldn't say no on a dark, windy night in Streatham, but he was in a different class. Sam was mooning about, telling me I was stupid, and should forget it. I think he fancies me, and I like him a lot. We danced until we melted, and laughed a lot, for some unknown reason. So Friday was flat, and I stayed in and watched the rain. Ricky rang to say there was a job going at some new clothes shop, but I can't be bothered with nine-to-five at the moment. Maybe I'll take some more photographs. Finished the weird *Orlando*, and fantasized about queening around in a huge Elizabethan mansion!!! Out for a drink, quite late, and saw Jon, who's taking a week off to go to Paris with his boyfriend.

THE OLD QUEEN REMEMBERS

I remember a sleazy basement in Soho, with pink flowered wall-paper and odd chairs from abandoned three-piece suites, where the most Bohemian of us met. There we sat, ladies' head-squares flowing from our pastel-coloured chemises, quoting Firbank and talking in a sort of Dada shorthand utterly unintelligible to an outsider. We certainly had style – something these people know nothing about. We surprised the ordinary man in the street with a splash of colour and choreographed footsteps. How else were they to know that we were real and not just fairy-tale? It was a terrible struggle, especially when all the world seemed to be dressed in navy, grey, or khaki – the male world, that is. Drab, drab, dingy dreariness. But the soldiers! They looked so handsome in those uniforms. I remember them on leave, coming into the pubs at weekends – quite shy some of them, except the merchant navy boys. And after having a few, they would let their hair down and start messing about a bit. Most of them were very polite, charming men, just looking for new company. Even the rough ones were a challenge we adored – usually unhappy lonely boys, unsure of themselves in a cruel world. I suppose they felt threatened in a way, as if they thought we compromised their masculinity. But we reinforced it, really. And we were men, after all. Just different men from them. The gentle ones understood that, and really needed what we could offer. Lonely for love. It can be lonely in the army, after all. But not one of them didn't love his best pal like a brother. They had big hearts for friendship. Ah! If only they had let me into the army. Not the navy, because I can't swim! But the army, with all its comradeship. That's what's missing these days – friendship! And manners. Sex-mad, most of them. And they start so young.

I didn't dare even think about it until I was twenty-two, and I could never have told mother. She might have thought I was rather flamboyant, and I suppose she wonders about me — even now. But still. I couldn't tell. It wouldn't be right, somehow. Like bad manners. Anyway, we tried to have a happy time. Secret places; special names; like being another person. Everything's so obvious nowadays, and too easy. So many of us had to live a lie. People were afraid to 'come out' for fear of losing their jobs, and one or two of the more obvious ones were actually dismissed on some silly pretext. For most, though, it was a case of pretending to like girls and hate 'queers'. Dreadful! I dare say that the fear of being discovered reduced a terrible number of men to despair, and even suicide. There were quite a few of those when I was young. And there was prison. People were terrified of being caught, or blackmailed, or even just beaten up. No wonder so many stayed in the closet. They didn't have much option, did they? I'm sure that's why so many of the older set are bitter. After a lifetime's conditioning — being made to feel warped and sick — it's not surprising they're lonely, and frustrated, and full of regret. Well, *I* was never ashamed of the way I was. Some of us had to have the pioneering spirit. And not like this 'Glad to be Gay' and pink triangles everywhere. It's like a gimmick now. They haven't suffered like we did. And they call it a revolution, when actually it's just a free-for-all. People aren't friendly like they used to be — that's what it is. They don't have anything to say. It's just sleeping around without even knowing who it is . . . they just come in here to find somebody new, without even caring what a person's like. It's not the same any more. Something's gone for ever. I don't know whether it's age — I suppose it is — but I feel like a stranger, even here, where I've been coming for over twenty years. Just like a stranger! People come and go. And they call it the 'scene'. All I can say is it's not what we were hoping and struggling for. It's easier than it was, but for all the clubs and discos and things, there's still no love. None!

HEAVEN

HEAVEN

The beauty of Heaven is its size. Despite the mutterings of cosy little queens who prefer fifty square feet so they can keep tabs on the trade, the advantage of space is very great. It holds more, and therefore there is more to choose from. It is possible to escape from a larger bar to somewhere smaller, and the desire to escape is quite frequent among queens. Cuddling couples can perch on the many stairs, whilst the serious solitary cruiser will find a good vantage point in the entrance, spotting the goods as they arrive. Best of all is not having to watch the disco queens dancing. There are coloured lights and a lot of smoke, and much of the time the crowds are in silhouette, which is a blessing. It is the perfect setting for fantasy, whether it be the last act of *Götterdämmerung* or a Roxy Music spectacular. Perhaps the only questionable thing about the place is its name.

Heaven is the queen's paradiso, and she likes to spend as much time there as possible. It is really a giant fun-palace full of the most arrogant people in Western Europe, all desperately trying to enjoy themselves. Almost every type of queen is represented in this noisy firmament, and if you go it is absolutely imperative to be able to survive the perils which await you, chief of which must be the competition. Being an expert on eighteenth-century French furniture styles or having a passion for collecting *Astérix* books count for nothing unless you look good. If the effort is frequently transparent, that is because some queens prefer theatrical intensity to natural ease. So many lead such ordinary lives that any opportunity to dramatize and costume a fantasy is necessarily grasped with terrible commitment.

There are those who treat the whole setting as Miss World's catwalk, gliding up and down with a silly conceited expression fixed on their faces, a trace of intelligence nowhere to be seen, but always looking around. The young and trendy are very keen on this notion of life as a parade – cruising as perambulatory performance art. It is most tedious for the static queen, who may be treated to the same fashion show perhaps a dozen times in one night. The young are also fairly incontinent, and many of these seemingly poised little wanders are actually journeys to the loo. At other times they linger beneath fluorescent light, thinking it makes them look tanned and glamorous – especially if they are wearing white. These areas are avoided by queens with dandruff. Otherwise they would have to endure remarks like 'Is it snowing outside?' The ugly are remarkably prone to delusions of beauty and, with pitiable arrogant abandon, trot about as if mere repeated showings might be enough to create an impression of dazzling beauty. Still, grotesques do have a tradition of appearing in side-shows, and under the right circumstances some of these bearded ladies and legless monsters could earn a fortune. As it is, they give intense pleasure to those queens who love to be reminded of their own good looks. So ugly queens are oddly popular, and usually flutter around some handsome man whom they cajole, amuse and entertain. All of this is very disturbing to watch. No queen likes to see beauty pursued by the beast, especially when beauty is so flirtatious and apparently intimate. But Heaven is a fun place and the pleasure principle brings harmony where many queens would like to sow seeds of discord.

Barmen are the most popular queens in Heaven, and their queenery knows no bounds. Like all people in a position to serve, they can choose to oblige or not, as the mood takes them. It is this aspect of the job which they relish. The slightest offence may be taken, whether it be at your waving a twenty-pound note, or informing him that you have been waiting ten minutes and the guy he is serving has just walked in. The fact that the lucky guy is some American porn star's double explains but does not help matters. Nostrils flaring, your public servant will either make very heavy weather of slamming down a can of Colt, or simply never look in your direction again and go about his chores. These involve emptying ashtrays and wiping down the counter, neither of which is done too frequently, unless he likes domestic order. Some barmen are trained little housewives, some are not. But if their lacking efficiency does not commend them, which is quite unlikely since they all turn into efficiency queens, their looks cannot fail. Almost all the barmen are handsome, chunky or cute. It is a prerequisite, and accounts for some of their arrogance. If you are going to trap a few individuals behind a bar knowing that everybody is going to have to look at them at least once in a night, it shows impeccable taste and good business sense to employ attractive men and boys. Given the amount of attention they receive, it is hardly surprising that it goes to their heads, along with the power they wield. Most of them would gladly wear T-shirts bearing the slogan: 'If I'm not perfect, throw me away' – some with more justification than others.

The regular queen is absolutely *au fait* with all their names, from Mike to Chuck, to Todd the new boy who only started tonight and who has already been set up by that nauseatingly slick and familiar queen, the one who never misses a night, and tries to be funny but never is. The handsome regular, the one in the blue T-shirt with the thick wrists and much-loved biceps, probably knows most of these queens and has certainly slept with the best of them. His easy familiarity is envied by all those who lack it. He never messes about when a tall dark stranger walks into the crowded bar, however far away he is. He is like a beacon of charm and smiles and straightforwardness. Queens want to be his friend after it is all over, whether a one-night stand or two weeks in Morocco. And he has a lot of friends. He is nothing special, just a car salesman, not a model or pop-star. He is ordinary, but has a natural quality which is very special amongst so much pretension. He is also rather smug, and thinks he is straight-acting and not a queen at all. But vanity gives the lie to this attractive simplicity, and makes him a knowing flirtatious tart. A fan club of queens is a dangerous thing. Like the middle class, they absorb the most unlikely pin-ups through sheer ubiquity, and through a seduction by manner which is hard to

97

resist. Once a guy is made aware of what he has got, when he knows he is a heart-breaker with a great body, then he becomes at the very least a princess. Being attractive does not make him a queen, but revelling in his powers of attraction does.

Heaven brings out not-so-hidden fantasies. A boy who appears in a talent-spotting competition and hears the applause will never be content without it. Some boys dream of Shirley Temple, and some act out that dream. The girly queens flock to Heaven like toddlers to a sweet shop. They flounce about the place, giggling and shrieking, hands and arms flung about in a wild sign-language embellishing eloquent phrases like 'She never!' and 'Ooh, Gloria – *don't*!' They like to call each other bitch and never ever stand alone. Once out of the pubs and set free in Heaven's wide-open spaces, their hysteria feels no restraint. Lacking androgynous beauty, they daub themselves with Boots' blusher and eye-liner, and bat their eyelashes like Sixties sluts. They are great favourites with the uglier butch queens, who use them as trash cans, but many of them prefer 'sisters', or well-groomed queens, very suave, with a bit of *hauteur*. Like so many queens they have no shame in public, but can be quite suburban and prudish in private. This is always an annoying reversal and lets them in for a lot of abuse which, because they are so desperately inadequate, they enjoy. Some of them have very old-fashioned ideas about what men are: all muscles, hairy chests and big pricks. But unlike clones, who have similar ideas, girly queens are little women *manquées*, trying their hands at the role of conventional 'pussy'. Although impressed by money, they are unlike rent boys, and want sex more than cash, more than stardom even. And by sex they mean big cock. Heaven is where they hope to find love one day. Love, of course, is the same regular big cock. The problems these girls face in life are enormous and they deserve pity. An incestuous relationship with Uncle Brian probably made them what they are, along with a little love from mummy, and too much time spent playing with their sisters' toys and friends.

Heaven is addictive, a perfect fix for the energetic floozies who are too vacuous not to enjoy themselves every repetitive minute of the time. Occasionally, though, you might spot tired little huddles of glassy-eyed butterflies, their gaudy wings trembling with nervous exhaustion, minds coloured with a slight momentary awareness that all their efforts are for nothing. As the night progresses the walls are lined with unlovely victims of disenchantment, whose expressions vary from that of one whose house has burnt down, destroying every personal record of his existence, to a stony tight-lipped glare at anyone still appearing to enjoy himself. Queens are notoriously bad in defeat, especially when they are drunk.

The pissed-off look is not necessarily genuine, however, since the advent of the Islington and Camden Town rockabilly queen. The rockabilly might wear a slick suit, or look like a tastefully arranged mess: bits of black paramilitary gear draped about with careless flair, perhaps a donkey-jacket and duffel bag, topped with an ice-cream mop and tapering away to huge black boots or dainty canvas slip-ons and thin hairy ankles. They see themselves as avant-garde skinheads, and have a close-shaven contempt for queens who are not as extraordinary as they are. Some keep this unjustifiable contempt to themselves like a worry bead, feeling for it every now and then – a shot of reassuring superiority. They are often very insecure. Others etch it in their serious expressions with all the overrated talent of a first-year exhibitor at St Martin's, where many of them are on permanent exhibition, occasionally loaned out to the Bell and the Asylum. (The Asylum – Heaven on Thursday – had to be created by a shrewd collector in order to hang this contrivedly bizarre series of self-portraits.) Where the old queen overkills with gentility, most of these ostentatiously modern queens have almost no manners at all. Mannerlessness is as fashionable as little black leather caps, and may have some deeper origin in an ideological and revamped contemporary desire to be classless. Since this tiny island is once again governed by the affectedly moral and well-bred brigade, art students and other young queens seriously engaged in the appearance of things project an earnest rejection of night-life as a reliable sequence of pleases and thank yous, excuse mes and after yous. When you are being shoved about and having your pint slopped over your favourite jeans, try to remember that these queens have a vision of contemporary life as a mess. The more mess, the more modern.

Looking pissed-off is 'cool', and an essential feature of the soulless appraisal of things. If beneath it there lurk enthusiasm and keenness, they are tell-tale evidence of sensitivity and must be kept in a dark room – speaking of which, some of these boys are ambitious photographers. It is in their photographs that the assumed anti-romantic attitude blinks its shutter and, like a chameleon, takes on a different colour. The rockabilly queen is seriously engaged in the art of concealment, because he wants to toughen the stereotyped idea of the queen as a warm sensitive person with artistic leanings. So he looks dead bored, chews gum, smokes a cigarette and drinks lager all at the same time, often screwing his face up into a scrumpled rag of rubbishy disregard. Whilst there can be something winning and attractive in this wilful disfiguring it is also a pain in the neck, since for all his affected singularity the rockabilly in repose is just another sensitive little queen.

One thing which does give the lie to these apparently cold-blooded *poseurs* is their need and love for friendship. They cling to each other, not merely because they prefer their own kind and thrive on mutual self-congratulation. It is also because they have a sincere loathing for the traditional round of promiscuous indiscretion and dumb animal contact. Nor do they want to be sullied with the un-chic queens. Sincerity gives the lie to their image as much as their valuing friends does. If you are used to offering a cigarette, saying you live in Battersea, and leaving with a pick-up, they will elude you. If you see them in an ordinary leather queens' bar, they are rarely looking for sex – just checking out the place to confirm their worst suspicions that a lot of queens are still huddling together in subcultural herds looking for a very temporary mate. They forget, of course, that they huddle in herds themselves. They cannot function in an atmosphere where

100

the principal motive is lust, and some of them like sex least of all. They prefer to meet people at parties, where they can talk to strangers because the social framework permits the interchange of ideas. This represents that commonplace belief which insists that what a person is like in his head will lend quality to any sexual adventures you have with him. They are not all like this, but those many who are show a blithe awareness that sex is one of several modes of self-expression. They may have something to say worth hearing, but can be so shy that no amount of flattery will lure them into a committed performance for your strange delight. They tend to be lost without their friends, so although dead to strangers' advances, they have a distressing lease of life when one of their own kind, whom they always know, comes up. The problem of breaking into coteries is not peculiar to queens, but unlike leather queens and clones, this herd is strongly defined not only by fashion, but also values, friendship, and generation. So the difficulties appear unusually insuperable. You may be tempted to buy a costume and get a funny haircut, but you will doubtless find it easier and more natural to despise their insularity. They are not like queens who relish your exclusion. They may even like the look of you, if you are young. But they are queens about style and creative talent, which you either have or do not.

Many of them are also conceited shits, and their fake cameraderie is not worth a moment's envy. They know a lot of clever people who live and work in Soho, and enjoy having lunch with them in the Pollo, or tea in Valerie's. They can introduce you, if you like, to poets and painters and film directors. They are the new Bohemians and like to drink in the French, where all manner of talented character goes. Heaven is their time off from ambition, which otherwise influences their every contrived gesture and studied throwaway remark. Some of the coteries are more distinguished than others, and when *they* enter in their pyjama bottoms and Oriental kimonos, pretty but disdainful, slightly nervous of their dreadlocks' effect, there rush up similar if less accomplished types, eager to flatter. To the rockabilly queen with a sense of hype, the choice of dress is made in the knowledge that others will want to be seen with him if he gets it right. They treat each other like celebrities, and when graceless, they ape the style of the celebrity who can get away with any kind of bad behaviour. How they look at home in the Asylum, being so clever and contemporary, and couldn't-care-less when they could: dissident inmates with shaved back-and-sides.

Queens care so much about appearances because there is always competition, and the chance that on a bus or in the late-night shop there may be someone worth impressing. In Heaven it is the purpose of appearance to usurp the dismal insistence of reality. But as with Cinderella, the illusion can last only a few hours. When the bright ordinary lights go up and the rubbish is put out, the glittering assembly turns to a motley collection of tired drawn faces, like a crowd of extras when the director calls 'Cut!', or mass of insects taken by surprise when a stone is lifted. If there is one queen who survives this illumination better than all others, it is the guy with the beautiful body, most of which is exposed. Whatever misgivings you may have about the manner, which is all Ultrabrite smiles and 'having a ball', the body needs no apology. The entire ethos of letting hair down would go for nothing in a place where English dullness and puritanism insist on decorum. There are still raised eyebrows in English life, but in Heaven take your shirt off if it is hiding prime beefsteak and watch those hungry eyes feed.

Some queens complain about bars and clubs being too like meat markets, which is usually a case of the hamburger resenting the T-bone steak. Perhaps they cannot break into the buyer's market or, like vegetarians, have some principle about the degradation of animal life. Whatever the complaint's cause, it is certain that these suburban campaigners for more real human beings have an unrealistic attitude to the demands of sexual hunger. When hungry, it is natural to eat. For some, sex is an integral part of everyday life; for others it is not. Some queens were created to have midnight conversations about *Parsifal* and Genet, others about house-plants and wall-paper patterns. Some were created to be manna from Heaven. Of course it can help to show an interest in his career as a ladies' hairdresser, but his body is what he is, and that is what you are really interested in. There is one problem, though, which is frequent and tricky to solve. It is, like so many others, essentially tribal. Good bodies like other good bodies, attracted by the competition being on a higher level than usual. Trials of beauty and strength go on across the bar, on the dance-floor, in the loo, at the pool table – anywhere, in fact, where another semi-naked queen has established territory. These are the queens the barmen love, quick with a lager when they come sweating from the dance, smiling and confidential with their private jokes and sexy exclusiveness.

They are always there, these bodies, and for simple visual pleasure they have no equal. Their virtue lies in being straightforward clean-cut objects. Their inhabitants rarely have mystery and are usually profoundly uninteresting. Although their vanity is a pain, most queens are vain and at least these have some justification. At the summit of the queen's world-view is the widely held belief that physical beauty is the only form of transcendence. In Heaven, therefore, these creatures are archangels appointed to reveal that not all human beings are miserable ugly animals. When the lights go up they have nothing to lose, splendid literal statements of what most queens imagine to be an impossible ideal. They have their imitators, and because of the heat in the place some of the stringier queens discard garments to no good effect, more like stick insects than people. As is often the way with unfortunates, they have no idea of the aesthetic offence they give and, blissfully ignorant in all respects, have a heavenly time showing off their wares. The younger ones behave more like naked little children than Salome, and if there were a swimming-pool instead of a dance-floor would be splashing water at each other. Of course, the leather queen is an obvious dissenter, and there are always queens who would like to take something off but feel they look so good in donkey-jacket and black cashmere scarf that no amount of heat would induce them to.

Skinheads have the most primitive attitude towards showing their bodies. Their inverted aesthetic idealizes looking like a slob, so beer-guts are as prestigious as biceps, and scrawn as muscle. Boasting scarred and tattooed torsos, their necks and shoulders bruised with cancerous love-bites, they lurch from level to level like half-shaved apes. Rough and ready, they proclaim violence and strength rather than the superficial tone and sheen of beautiful bodies. Their muscles are usually an acquisition of labour, not self-love, and if they body-build, they do not do it at the Y. Their pride is in arm-wrestling, not passive genuflection. The utilitarian appeal of this aesthetic finds most admirers among the rockabilly queens, who tend towards the more sophisticated idea that ugliness and strength are quintessentially beautiful, whereas YMCA queens' immaculate bodies are nothing more than manikins for advertising and publicity. The naive brutish ideology of most skinheads is far less queeny than the codified and theatrical sado-masochism of most glossy leather queens. In fact skinheads stimulate the queenish obsession with commonness and low life, another reason why rockabilly queens worship them.

The desire to have a bit of rough – slumming it – is an obvious form of inverted snobbery, often found among queens. Chelsea queens adore the influx of young East Enders at the weekends, for the same reason that Wilde liked working-class boys: the sex is good, and it is good for kicks because it is with a social inferior. Such snobs never realize that the East Ender despises them far more deeply than they could him. Nor are they paying. Snobbery is one of the chief symptoms of queenery. For example, the searing desire to get the arty-looking guy with green eyes and blond-tipped fringe may be as much the wish to be seen getting him as it is the need to get the one you want most. So it is that there are not only heavenly bodies with whom it is important and prestigious to be friendly, because they know the proprietor, the doormen, the barmen and the cutest boys; there are queens whom it is worth picking up because your success will be noted and envied by a cast of old and young hopefuls. Heaven accentuates this self-conscious pride in conquest. There is no better audience than there. Queens watch whatever will stimulate them and pass a little more time. Getting a superior catch makes for very superior feelings. This kind of snobbery is articulated by the facial expression of possessive warning — 'Hands off, dear, it's mine! Yes, I know it's fabulous, so eat your heart out!' Proud possessors usually finger their goods a lot, to demonstrate the owner's prerogative — often a bitchy little performance intended more to burn off competitors than to express any spontaneous physical affection. Snobbish queens tend to treat generally desirable consorts in the same way as many men treat beautiful women. They are trophies, hung on the arm with smug materialistic conceit. These temporary couplings are often propelled by the less attractive partner from bar to bar, a sort of royal walkabout. Whereas most queens would leave once they have a good catch, the snob is not content with believing he has the best. He also wants the self-satisfaction of rubbing other queens' noses in it.

It is snobbery which calls out the barman's name, and purrs all the more when the barman refers to you by name — so long as a few nameless nonentities can hear as they wait to be served. Heaven is filled with this tiresome one-upmanship, even to the clichéd notion of some queens behaving as if they own the place. Some even relish the opportunity of directing others to the loo, giving the information with bored peremptoriness, experience patronizing innocent ignorance. Ordering bitter usually turns some scowling face in your direction, sneering at the new boy who does not know they only serve lager. It is so English and middle-class, being ridiculously proud of simply knowing what to do and where, all of which any fool can learn. Such queens try to perpetuate the mystique of heaven on earth by creating the snobbish illusion that it is an exclusive world to which you may or may not be admitted. And they do this out of anxiety and insecurity, those two archetypally queeny bedfellows. The worst of them derive some pleasure from seeing others make fools of themselves — even going so far as to engineer it. It is as if there are petty tests – you do not know what they are, but sense you have to pass them. Snobbish queens are also very middle-class about blindly insisting on their little world's rituals and status quo. For all the glamour and exhibitionism, it is snobbery which makes so many of them unreflective and ungenerous.

Appearances are the first things which receive the snobbish appraisal. You may be wearing a Giorgio Armani jacket, the best piece of slick style in Heaven, and feeling a little snobbish yourself. But snobs also enjoy undermining the snobbery of others, especially when its prize is more enviable than theirs. It will not be long before a couple of semi-chic queens start staring in your direction, readable minds saying 'Who does she think she is?', or more generously, 'Fabulous jacket, but she looks a mess in it. It doesn't suit her at all!' You may dismiss them as envious scrubbers, but matters get more complicated if you are feeling a bit unsure of that beautiful, stylish expensive jacket which creates the impression that you are making an effort after staying in all week. Very un-chic! Is it really that bad? Where can you put it without it being stolen? Who cares what anybody thinks? The truth is that you might well care. A feeling of insecurity about clothes can ruin a queen's evening, and Heaven is particularly plagued by fashion critics hell-bent on deriding your notions of *haute couture*. Dressing up is best for the Hippodrome. The critics are many but the effort is at least appreciated. In Heaven it is better to be dressed with uncontrived ordinariness, unless you are a rockabilly, or a ditzy queen perpetually ornamented with rhinestones and frills. If you can have a 'look' which is ordinary, but not a typically gay uniform of ordinariness, as are jeans and a white wrestler's T-shirt, you will have a singularity which unsettles the uniformed brigade and has snobbish curiosity for the vanguard of the avant-garde. Of course, some queens are never impressed and scowl at everything from denim to tulle.

Snobbery is always born out of some sense of inadequacy and fear of exposure. It is worth noting that the simplicity of a damning critical glance or superior disdainful stare may quickly turn the more tawdry and defensive queens from snobbish caricatures to the lily-livered nobodies they are at heart. Because such a premium is put on appearance and demeanour, many queens tend to have masks rather than faces, affected posture rather than natural and relaxed presence. Dealing with them is largely a question of realizing that they are nothing more than the sum of a few meagre stock theatrical gestures, and telling them if need be. A confident look, tinged with pity, can sometimes communicate to them the essential and saddening fact: that you are a real human being with intelligence and a sympathetic nature, whilst they are little more than lifeless stereotypes. Many of them cultivate snobbery because they have known its condescension; many because the put-down is their favourite form of expression; many because they carelessly regard affected superiority as something admirable and winning; and many because England has infected them with the pernicious notion that class is important, and the higher the better.

The worst type of snobbish queen is the sensitive homosexual, favoured by the gods and disenchanted with his own kind. He is not as common as he was, but the whimpering of Sebastian in *Brideshead Revisited* has spawned a waxwork generation of look-alike English queens, playing with vowels, wearing cricket sweaters like social emblems, pouting and mooning as if mother had scolded them. They are mostly lower-middle-class pretenders, enchanted by the idea that commoners – like most of the queens in Heaven – will swoon if they upper-middle their classy appeal. They lounge about as if in some country house, blond hair falling carelessly over their brow, horn-rimmed spectacles at the ready in case something interesting is said which merits their being worn. Some have double chins and try to have an awfully good time, but mostly they have a patronizing involvement with whichever *Brideshead* addict they have cornered. There is an icon of snobbish appeal for those who are genuinely involved in the business of social climbing. If it is not the young English aristocrat look, then it is the businessman in his pinstripe suit. And since so few of them go to Heaven, and since the general preference is for youth and a kind of rich bored look, the queens who are easily won by potential chandeliers and thirties romanticism giggle and perform for these snobbish malformed impostors because they are snobs themselves. The sight of two snobbish queens, craning and sneering in their bow-ties and cravats at the leather and denim about them, is a symptom of the way in which Toryism goes hand in hand with closeted queenery and public-school fiction. It is a bizarre riposte to the American preppy look, which is usually handsomely presented; indeed, the Ivy League boy is much more a credible aristocratic ideal than these bloated English types who proclaim their university education as some guarantee of a socially desirable screw. Those boys who have legitimate reason to wear such clothes can be queens, but they marry and live with Sloaneish wives in South Kensington, getting awfully drunk with their male friends and talking about bum-boys. Appearances are deceiving, and this archetypal *poseur* – child of Thatcher's England – is an insidious idiot, almost always bad at sex and socially very far removed from his second-hand wardrobe's implications. Posy queens have bankrupted themselves for the sake of collars and studs, even tailors and shoemakers. If there were any discretion in Heaven it would exclude such reactionary twits, except that some queens wear these costumes with a sense of irony.

If queenery enjoys some status as an art of exaggeration, then its qualities are fewer when it is practised without irony. Without irony it is little more than an exercise in self-advertisement and -regard. Queens without irony are like performers with no off-stage personality of their own. They can easily be fucked, but their lack of inner life and any capacity for self-reflection makes them easily forgotten, whatever the performance's quality. So many queens take Heaven and themselves seriously. It is one of their greatest undoings. The most memorable queens satirize themselves as well as the world at large, seeing themselves as part of the human condition, and not above it. Those queens who preserve their glib, witty and brittle surface without any sense of irony merely reinforce the stereotype: the queen as bitter, meretricious outsider. They do nothing to encourage or improve social awareness and acceptance, merely feeding bigotry and oppressive intolerance. Traditional camp is one of the more baroque styles characteristic of queenery's exaggerating art. But whilst it may be amusing and distinctive, it is also a sad product of society's unjust repression of queens. It perpetuates the complacent subcultural mentality of much gay life, ensuring that popular opinion will continue to keep its back to the wall and maintain that queers are all lisping, limp-wristed nances. The gay vaudeville is an exuberant wasting of time, but mostly lacks the pathetic wisdom of comedy. It rarely reinterprets, and is ultimately a tiresome and indiscreet barrage of embellishment. Many of its amateur stars go to Heaven, but they give no lasting or memorable pleasure. They are unable to laugh at themselves because their hearts are rotten with resentment. Usually, they are manic-depressives masquerading as influential critics of human behaviour.

One of the things which most interferes with the enlightenment of queenish disdain is resenting the apparent happiness of others. Bitter queens look around Heaven like Satan envying Paradise, outcast angels preening their wings but never flying. But of course, because Heaven is a fun-palace, many queens feel obliged to look as though they are enjoying themselves. The spectre of depression and misery is so close to the surface of gay mentality that jokes and smiles are generally considered attractive recommendations of positive thinking. Nobody likes a miserable-looking queen, and it is always better to grin and be sociable than frown and look superior. This is particularly advisable if you are there to cruise successfully. Yet it is another indication of the superficiality of queens that they cannot appreciate or understand the thoughtful expression. If a queen's face is in repose there is either nothing going on inside the head, or it is full of frustrated misgivings. In Heaven most queens are either up or down. Perhaps a few are thinking about something other than cruising, having lots of fun, or wishing that they had never come. But if you sink into thought about this or that, there always comes up some presumptuous queen, telling you to cheer up, it might never happen, spend some time with him and you will have a bundle of fun.

The sight of hundreds of queens typifying virtually every aspect of a subculture at play is rich food for thought. It is a mystery why so few of them have a general inquiring interest in such a revelatory microcosm. They are like actors whom the part takes over, feeling that they do not exist unless speaking queens' lines and thinking queens' thoughts. Perhaps thinking about it would be too depressing, since they would invariably dwell on the gap between expectation and fulfilment. One does not go to a fun-palace in order to ponder on the nature of existence. But looking around, you have the unavoidable impression that despite the variety of types there is a consistency of manner, that an attractive appearance will be blighted by some queeny mannerism. And it almost always is. Some are worse than others, and not too hard to ignore. But some are catastrophic full-blown operas, impossible to listen to and intolerable to watch. It is reasonable enough to expect a masculine figure to behave like a man – but watch it walk. You do not even have to hear it to know from the falling jaw and lip-movement that it is a well-built lady. There is one solution to this disappointment. Silence. So it is that sex with a queen is frequently and necessarily performed without talking. This may well be why conversation has such a low premium in Heaven. Even if he had something interesting to say, it would be so irritating to hear it intoned like a fish-wife's gossip.

There may be individuals around, but it will take hours of scrutiny before you spot a potentially straightforward type who has not acquired the habits and characteristics of a thousand others. And although he might have read Proust and like Mark Rothko, he is more than likely to be boring about them. There are such pitfalls in searching for a charming rounded human being that in Heaven it is better to focus your attention on physical beauty rather than quality of mind. However idealistic and prone to romantic yearning, you will deprive yourself if you cling to principles about needing to like the person as much as his body. There is always the possibility of that surprising development, but the chief object is to have fun and find somebody attractive to sleep with. And that involves suffering numberless fools gladly, and enduring countless disappointments. In Heaven it is all there for the taking — a jumble sale full of cast-offs and other people's property. The rummaging may get rather depressing, but somewhere there is something you want.

THE ASYLUM AT HEAVEN
LATER THAT NIGHT

IN THE LOO

MAVIS. You make me sick, you do!

DORIS. What have I done now?

MAVIS. It was just the same in the bloody pub.

DORIS. Listen, dear! If you want to get it together, carry on.

MAVIS. How can I, with you staring in his direction every time I look over?

DORIS. But he's cruising me, Mavis. He wants something a bit glam, dear – not all over the bloody place, like you're looking tonight!

MAVIS. Get you, dear! Who do you think you're kidding? Have some more liner and find your own bloody trade.

DORIS. Some of us don't need 'slap', Mavis.

MAVIS. Hark at her! Why don't you try that one over there, dear?

DORIS. Which one?

MAVIS. In the corner – the clone – he's been there ten minutes, Doris. He keeps looking at us in the mirror, dear!

DORIS. Is he wanking?

MAVIS. Well, he's not been pissing for ten bloody minutes, has he? Honestly, what do you think he's doing – admiring the scenery? Sometimes, Doris, you're as blind as a bat.

DORIS. I don't think I want to. I'm trying to be ladylike tonight.

DORIS. Who are you kidding?! Go on! It'll only take five minutes. She's been ready to come for ten, dear. If one of us doesn't do it, she'll die of exhaustion!

Gloria arrives as Doris goes to stand at the trough.

GLORIA. Hello.

MAVIS. Hello, Gloria. Where've you been?

115

GLORIA. There's this fabulous hulk playing pool, stripped to the waist, with tattoos all over his arms. You should see the biceps, Mavis! I've never seen anything like it – not since that lorry-driver from Newcastle. And this one's a skin, too. I didn't know whether I was coming or going, really I didn't. So I just leant against that pillar thing, looking gorgeous. If only we'd been in the sauna . . .

MAVIS. So what's happened? Did he speak?

GLORIA. Don't be daft, Mavis! They don't speak, skins don't. They just look at you really hard, as if they really hate you. It's fabulous. Where's Doris?

MAVIS. She's in the corner, trying to pick that clone up . . . well, she was. They both were. She must have dragged him in the lock-up when I wasn't looking. She's anybody's, our Doris. Do it anywhere, she will! At least it'll keep her off my pitch. Come on, Gloria. I've had enough of this. There's nothing in here, that's for sure.

GLORIA. It's crowded, though, isn't it? I think I might hang on a bit. You never know.

MAVIS. Well, there's nobody my type! All bloody student trendies, pretending they want a shit. Don't fool Mavis, though. Those two have been standing there for hours. They were there the last time I came in.

GLORIA. Oh! He's nice.

MAVIS. Which one?

GLORIA. Next to the black guy, near the corner. Nice bum. Big, too! I wouldn't mind a bit of that.

MAVIS. Honestly, Gloria, you're just sex-mad, you are. What about the skinhead?

GLORIA. I can have them both, can't I? Anyway, I'm going to have a piss. See you later, Mavis.

As Gloria goes to the trough, a lock-up opens. Doris comes out alone, and someone else goes in.

MAVIS. The cat got the cream then, did she? Looks like somebody

116

else wants some too!

DORIS. There's plenty to go round, dear! Fabulous!

MAVIS. She's probably got AIDS. I'd wash your hands if I was you!

DORIS. Listen, Mavis! If anyone's dying of AIDS round here, it's you. Who went with that American clone at the Coleherne? The seven-foot-tall one!

MAVIS. I told you, we didn't do anything. He just wanted to talk, that's all. And he was six-foot-six, if you must know.

DORIS. Talk! Who're you kidding, dear!? You told me he was hung like a donkey. Didn't do anything! Anyway, I couldn't have done it. He was like a bloody lamp-post!

MAVIS. Well, I'm not changing my life just because the papers say there's a gay plague. At least I haven't got crabs!

DORIS. What's that supposed to mean? Mine died weeks ago. You're the one who's never out of the bloody clinic, dear. God knows what they'll find when you're dead.

MAVIS. You've no room to talk, Doris Richardson. For someone who's had it with a length of scaffolding, they'd probably find a bloody kitchen sink if they had a good look. There's enough room for one!

DORIS. Bitch! Where's Gloria?

MAVIS. Jerking off that wanker in the leather jacket!

DORIS. Nice! I wouldn't mind the big black number – he seems very turned on by Gloria's wrist-job.

MAVIS. Come on, Doris! You've just had something. Can't you stop? Go and read some graffiti, or something.

DORIS. But it's so big, Mavis! Look at it! I'm hanging around for a bit.

MAVIS. Oh, I'm going back. It's too crowded down here. As if there's anything worth having. Oh, hello Gloria! Who's your friend?

GLORIA. Marco! He's Italian. That's Doris and that's Mavis.

MARCO. Marco!

GLORIA. Cute, isn't he? Come on, Marco. Let's get a drink.

MARCO. Eh?

GLORIA. *Drink*! You know – *bierro*!

MARCO. Sorry! Me speak no very good English.

GLORIA. 'Course you do. Come on. See you, girls!

GLORIA. What do you want?

MARCO. Sorry?

GLORIA. *Bierro*?!

MARCO. Ah – to drink! Please, orange.

GLORIA. Are you sure? Don't you want a Pils or something? (Might have the clap, drinking juice!)

MARCO. No Pils, please. Just Coke, yes?

GLORIA. You wait for ever at this bloody bar! Can I have a Pils and a Coke? What? I've been waiting ten fucking minutes already. You want to get your act together, dear. Nobody's been down this end for hours! Honestly, they're fucking hopeless.

MARCO. Sorry?

GLORIA. Nothing! Whereabouts do you come from, then – in Italy?

MARCO. Italia!

GLORIA. Yes, I know you come from Italy – but whereabouts? Is it Rome?

MARCO. *Non capisco – scusi.* Sorry!

GLORIA. Fuckin'-'ell! Where you *live*? *Roma*?

MARCO. Ah! You want my home – yes? Is Firenze, I *live*, yes? *Sono di Firenze.*

GLORIA. Very nice, I'm sure. Where's that?

MARCO. Sorry?

GLORIA. Oh, it doesn't matter! Marco's a very nice name!

MARCO. Is my name – Marco!

GLORIA. I know it's your name. It's very nice. Unusual. Do you know what I mean? Marco nice name!

MARCO. Ah! You are Marco *anche*?

GLORIA. You what?

MARCO. Sorry! *Non capisco.* Er, I 'ave *libro* – book.

GLORIA. Oh, you've got a phrase-book. Let's have a look. Bloody languages. Why can't everybody talk in English!

MARCO. Sorry!

GLORIA. Just a minute. I'm looking, OK? Ah! What about '*Lei e molto bella, signor!*' Was that right?

MARCO. *Molto bello! Io? Tu parli bene italiano – ma non è vero.*

GLORIA. Fucking hell!

MARCO. Fucking?

GLORIA. Yeah! Fucking! Know what I mean. What the fuck's the word for fucking?

MARCO. *Che cosa vuoi?* I no understand. You are . . . ah! *Non capisco. Come faccio? Che cosa dici?*

GLORIA. Shit! This is a real waste of time! You want to come home with me after here, yes? My place? Understand? Fucking? You know – sex!

MARCO. Ah! The sex – you want, eh?

GLORIA. 'Course I fucking want it. What do you think we were doing in the loo – having English lessons?

MARCO. Please – the book!

GLORIA. Yeah, why don't you have a go, dear.

MARCO. *Mi dispiace ma sono stanco, molto stanco.* I am – tired, please.

GLORIA. Not half as tired as I am, love!

MARCO. *Capisci?* You understand?

GLORIA. I understand the brush-off in bloody *Chinese*, dear. Don't you worry!

DORIS. Hello, Gloria. I wondered where you'd got to.

GLORIA. Fuckin' 'ell, Doris. I've got a right one 'ere.

DORIS. Hello, Marco.

MARCO. Ah! *Che bruta!*

DORIS. You what? What did he say, Gloria?

GLORIA. Don't ask me, dear. I've just had half-an-hour of it! Trust me to jerk off a bloody 'Eye-tie'! Who've you been up to?

DORIS. This fabulous black guy. He was so fuckin' big. And we

120

had to wait hours for a lock-up. It's so crowded down there! That vile queen from Mile End – the one with the eye-shadow, and fat bum – she was tarting around. Not a soul pissing; just standing around waiting for the lock-ups. Like that cottage in Clapham!

GLORIA. Which queen from Mile End?

DORIS. You know – the one with the purple nylon wig, and stuff. They call her Cilla Black at the Vauxhall. She puts her drag on in the cottage!

GLORIA. Oh, that little cow. She once got one I was *really* after. Bitch!

MARCO. You like drink – yes?

DORIS. Thank you very much! I'll have a Pils.

GLORIA. Yeah, I'll have a Pils too, Marco.

MARCO. Pils?

GLORIA. Pils lager. Just say two Pils. They'll know what you mean, dear, if they stop fucking about and serve a few down here. Do you know, Doris, I waited – it must have been nearly twenty bloody minutes – while she served queens who hadn't been waiting at all! They're so fucking full of themselves here. Twopence-halfpenny models, the lot of them. Picking and choosing as if they were God's gift. Queens!

DORIS. Oh, but this black guy, Gloria! Something else! I've never seen anything like it!

GLORIA. What do you mean, 'seen' dear? Sucked, more like!

DORIS. Gloria!

GLORIA. Well! That's what you did, isn't it?

DORIS. Actually, we did everything!

GLORIA. You dirty little bitch! You didn't!

DORIS. We did!

GLORIA. The state of you, Doris. One day you'll be found dead on the job in a fucking cottage.

MARCO. Pils.

GLORIA. Oh, he's actually got served. Little Marco! Well done, dear!

DORIS. *Grazie*, Marco.

MARCO. *Prego!* You speak Italiano?

DORIS. Oh no! Just the odd word, here and there.

GLORIA. She's been going to night-school, specially for you, Marco. Haven't you, Doris?

DORIS. There's no need to be nasty, Gloria. I was only saying thank you!

GLORIA. Christ! You've already had a clone, and a fucking black man, and now it's the 'Eye-tie'! Shall I ask everyone to form a queue? Slut!

DORIS. Right! That's it. I've had enough. I'm going to find Mavis.

GLORIA. Where's she?

DORIS. Down the cottage! Where do you think?

GLORIA. Well, hang on a bit. I'm coming. See you around, Marco.

DORIS. *Ciao*, Marco! Come on then. We might be missing something!

MARCO. *Ciao. Ciao. Che bruta!*

¶ SATURDAY: Bought a black PVC coat and hated it when I got back. Good for the rain, though, which hasn't stopped for days. No point in washing the hair, which is filthy and looks really good. Went to see Visconti's *L'Innocente*, which must be one of the best-dressed melodramas on film. Wonderful sad music, and the women devastatingly beautiful. Rainy afternoons should be spent in the cinema, or in bed with someone sleepy and handsome. Went to Ricky's party, which was better than I thought it would be. Met a cute guy from St Martin's who doesn't know whether he's gay or not. He's into Wagner and mythology, and looks like Puck. I banged on about why it's always better to wear black, and how people aren't mysterious enough. Actually he was like a scaled-down version of the guy from the Bell, which is probably why I was into him. After too much neat vodka, we left together and he came back. We kissed a lot, but nothing too complicated because he got a bit nervous. Still, it was nice to cuddle, and his body was like a dancer's — everything quite small and firm, and exactly where it should be! He's two years younger than me, and slept in my arms, which made me feel older for some reason. Life isn't so bad, after all.

THE STRAIGHT-ACTING QUEEN
MEETS SOME FOREIGN QUEENS

STRAIGHT-ACTING QUEEN. (I could just do with something to take home tonight. After missing the blond guy in the pub, it's almost a question of pride. How he could have gone off with that wizened old trendy is beyond me. I stand around, trying to work out whether I like him or not, and after too much bloody thinking I decide I do and he's already been nabbed by a monster. Next time I'll take first and think later! I wish Sam or somebody would turn up. Heaven's such hell when there's no one to talk to. Maybe I should have gone to that party in Old Street — I suppose they're all there, stoned out of their minds! I'm sick of all that. I can see Jeremy over there, pretending he hasn't seen me — queen! God! I remember him when his only sex was with porn mags! Still, once you're a regular on the bar and club circuit, it's only a matter of time before something gets spoiled, and little queeny techniques take over where there used to be charm and shyness. Thank God it's never happened to me, although I was never shy to begin with. Pretending you haven't seen a friend — pathetic! It's a different story if there's no one else around — he's all over you then, as if no one else existed! Look at him — craning around. Who's he with? Shit! He's got that big American I liked. What a pain!)

SAM. What are you standing around looking pissed-off about?

STRAIGHT-ACTING QUEEN. Hello, Sam.

SAM. One of those rockers just tried to pick me up. Crazy!

STRAIGHT-ACTING QUEEN. They look really good, though. Great jackets!

SAM. Yeah! Too pissed, though, and I bet they're into wee-wee and things like that.

STRAIGHT-ACTING QUEEN. Well, you're not proud, are you? It's only water!

SAM. Dirty water, you mean. Honestly, the thought of it makes me feel ill! And they probably bash you about a bit, so the whole thing would be a bit risky.

STRAIGHT-ACTING QUEEN. What are you up to?

SAM. Just some boring part in a one-acter – it's Shakespeare next term, though, so that's all right.

STRAIGHT-ACTING QUEEN. I'm sick of college, actually. I made quite a good black suede jacket for the assessment, but the fucking sleeves went wrong and I can't find any more suede the same. It would be fantastic, though – one silver buckle at the front, and one slung across the back, at the waist. Simple. Original. Stylish. But I've fucked it up!

SAM. Have you heard about Jeremy?

STRAIGHT-ACTING QUEEN. What about him?

SAM. He was picked up by some middle-aged dilettante, who's taking him to Monte Carlo.

STRAIGHT-ACTING QUEEN. Doesn't surprise me. He's no pride. None! Just uses people, then drops them like stones. He's over there, pretending he hasn't seen me, doing his 'Don't talk to me, I'm with a fabulous boy' bit. So incredibly rude!

SAM. I know, but I think the American guy is into Ben's new one.

STRAIGHT-ACTING QUEEN. Who's that?

SAM. I don't know his name. He's fantastically handsome, though. You've probably seen him in the Bell.

STRAIGHT-ACTING QUEEN. Is he here?

SAM. Sitting on the steps, over there. Can you see – drinking now.

STRAIGHT-ACTING QUEEN. Jesus! Ben's probably installed a nuclear warhead to ward off competition, though. It's not like him to risk a catch like that in public!

SAM. Oh, I don't know. He gets a kick out of everyone being after it. And why not? He's better than anything else here, except my French boy.

STRAIGHT-ACTING QUEEN. French boy? Where's he gone? If I know French boys, you'll probably never see him again. He'll get kidnapped or lost!

SAM. God! I hope not. He's here, anyway. Just coming. Pierre – this is Alex.

STRAIGHT-ACTING QUEEN. Hi!

PIERRE. *Bon soir!*

STRAIGHT-ACTING QUEEN. Does he speak English?

SAM. Hardly any. Can you speak French?

STRAIGHT-ACTING QUEEN. A bit. *Ça va?*

PIERRE. *Bien, merci. Parlez-vous Français?*

STRAIGHT-ACTING QUEEN. *Un peu, mais trop mal pour les mots!*

PIERRE. *Mais non, monsieur. Vous parlez bien.*

SAM. I only know '*Je t'aime*', but it seems to work. And a bit of Molière we did at college. He keeps saying I'm beautiful, which sounds really cute with a French accent!

STRAIGHT-ACTING QUEEN. You're so vain, Sam. One day you'll be a wrinkled old queen, and then what will you do?

SAM. I shan't live that long. And if I do, I'll be stinking rich. The only solution to age is fame and money. You certainly won't see me standing around in bars, looking at what I can't have, all sad and frustrated.

STRAIGHT-ACTING QUEEN. Sounds like me!

SAM. No, Alex. You just look angry and unapproachable. You should try smiling – it works wonders.

STRAIGHT-ACTING QUEEN. I hate it!

SAM. It must be very hard work. Gnashing teeth and foaming at the mouth.

STRAIGHT-ACTING QUEEN. Well, it's better than pretending to enjoy standing around this place. And it stops all the wankers trying it on, apart from the 'Cheer up' routine.

SAM. Sometimes, I wonder why you come here at all. It's as if you really want to have a bad time.

STRAIGHT-ACTING QUEEN. I like being on my own, that's all. And it's quite weird, just watching it all. They all look the same – most of them.

SAM. So what makes you so different? They probably think 'Look at that miserable wanker, all screwed-up and lonely!'

STRAIGHT-ACTING QUEEN. They can think what they like, Sam, if they can think at all.

SAM. Well, you're obviously in a bad mood, so maybe we'll go and talk to Ben and leave you to queen around in solitary grandeur!

STRAIGHT-ACTING QUEEN. Do what you like.

SAM. Sometimes you're so bloody superior, Alex, it's a wonder you breathe the same air as everybody else.

STRAIGHT-ACTING QUEEN. I don't.

SAM. Come on, Pierre. *Allons!* See you later, maybe!

STRAIGHT-ACTING QUEEN. Yeah! Maybe! . . . (I can't start getting into a bad mood again! If I'd got that guy in the pub, it would have been different. There must be something here worth some effort – apart from the guy with Ben. The French boy was quite cute – a bit immaculate, though. I hate all those expensive off-the-peg leather jackets. Can't say I feel too good in this bike jacket, though, with those rockers falling about. One of them will probably come over and start banging on about scrambling in the Isle of Man! Quite like this guy leaning next to the bar – nice arms, and quite straight-looking. Seems to be into the clean-cut bartender. Same sort of thing – Lacoste T-shirts and jockstraps! Good fucks, though. Just thick, that's all. The dark boy standing on his own is all right. Looks a bit lost. Probably another French queen. Could be Italian. I always end up fancying the language barrier, probably because it cuts out a lot of talk. At least they're not jaded London queens I've seen thousands of times before. He's nearly finished his drink. Maybe I'll ask him if he wants another – don't think about it, Alex, just do it! Otherwise, it's a bad mood and home alone. OK?) Can I get you a drink?

MARCO. *Scusi?*

STRAIGHT-ACTING QUEEN. *Birra? Vuole berre?*

MARCO. *Ah! Parla Italiano?*

127

STRAIGHT-ACTING QUEEN. *Un poco — non parlo bene Italiano. Parla Inglese?*

MARCO. I no speak English very good.

STRAIGHT-ACTING QUEEN. Sounds OK to me. *Birra?*

MARCO. *Si, grazie!*

STRAIGHT-ACTING QUEEN. *Prego.* It's hard to get served here.

MARCO. *Scusi* — hard?

STRAIGHT-ACTING QUEEN. *Tempo longo comprare birra, capisce?*

MARCO. *Ah, si!* Long time for waiter.

STRAIGHT-ACTING QUEEN. Exactly! *Bene!* Are you here in England on holiday?

MARCO. I am in England — yes? — *per la vacanza.*

STRAIGHT-ACTING QUEEN. How long for?

MARCO. *Scusi* — sorry?

STRAIGHT-ACTING QUEEN. *Quanto giorni nel Inghilterra?*

MARCO. Ah! — for one week. I go *sabato.*

STRAIGHT-ACTING QUEEN. (God! I think this is just a bit too like hard work. Maybe I'll just have a drink with him, and then move on! — *prestissimo!*) And where are you staying? Where's your hotel?

MARCO. Is at King's Cross.

STRAIGHT-ACTING QUEEN. Are you here alone, in England I mean?

MARCO. Alone? *Scusi* — my book.

STRAIGHT-ACTING QUEEN. (Phrase-book time! As if we had anything to say. Just another silent screw! Wouldn't mind Sam's French boy, though. At least I've got that O-level! Maybe I just give this one my number and then see if I can't do something about the French boy. Be good if I could find somebody who speaks English in this place!) I'll never get served here. I'll try downstairs, and come back. OK?

MARCO. *Scusi?* — sorry?

STRAIGHT-ACTING QUEEN. Downstairs. I go for *birra.* Then *ritorno.*

MARCO. *Si! Capisco. Ciao!*

DOWNSTAIRS

STRAIGHT-ACTING QUEEN. (That's more like it — the guy in the grey jacket, looking a bit dapper in his 'Rayban' shades. It's such a drag when they're always with friends, though! The usual boring thing of standing around trying to catch his eye; you can never work out whether they're friends, or sleep together, or what! Must be friends — they keep looking around to see what's worth having a little natter about. He looks bored, though. Why the hell do people stand around with nurds, wanting to escape but never getting it together? At least he can see my good side, and it's dark enough to look good down here. Everything's so obvious, really, and so exhausting! Why can't they just get the message, and spare us this tacky little drama of glances and smiles. It's OK as long as it's sexy and gets somewhere. It's when nothing happens, and it's just been time wasted and beers drunk. Ah! He's coming to the bar. Well, that's all right then!)

FRENCH QUEEN. 'Ello!

STRAIGHT-ACTING QUEEN. (French! We've been invaded.) Hi! Can I get you a drink?

FRENCH QUEEN. Please, I would like an orange juice!

STRAIGHT-ACTING QUEEN. Is that all!

FRENCH QUEEN. Oh yes! I don't drink, actually. I don't like it.

STRAIGHT-ACTING QUEEN. I see. Very sensible.

FRENCH QUEEN. Sometimes. At Christmas, maybe.

STRAIGHT-ACTING QUEEN. I thought all the French were drinkers.

FRENCH QUEEN. Not really, actually. Not like you English, with your beer and fish and chips!

STRAIGHT-ACTING QUEEN. Do you come from Paris?

129

FRENCH QUEEN. Yes, actually. You have been there?

STRAIGHT-ACTING QUEEN. A few times, yes.

FRENCH QUEEN. You like?

STRAIGHT-ACTING QUEEN. It's very beautiful. I prefer the South, though.

FRENCH QUEEN. The sun, yes? I like very much the sun. It never shines in England. That is why you are all so white – you say white?

STRAIGHT-ACTING QUEEN. Pale, you mean. Well I suppose we are!

FRENCH QUEEN. I like this. You are a bike-boy, yes?

STRAIGHT-ACTING QUEEN. Well, I don't actually have a motor-bike. The jacket was given to me by a friend.

FRENCH QUEEN. Ah! Is an image, yes? You don't speak like the leather queen, actually. But your look is very –

STRAIGHT-ACTING QUEEN. Scruffy? Untidy – yes? *Comme mon âme!*

FRENCH QUEEN. *Votre âme.* You are very strange. What is your name?

STRAIGHT-ACTING QUEEN. Alex.

FRENCH QUEEN. You are English?

STRAIGHT-ACTING QUEEN. Of course. What's your name?

FRENCH QUEEN. Gérard.

STRAIGHT-ACTING QUEEN. You are very beautiful.

FRENCH QUEEN. *Merci* – but why do you say so?

STRAIGHT-ACTING QUEEN. What?

FRENCH QUEEN. Already, you are saying I am beautiful. You are very fast!

STRAIGHT-ACTING QUEEN. Not really. Just saying what I think, that's all.

FRENCH QUEEN. Your eyes are beautiful. But I think you are a little frightening. It is an image, yes?

STRAIGHT-ACTING QUEEN. I suppose so. What are you doing tonight, anyway?

FRENCH QUEEN. I am with my friends.

STRAIGHT-ACTING QUEEN. Ah!

FRENCH QUEEN. But I can stay with you, if you like.

STRAIGHT-ACTING QUEEN. Whatever you want.

FRENCH QUEEN. Well, if you don't like, I can go back to my friends.

STRAIGHT-ACTING QUEEN. I'd like you to stay – all right?

FRENCH QUEEN. Yes. OK. Where do you live?

STRAIGHT-ACTING QUEEN. Islington. It's not that far.

FRENCH QUEEN. OK! Now a drink, yes?

STRAIGHT-ACTING QUEEN. Yeah! Why not!

NARCISSUS MEETS A STRAIGHT
MALE STRIPPER

NARCISSUS. Hi! Can I get you another drink?

STRIPPER. Eh?

NARCISSUS. Do you want another Guinness?

STRIPPER. No, it's all right mate. I've got to go.

NARCISSUS. You've got to go? Why? It's just a free drink. I mean, if you don't want . . .

STRIPPER. OK then. Cheers. Well, like I thought . . .

NARCISSUS. What?

STRIPPER. I say, I'm a stripper.

NARCISSUS. Really! You're a stripper! I see.

STRIPPER. I'm tryin' to get some work, see. I was in a gay pub earlier.

NARCISSUS. Oh really!

STRIPPER. Yeah! Well it's weird. This is the first club I've tried. Gay, I mean.

NARCISSUS. I see. Are you a good stripper? I mean, do you do it well?

STRIPPER. Eh? OK!

NARCISSUS. What on earth made you be a stripper?

STRIPPER. Money!

NARCISSUS. Money?

STRIPPER. Yeah! You're from the States, aren't you?

NARCISSUS. No, actually. I'm from Parson's Green.

STRIPPER. Yeah, but it's not English, is it?

NARCISSUS. What isn't?

STRIPPER. Well, you've got a bit of an accent then.

NARCISSUS. Yes. Where do you come from?

STRIPPER. South London. Streatham.

NARCISSUS. Streatham. I see. And now you've fallen on hard times and become a stripper, trying to get work in a gay bar. Yes?

STRIPPER. Yeah, well . . . I wish there was some women. Know what I mean? I mean gay boys, they try to be women, don't they?

NARCISSUS. Some do, I suppose.

STRIPPER. Actually this bloke I know – he's in the media – well, he's the fella who's going to put me in this film. Mud-wrestling. Well, he said there was sex in the dressing-rooms. You just grab one of the birds and fuck in the dressing-rooms. He told me a few things about London. I was in this club, see. Earlier on. And this bird, she says to me 'Give us a good strip and I'll give you a good fuck!' Well, I was pissed-up – well, I wasn't pissed. I'd had a few drinks, know what I mean? It was a posh place, you know. Anyway, I thought I'd send her up, so I says 'What kind of anus have you got?' It's only women in these clubs, see. They don't let men in. What do you do, then?

NARCISSUS. I'm a model.

STRIPPER. Oh, yeah? You into the American gear, then?

NARCISSUS. What? You mean clone gear?

STRIPPER. Dunno? What's that?

NARCISSUS. Checked shirts and 'taches. Like the guy over there. But I'm not into that.

STRIPPER. What you into, then? Body-building. The gym. All that lark?

NARCISSUS. Yeah! I do a work-out every day. I like it.

STRIPPER. Yeah! You look in good shape. Me – I used to do all that, you know, the bull-worker and all. But I never kept up with it.

NARCISSUS. You look OK to me.

STRIPPER. Oh, yeah. I'm in good nick. You've got to be – for the stripping. They won't have you if you've let yourself go.

NARCISSUS. Well, you haven't, have you?

STRIPPER. Well, the girlfriend wouldn't like it – see?

NARCISSUS. Right! Shall we just go round there?

STRIPPER. What, mate? Where?

NARCISSUS. The back of the stage. It's less crowded, behind the stage.

STRIPPER. What for, then?

NARCISSUS. I just thought . . .

STRIPPER. Yeah, well I don't know. I've done a few massages, like. But nothing else. Know what I mean? Not with another bloke.

NARCISSUS. Yeah! Well, it makes no difference to me. I mean, I've had as many straight guys as gay. It doesn't mean you're gay, does it?

STRIPPER. I'm not, am I?

NARCISSUS. It's nothing, really. Do you want some gum?

STRIPPER. No thanks! I've got some photos here. Do you want to see?

NARCISSUS. Sure!

STRIPPER. Well, they're for an agency. I've got this agent, see, but he doesn't get much work for me. But that's the smooth look, suit and tie job.

NARCISSUS. They're pretty good.

STRIPPER. And I had these done, too. Not dirty, like, but the guy said I needed a few nude photos for special jobs, like. Underwear — that kind of thing. They like to see a bit of cock. Anyway, that's them.

NARCISSUS. Have you got a hard-on there?

STRIPPER. Well, in-between like. The guy said you've got to make a point. If you've got it, that is. I didn't mind. So I take them around, to show the geezers in charge. They're all right, aren't they?

NARCISSUS. Fabulous!

STRIPPER. You done modelling, then?

NARCISSUS. Yeah. Quite a lot, really.

STRIPPER. Nude and all? I mean, porn stuff?

NARCISSUS. Once or twice.

STRIPPER. Well, why not? You're a good-looking bloke.

134

NARCISSUS. Thanks! Shall we go round there? I mean . . .

STRIPPER. If you like. But like I've said, I've done a few massages. That's all. Just a few massages.

NARCISSUS. And you're a stripper.

STRIPPER. Yeah – that as well.

NARCISSUS. Come on, then.

STRIPPER. All right. I can't like with a bird, though. Know what I mean?

NARCISSUS. What?

STRIPPER. Kissing. I can't do that, mate! Christ! There's a lot going on back here, yeah?

NARCISSUS. It doesn't matter. Nobody's looking. You just stand there while I – that's better, so I can get this one out. Shit! It's better than the picture!

STRIPPER. Yeah?

NARCISSUS. Yeah!

STRIPPER. I don't have to do anything. Is that it?

NARCISSUS. You can have this if you want. I don't know. Maybe you're too shy.

STRIPPER. Yeah. Maybe! I don't suck cock, mate – that would mean I was queer, wouldn't it?

NARCISSUS. Anyway, I'll just carry on. OK?

STRIPPER. If you like. Like I said, I haven't done it with another bloke. Not anything like this. Oh! Careful, yeah? That's better. Nothing like this. Just a few massages.

135

¶ SUNDAY: Sat around reading papers and watching TV. Jules left at tea-time, and I felt a bit sad as he wandered away in the drizzle. An empty, grey, drizzly Sunday somehow summed up the pointlessness of this brief encounter. Not pointless while it's going on, but afterwards the experience starts its new life as a half-remembered statistic. Anyway, I was still thinking about the Bell guy, and wondering whether he'd be there tonight, and what to wear, and how to start a conversation, etc., etc. . . . The extra hour before the pubs open is almost the worst thing about Sundays. I had a shower and washed the hair, which was a mistake. Maybe I should get it cut, though the last time I looked like a Russian dissident. I'm sick of looking like all the others, but it's a look that works as far as pick-ups are concerned. Since I started growing it, the success rate has gone down. Or perhaps it's me! I think I spend more time thinking and talking about my hair than I do about anything else. His hair was quite long, though. That's a sort of start. Had something to eat, against my principles, and wasted a couple of hours until it was late enough to go. Tried on virtually everything I possess, and chose the same old black look. Whatever else, it's comfortable and easy to relax in. The PVC would be a bad idea if he was wearing his. I decided I was looking OK, and arrived in a good mood. Ricky was there with a couple of cute career boys. It got quite crowded, and getting a drink took ages, which put me in a bad mood. Maybe they do it as quick as possible, but why can't they remember who's been waiting longest? I turned round with a pint, and there he was. Same clothes, expression, and just a million times more stunning than I remembered. And alone. Half a minute earlier and I could have bought him a drink. Shit! I hung around while he got served — a Coke — which took another age. Then he moved down to the dance-floor, so I followed. Standing in the shadow, on the edge, he looked angry and superior, and impossible to talk to! I stared a bit, then went to the loo. When I came out he was just on the left, so I asked him if he wanted a drink. Imaginative! The music was really loud, so he couldn't hear. Why does an opening line sound so bad when you repeat it? Anyway, he said OK, and I got a Pils and felt incredibly nervous. We moved away from the dance-floor, and he smiled for the first time. His name is Danny, and he's a freelance photographer and does some modelling. We talked about Robert Mapplethorpe, who he thinks is like Beaton only worse. He said he liked the black guys though, which made me feel like I wanted to be big and black! It was the skin, he said — like doe-skin. I kept thinking how I was going to ask him back, or would it be better to meet another time, or did he have a boyfriend. It was about 11 o'clock, so we must have talked about other things — England, I think, and what a dump it is, and how we're all meant to love it just the same — and I do! He says he wants to live in Paris for a year, because there's more interesting work, and French boys are so cute. That made me feel really odd, queasy somehow, although I reckoned I was as good as Paris could offer. He said English boys were boring, and I hoped I was an exception but didn't say so. I asked him what he was doing when the pub closed, and he said nothing really, just going home — Camden Town. Did he want coffee? No, he didn't. He had to work early tomorrow. So we swopped phone numbers, and he said he'd give me a ring. 'Tomorrow?' 'Why not!' He gave me a soft punch on the shoulder and said 'See you around', which pissed me off, although I felt really good. And after he'd gone I wished I'd walked him to the Underground, and felt angry and nervous — and lonely, which was somehow exciting and gave me a high. Ricky was still there, and we shared a taxi, me not talking much and him quite drunk.

TWO CLONES CRUISING

VERA. Mabel!

MABEL. Vera!

VERA. Where've you been dying, dear? They're organizing a funeral at the LA, with poppers instead of incense. All that's missing is that tired and rotten old body of yours! Drinky-poos?

MABEL. Cow! I've had 'flu, haven't I? And I've got a drink, thank you!

VERA. Well I hope you aren't looking for sympathy, dear, because you won't get it after what happened last week!

MABEL. When? What have I done now?

VERA. That gorgeous lumberjack from Canada. When we went cruising the zoo at Regent's Park. Remember? And you stole him from Aunty Vera. In front of all those reptiles!

MABEL. I never did! He looked very lonely.

VERA. This one had been cruising him for a good half-hour before you staggered in from the sea-lions, Mabel. You knew what you were doing, dear. But frankly, if she was willing to crawl into bed with a faded old pensioner like you, she certainly wasn't going to be my type. Teddy-bear cuddles, was it?

MABEL. Mind your own business! What I do is my own affair. I don't have to ask your approval.

VERA. Fucking hell! It's not as if I haven't put you in the way of some nice big butch numbers before now! Ingratitude, that's what I call it.

MABEL. Oh, come on Vera. Don't be horrid to me. Not tonight.

VERA. Why on earth not?

MABEL. Because I've put the wrong shirt on, and an opera queen tried to pick me up in the pub. So boring, too!

VERA. Opera now, is it? We are going up in the world, dear. I was going to tell you about an orgy in Fulham, but I'm not sure you deserve to know after stealing my lumberjack.

MABEL. Oh, go on Vera! I haven't been to one for weeks. Who is it? Anybody we know, or somebody new?

VERA. New! It's been around so long it's got 'Used' tattooed on each cheek!

MABEL. You don't mean Patsy?

VERA. Who else?

MABEL. I thought she'd had another nervous breakdown.

VERA. She's recovered, dear, so she can have another one after the orgy. Anyway, it's next Saturday night. Bring your own cans, and a wet-suit.

MABEL. But I haven't got a wet-suit.

VERA. Well, a roll of cling-film will do. I thought I might take the bus driver, that one we found in the Vauxhall that night, with the rug and biceps.

MABEL. But he was mad, Vera! Didn't he make you wear a corset and pose all night, with just a corset on, playing with yourself?

VERA. Well, what if he did? Think what he might do at an orgy. It could look like the Ziegfeld Follies! You'd like that, wouldn't you Mabel? It's your period, isn't it?! You could bring the opera queen!

MABEL. Thank you very much, but I don't think I'll come.

VERA. Why ever not?

MABEL. Well, to tell you the truth, Philip's arranging one, and I'm really cheesed-off about it, Vera. You know it's his birthday.

VERA. I didn't, love, no! But Scorpios can be real heels. Is he a rat?

MABEL. You what?

VERA. Chinese horoscopes! He's probably a rat.

MABEL. I don't know what he isn't! All I know is I arrange to throw a dinner party, and now it's all spoilt because he wants to have an orgy. I think he's too young for me now. It was all

139

right in the beginning, but now it's just rows, and him going off and picking up the younger crowd. I feel out of place, Vera.

VERA. Mabel! I'd no idea. If you want my advice, let him have his fucking orgy, dear, and go to one on your own. I always said he was using you, just to get somewhere to live.

MABEL. But I love him, Vera. I love him.

VERA. More fool you, Mabel. Stop being a *try*-sexual, Mabel. Have some *suck*cess, like Vera does. You want to get out and do a bit of shopping on your own. Let your hair down, and get your act together. No wonder you pinched the lumberjack! I'd never have said if you'd told me all this about Philip. Has he stopped sex?

MABEL. Yes, Vera. He has. In fact, I can't remember the last time! I'm frantic. I really am! And I've started wanking again, after all these years.

VERA. Poor old Mabel! Whatever shall we do?

MABEL. Well, I'm not going without, dear. That's for sure! I quite like that American-looking guy over there. Very nice!

VERA. 'Ish!! Bit young for you, dear. I thought you'd had enough of fickle youth.

MABEL. If it's a one-off, fickle doesn't come into it, Vera. I want some fun, that's all.

VERA. Well, give it a whirl, girl.

MABEL. But I hate this shirt, Vera. Is it all right? I need some reassurance, Vera. It's not too bad, is it?

VERA. Fuck the shirt, dear! If you play your cards right, it won't be on for more than an hour. Off you toddle, love. Aunty Vera will be up here, if there's a cock-up. Well — if there isn't a cock-up!

SCOTT. Hi!

MAVIS. Mind if I join you?

SCOTT. No sir!

MAVIS. You're American, aren't you?

SCOTT. Sure am.

140

MAVIS. Whereabouts do you come from?

SCOTT. New York.

MAVIS. Oh, I love Manhattan. London must seem very slow and boring in comparison.

SCOTT. Yeah! It's tamer than Manhattan. This place is good, though. Crazy!

MAVIS. It's a shame you missed the Subway, but it closed down.

SCOTT. Yeah, I heard about that from a guy who came over last year. That was meant to be a heavy scene, yeah?

MAVIS. It was, if you go for that sort of thing. Some queens thought it was too dirty, but that never bothered me. Mind you, I never went that much. But my other half loved it. He likes it in the dark. Says it makes him feel randier — the atmosphere. It's so nervy and dangerous, like. Well, it was! He liked it a lot.

SCOTT. Yeah?

MAVIS. It was so easy, you see. You could just go in the back room and get your rocks off, and that was that. No standing around enjoying a long romantic build-up. As long as you were in denim or leather. They wouldn't just let anybody in.

SCOTT. I guess not. We've had all that in Manhattan for years, though. You heard of the Mineshaft? Or the Anvil?

MAVIS. Oh, yes! I never went to them, though. Somebody took me to the Cell once. He was a Centaur or something — you know, those bike clubs. Trouble with us is we're all a bit backward here. What are you doing in London?

SCOTT. Studying.

MAVIS. You're a student, are you? I thought you might be an American footballer, or something. I mean, you're not small!

SCOTT. Well, I guess I was built on the big side. I play baseball at college.

MAVIS. I like a guy who plays sport. I mean, it keeps you in shape — trim. When you're not getting any younger, it's important to get a bit of preservation together.

SCOTT. Come on, man! You're not that old.

MAVIS. Well, I say I'm thirty-seven but actually I'm forty. I don't think I look it, though. Do you?

SCOTT. No, man! Not forty. No way.

MAVIS. You must be – now don't tell me. I want to guess. I'd say twenty-five, maybe twenty-four.

SCOTT. Twenty-four. I guess you think that's young, yeah?

MAVIS. A baby! I can remember twenty-four. I was still in the closet, selling insurance. A lot's happened since then. What's your name? Mine's Gordon.

SCOTT. I'm Scott. Glad to meet you, Gordon. I guess I'll be moving on, now.

MAVIS. What? You're going? But I was going to buy you a drink!

SCOTT. Another time, maybe.

MAVIS. Well, can't we arrange something? Have you got a number?

SCOTT. Well, that's kind of hard. There is a phone, but it's public like. I guess it's better to maybe run into each other here sometime.

MAVIS. But I'd like to spend some more time with you, Scott. Can't we meet for a drink? Tomorrow, say!

SCOTT. I guess you're not getting my drift, man.

MAVIS. What do you mean?

SCOTT. Like, I'm not interested. OK?

MAVIS. You mean – that's it? Just like that!?

SCOTT. It was good talking to you, but that's all there is to it. See you around, maybe!

MAVIS. Yes! See you around – maybe!

MABEL. Well, what can you do?

VERA. Never mind, Mabel. Plenty more fish in the sea. He wasn't your type, dear. Much too young. What you need is an older man; the experienced type. A doctor, or something. Somebody strong, Mabel, not a fresh American college boy with clean teeth and green gills.

MABEL. But he was big, Vera. And young. I just fancied him, that's all.

VERA. And what did he do, dear? He told you to piss off!

142

MABEL. He didn't at all. He said he wasn't interested — that's what he said. And it hurts, Vera. I mean, do I look like I'm prehistoric or something? My face is not bad, and I've got the tummy more under control.

VERA. Maybe he hates the moustache, dear. Some queens just aren't man enough to know what a moustache is — what it can mean to another man.

MABEL. Well, whatever it means, it didn't mean much to him, did it? What I don't understand is, we were getting on quite well. Do you know what I mean? Talking about things. A real conversation. Then suddenly he's going and I'll never see him again, Vera. It's not fair.

VERA. Always stick with your own kind, Mabel. I've told you before. Philip might be footloose and fancy-free at the moment, but at least he's yours, dear. He's going through a phase. And it's not as if you haven't had some on the side. Everybody does. And why not? It's only natural.

MABEL. But I want something else.

VERA. Listen, Mabel. You want sex. That's what you want. Well, it's all over the place, just there for the taking. Get your act together. Don't waste time talking about the weather. Get out there and squeeze a few balls. You'll be surprised how easy it is. There's not much here, mind. Just a lot of little trendies. Find a man. A real man!

MABEL. Sometimes, I think I've forgotten how to do it. I just don't seem to be able to pick them up any more. And it's not as if things don't turn me on. They do: bums, oily denim, forearms. I feel starved of them all!

VERA. Get a new face-cream, dear! Buy some nice new pants, and take a weekend in Amsterdam. That's a recipe from Aunty Vera which has never failed.

MABEL. You're probably right. Maybe I'll renew my membership at the Y.

VERA. Exactly. Get out, see new faces, meet people. That's what the gym's for.

MABEL. But Philip's always there. He'll think I'm trying to keep tabs on him.

VERA. Let him see you enjoying yourself, Mabel. Ignore him. Smile a lot, and make friends with a body-builder. There's nothing like a bit of jealousy to liven things up.

MABEL. But he's had all the body-builders!

VERA. Have a few yourself, Mabel! Give yourself a break, and have a muscleman. Now there's a well-made man, standing over there by the wall.

MABEL. Where?

VERA. There! In the red and green check. Lovely beard. Come on, Mabel. Let's get over there, and see if we can't do a bit of grievous bodily harm. But don't smile too much, dear. He might think you're a bit soft. Try the strong, silent approach. I'll just melt into the background — once you've made contact. Oh, Mabel! Look at him! Now that's what I call a real man. And Aunty Vera's being a good girl, and giving him to you on a plate. Look at those hands! They're what I call man-handlers. Get in there, chuck!

MABEL. Hi! I'm — oh, I'm sorry. I didn't mean to tread on your foot.

MIKE. Walk all over me! Tread on my balls!

MABEL. Well, that's what I call being direct. What's your name? I'm Gordon.

MIKE. Mike!

MABEL. Suits you. You look like a Mike.

MIKE. Yeah? What's a Mike look like, then?

MABEL. Well — like you do. Like a real man. Tall, dark, silent.

MIKE. That's me!

MABEL. Do you want a drink, Mike?

MIKE. Get me Colt. In the can, yeah?

MABEL. Sure! Don't run away, now.

MIKE. I'm not running anywhere. OK?

MABEL. Won't be long, Mike.

MIKE. Great!

144

VERA. Well?

MABEL. I thought you were supposed to melt into the background. That's what you said.

VERA. Fucking hell, dear! Didn't Aunty arrange it all? You're just a little bit ungrateful, Mabel. It spoils you. Do you know that?

MABEL. He's called Mike.

VERA. That's a nice name. What does he do?

MABEL. We haven't got that far, yet. Can of Colt and a lager. Thanks!

VERA. What has he said?

MABEL. He's not much of a talker, actually.

VERA. The silent type, eh? I knew from the moment I saw him. Strong! Silent! Oh, I can't wait to hear what it was like! Just don't let the side down, Mabel. Aunty Vera will be expecting a blow-by-blow account.

MABEL. You don't think we'll come to blows, do you Vera?

VERA. You never can tell, dear. Now off you go. And don't do anything I wouldn't do.

MABEL. I'm back.

MIKE. Yeah! Ta!

MABEL. How can you chew gum and drink at the same time?

MIKE. Just can.

MABEL. Don't you get tired? Chewing, I mean.

MIKE. No!

MABEL. Oh! Didn't you used to go to the Subway? I'm sure I've seen you before somewhere.

MIKE. That's right. Nothing's been the same since the Subway.

MABEL. I never went much, myself. You liked it, I suppose.

MIKE. Loved it. Easy sex, and lots of it!

MABEL. Well, there's no answer to that. I don't suppose you want to dance?

MIKE. I want a fuck!

MABEL. Don't we all! Where do you live, Mike?

MIKE. Earl's Court.

MABEL. That's nice and convenient. I suppose you go to the Coleherne a lot.

MIKE. Yeah!

MABEL. I haven't been for ages. Is it still the same?

MIKE. They've done it out. God knows why! But it's the same crowd.

MABEL. Cruising on the pavement after time. That was the best thing about the Coleherne. Not like the Subway, though.

MIKE. No!

MABEL. What are you doing tonight?

MIKE. Tonight? Tonight I'm taking you home and fucking you till one of us drops. OK?

MABEL. Well, I'm not sure about the dropping bit, but the rest sounds OK.

MIKE. Right then. Up yours!

MABEL. Cheers!

Ben's Diary

¶ MONDAY: Felt confused all day. Wanted to go out and wander, but kept thinking he would phone. He didn't. I should get an ansaphone for things like this! In the evening I sat around watching TV and trying to work out something to say when (and if) I rang him. After dithering about, I rang. No reply. Obviously I couldn't go out in case he rang later. Anyway, I didn't want to. What's the point when you're thinking about somebody in particular who won't actually be there? Rang just before going to bed, but still no reply. I feel as if I've got stomach-ache when I haven't.

A MIDDLE-AGED TRENDY HAS
SOME LUCK WITH KEVIN FROM
LEEDS

ADRIAN. Hi, hi, hi!

KEVIN. Hello!

ADRIAN. That's a nice furry haircut. Can I stroke it?

KEVIN. You what?

ADRIAN. Can I have a little stroke?

KEVIN. I suppose so. If you want.

ADRIAN. Mmm! Furry, furry, furry. Like a little rat!

KEVIN. Do you mind! I don't like being called a rat!

ADRIAN. What do you like being called, then?

KEVIN. Me name's Kevin. What's yours?

ADRIAN. Adrian. Are you just passing through, then?

KEVIN. You what? I live 'ere.

ADRIAN. But you don't come from London, do you?

KEVIN. I come from Leeds, actually.

ADRIAN. Leeds! No wonder you've come to London. And what do
you do, Kevin?

KEVIN. Not much. I haven't got a job yet, but I want to be a
model.

ADRIAN. A naughty one?

KEVIN. 'Course not! Do you know any models?

ADRIAN. A few, yes! Maybe we can sort something out. I could
ring a few people up, do you know what I mean? Try and sort
something out for you. We'll need to get you photographed,
but I can do that, or get someone to do it. We'll see who's
around.

KEVIN. I've got some photos me boyfriend took, but you seem to
know all about it. I can't afford to pay, you know!

ADRIAN. Well, we'll sort something out.

KEVIN. What do *you* do, then?

ADRIAN. I'm a painter – among other things.

KEVIN. A painter? You mean pictures and stuff?

ADRIAN. Well, I'm not a decorator!

KEVIN. Are you famous, then? I bet you are!

ADRIAN. Not really.

KEVIN. I've never met anybody famous before. Have you been on the telly?

ADRIAN. A few years ago, yes.

KEVIN. You don't look rich, though!

ADRIAN. I'm not! Artists aren't rich, you know. They starve.

KEVIN. Starve? You look a bit fat to me! I bet you're quite old, aren't you?

ADRIAN. Thanks, but I'm not that old!

KEVIN. You look older than anybody else. I'm not being rude, but you do!

ADRIAN. Well, I'm still capable of doing the odd thing, do you know what I mean?

KEVIN. Sex, you mean? Dirty old man!

ADRIAN. I'm not that old. Only forty. It's not so incredible, is it?

KEVIN. Well, you're an old trendy, aren't you? I mean, your clothes are really trendy. Are you trying to look young or something?

ADRIAN. You're a bit personal, aren't you?

KEVIN. What do you paint, then? Modern stuff, I bet. Have you got any people in 'em – these paintings?

ADRIAN. 'Course they have – boys, mostly.

KEVIN. Are they dirty, then? I bet they 'aven't got any clothes on, 'ave they?

ADRIAN. As a matter of fact, they haven't. That's the point.

KEVIN. Do you 'ave models, then? Is that why you came up to me? I bet it is! Well, I'm not taking me clothes off for no bloody painter, I can tell you that. Not if you paid me!

ADRIAN. I wouldn't.

KEVIN. Thanks very much! I wouldn't mind a drink, if you're offering!

ADRIAN. All right. In a minute.

KEVIN. Do you come 'ere a lot?

ADRIAN. Only on Thursdays. It's best on Thursdays.

KEVIN. Well, it's trendy, isn't it? And there's lots of boys – that's why you come 'ere, if you ask me. Looking for boys to do modelling and things for you.

ADRIAN. Believe it or not, some boys actually come up and talk to me.

KEVIN. Just because you're famous, that's why. They wouldn't if you weren't, you know. They're just impressed. That's all. I bet they don't fancy you. Any of 'em!

ADRIAN. You'd be surprised, actually. Boys have been known to sleep with me!

KEVIN. Some queens will sleep with anybody. Everybody knows that. I bet you promise all sorts to get 'em into bed. You don't fool me. Like all that stuff about getting me photographed, and knowing models and things. It doesn't fool me. You're just a bullshitter, you are!

ADRIAN. Actually, I meant it, Kevin. But if you don't want, then I shan't bother. What makes you so rude? I don't understand it!

KEVIN. Well, if you must know, I'm sick of queens promising this and that! I've been in London a few weeks, and you all talk a lot of rubbish. Just trying to get me into bed. Nobody really cares about you down 'ere. You're all a lot of lying phoneys. Painting! I bet it's a load of rubbish. You're probably a bloody bus conductor!

ADRIAN. Well, I'm sorry you don't believe me, but it's true. You could come back and see, if you want.

KEVIN. What else do you do? You said you did other stuff as well.

ADRIAN. Oh, photographs, films and things.

KEVIN. Really? You do a lot, don't you? I could be a star, you know! I've always wanted to be in the films. Hollywood, and all that! Anyway, Eric – that's me boyfriend – well, he says I'm better-looking than a lot of pop-stars. I wouldn't mind being a pop-star either. There's a lot of money in it, you know.

150

I've always fancied Sting, actually. He's my ideal. Really gorgeous! I like blonds. Always have.

ADRIAN. He's all right. I've met him.

KEVIN. You haven't! Really? Oh, I'd die! What's he like? I bet he's really sexy, close up. Who else 'ave you met? I never thought I'd meet somebody who knew real stars!

ADRIAN. Drink, drink?

KEVIN. If you're offering. A Pils, please. You're quite interesting, really! Except you're a bit old. Do you like me, then? I mean, do you fancy me? I bet you do! I don't mind, you know. I can take care of myself. Are you butch or bitch? Not that I'm interested!

ADRIAN. I'd like to take you home and cuddle you, Kevin. It's this furry little head. I just want to stroke it and stroke it. And we could watch a video, and have a joint.

KEVIN. Oh, I'd love a joint.

ADRIAN. Where's Eric, then?

KEVIN. He's working — at a pizza place. He's not coming out tonight. We 'ad a row, you see. Well not so much a row as a fall-out. I spent me dole, and he wanted the rent. Well, I'm hopeless with money. So we fell out. It's hard sharing a room. You get on top of each other, you know. And I don't want him to go off me. Well! You've got to have a boyfriend, haven't you?

ADRIAN. I can lend you some money if you like.

KEVIN. Oh, I couldn't. I don't know when I could pay you back, and you always get into trouble when you borrow. I stole twenty quid off me mam when I came down to London! Terrible, isn't it?! Fancy you knowing Sting, though! I've got a poster. Could you get his autograph for me? I'd be ever so thrilled!

ADRIAN. I'm not sure about that! Furry little thing! A Pils, then?

KEVIN. Please! But don't think buying me a drink means I'll jump into bed with you, because it doesn't!

Ben's Diary

¶ TUESDAY: He rang. At lunchtime. Whatever else I did today I can't remember, except wanting to buy new clothes. We arranged to go to the cinema tomorrow, so I stayed in and wrote a long funny letter to Christian, telling him I'd fallen in love!! I wonder if I'll ever be able to say 'We've fallen in love.' Probably better not to dramatize, although it's hard not to. Had the first dream about him I can remember, in which we were in a school playground, surrounded by school-kids. We were sliding on a shiny strip of ice with snow everywhere.

ELSEWHERE, IN-BETWEEN TIMES

CRUISING AT THE OPERA

GEOFFREY. Hello! How are you?

FRIEND. A dream, dear. And you?

GEOFFREY. All right, I suppose. Not very well, to tell the truth. Still, you're looking well. Have you been away?

FRIEND. A weekend in Hull with lover-boy. Exercise and vitamins, all in one passionate parcel. Plus a dab of Estée Lauder, of course!

GEOFFREY. I can imagine! What do you think of this lot?

FRIEND. Well, apart from a divine figure of manhood sitting in the next row, I'd have left in the first interval. Ghastly! I don't know what she thinks she looks like, but a brown paper bag would be more glam than that faded bit of tinsel. As for the wig – like a mop of cold spaghetti!

GEOFFREY. And it's such a gift!

FRIEND. Oh, it's a fabulous part! I've been the Marschallin in more dreams than I can remember. Talk about drag queens. She looks like something out of the Vauxhall.

GEOFFREY. Well, she's getting on a bit, isn't she?

FRIEND. I thought she'd died! I couldn't believe it when I saw the cast-list! As for the orchestra. Talk about the pit – it's the pits all right!

GEOFFREY. And what about the entrance with the rose!

FRIEND. What about it! They just blew it! Totally blown. She was about four bars late, and looked like one of the ugly sisters! No poise at all. And I never like it when they stand too far away. And all that bowing and curtseying. It was like a PT class.

GEOFFREY. Did you see the Britten?

FRIEND. Can't stand him, dear. Never could! All twing and

155

twang, and hours before a tune. Nothing happens at all. Give me Verdi every time! I want all Verdi at my funeral. Chorus after chorus. Or just '*Va pensiero*' — very beautifully sung.

GEOFFREY. Where is he, then?

FRIEND. Who? — oh, the paragon. He's over there, with the pinstriped queen, who's obviously head-over-heels. Who wouldn't be, though? I just don't understand why he doesn't come straight over and give me a blow-job on the spot. The state of that one, dear. Talk about obvious — she's like a jubilee beacon. The crush-bar cruiser strikes again. I've never seen her talk to anyone — just lolling about, gawping at the multitude, like a praying mantis, thinking people fancy her when they don't. She goes to them all, you know. Wexford, Cardiff, Leeds — you name it! And when it's not opera, she's on the South Bank cruising Level Five in the Festival Hall, and tapping her foot through Mahler! Apparently she's into dildos, so someone told me!

GEOFFREY. Terrible skin!

FRIEND. That's not skin, dear. It's rubber. The elephant queen, that's what she is!

GEOFFREY. Are you going to the celebrity do?

FRIEND. I wouldn't miss it for the world, dear. Not for the world! All those Joanettes throwing puce tulips on the altar! Now he's a sensation! Near the bookstall!

GEOFFREY. I think he's with his wife.

FRIEND. Wife, daughter, drag queen! Who cares? They're all a smokescreen. You can tell that one's a bender, dear, from the collar and tie.

GEOFFREY. How's work?

FRIEND. Don't talk to me about work! If I get another nuclear family wanting two weeks in Ibiza, I'll unplug the computer or send them to Siberia. I'm always as rude as I can be, in between the smiles and 'Yes, madam' and 'Would madam like a double or single beds?' You'd be surprised how many of the older ones have a double. It's disgusting at their age! But last week I met this heavenly courier from Australian Airways.

Built like a sheep-farmer, and screwed like an animal. Bliss!
He wants me to go to Sydney in the summer, and meet his
folks and all that. Imagine! Still, if Rita's doing another
colossal Verdi, I just might. How's the shop?

GEOFFREY. Dreadful! I sold one three-piece last week, and two
bean-bags! I've asked for a move to cosmetics, but they like to
have women selling the after-shaves, so what can you do?

FRIEND. Just look at those diamonds! Look at them! She must be
rolling in it! Probably some international celebrity. She looks a
bit like Margaret Dumont, don't you think?

GEOFFREY. Some women are so camp, aren't they?

FRIEND. What! They're hysterical! Talk about camp, dear! Just
give me *Eleanor Steber at the Continental Baths*! Have you got
that album?

GEOFFREY. Oh, I've tried everywhere. Everywhere! Deleted now!

FRIEND. Oh God, yes! I found mine in New York, actually. Ten
dollars. I can't remember when I was so thrilled! Shall we have
a little troll upstairs? You never know what you're missing in
this place!

GEOFFREY. I love walking up this staircase. It's so Joan Crawford,
isn't it?

FRIEND. Isn't it just! So many foreign queens, aren't there? Look
at that Arab princess! The state of that nose! She'll bang it on
the chandeliers if it's stuck any higher. Silly queen!

GEOFFREY. I don't know why those leather queens can't hire a
suit, or something. It's just ridiculous, poncing around in all
that tat on a first night. Some people have no idea at all!
Imagine what it's like, sitting next to them sweating and
squeaking.

FRIEND. They certainly let the side down, dear. I've never liked it
myself. Give me a stiff collar and silk tie. The manly look –
that's what I go for. Some of these fish don't know how lucky
they are!

GEOFFREY. I know. I went to the pub in the first interval, and got
talking to this clone. He looked nice, actually, although I
don't usually go for that type. Anyway, he was so rude about

157

suits and ties, I just thought to myself 'Up yours, dear!' I mean, it's all the same between the sheets, isn't it? I've never believed in that obvious look. What's the point of walking about with 'Queen' stamped all over you? It's American, if you ask me. Marlboro and moustaches!

FRIEND. Well, I've always said that they grow 'taches because they're all big girls trying hard to be men. As if a moustache ever fooled anybody!!

GEOFFREY. Exactly! They just don't have any discretion. I suppose we should go in. God knows what the last act is going to be like! I think I'd rather listen to the records than this dreadful noise.

FRIEND. The old Kleiber, dear! Nothing can touch it. Mine's hardly got a groove left.

GEOFFREY. Shall I see you afterwards?

FRIEND. Why not?! We could go back to my place and have a little pasta and fresh fruit. Would you like that?

GEOFFREY. Love to!

FRIEND. Well then — at the bottom of the staircase, yes? Better fasten your seat-belt, dear. This one's going to be a bumpy ride.

THE STRAIGHT QUEEN AT
A DINNER PARTY
IN HOLLAND PARK

DORA. We thought you'd been mugged, darling! Whatever happened?

CHRISTOPHER. I'm awfully sorry, Dora, but I had so much to do in the library it was impossible to get to the gallery before eight-thirty, and by that time I thought it would all be over.

DORA. Nonsense! You've been drinking, Christopher. It's that glamorous agent of yours, plying you with gin. Bitch! I've never liked her, not since she stole Perry's idea for a book of the world's great exiles. And it was really my idea, like all his ideas. Now come and meet people. You know Cressida and Tim.

CHRISTOPHER. Hello.

TIM. Hi!

CRESSIDA. Naughty boy! Been discussing chapter revisions with Vanessa?

CHRISTOPHER. Just the order of the index, actually. We thought it might be fun to begin with 'W'.

CRESSIDA. Very funny, I'm sure!

DORA. Now, Cressida! Don't carp, dear, or Tim might let Perry have his evil way, and disappear to Firenze for a wicked winter break.

CRESSIDA. Stop stirring, Dora, and leave Timbo alone. Some men are completely straight, darling, not that *you* know very many!

DORA. Don't say I didn't warn you. I'm only trying to soften the blow, dear. After all, you do bore him dreadfully, and Wykehamists have been known to bend with a little encouragement. Haven't they, Tim?

TIM. Now look here . . .

159

DORA. Where, darling? What do you want to show me? Funny boy! Now this is Christabel, and that's Lulu, and the love-birds in the window-seat are Jasper and Rupert. Beautiful, aren't they?! Who have we missed? Oh, yes. Lucinda and Johnny, squabbling in the corner, and Hugo here, our cherub for the night. He has absolutely nothing to say, but I adore watching him eat! And finally — I nearly forgot you, darling — this is Willy, our sparkling columnist for the night. He's a bit of a shit, but you won't mind that, will you darling? You'll have forgotten all their names before the main course, so all of that was a complete waste of breath. Oh! I almost forgot. This is *Christopher*, everybody — our guest of honour, who had enough taste to ignore my little opening, and loves me for myself, and not my male nudes. Shall we go through?

CHRISTOPHER. This all looks very lovely.

DORA. You're here, darling. The rest are placed. Please start, won't you? I never eat artichokes myself. They're such a chore.

CHRISTABEL. Well, actually, I model gloves. Mummy thinks it's frightfully vulgar being in the glossies, so I compromised and we agreed on gloves. It's awfully lucky, really, because I bite my nails, which meant that close-ups were rather tricky when it was all of me. Now they're covered up, though, and nobody knows. It's my professional secret. All models have one, you know.

CHRISTOPHER. One what?

CHRISTABEL. Secret. Some of them are bald, would you believe it. Well, not quite bald, but wigged. And one girl has somebody else's legs.

CHRISTOPHER. Whatever for?

CHRISTABEL. Because she's so good up top! She was head and shoulders for a whole year, and a stunning success. And then Fiorucci wanted all of her, legs and all, so she had to borrow some.

CHRISTOPHER. I see.

CHRISTABEL. Do you like women's legs?

160

CHRISTOPHER. I'm sorry?

CHRISTABEL. Legs! Do you like them? Some men don't, you know. They prefer feet. Bisexuals always prefer feet. Don't ask me why. They just do, don't they, Willy?

WILLY. What?

CHRISTABEL. Bisexuals always like tootsies and instep. I was telling Christopher.

WILLY. Bisexuals like men and boys, don't they? And Mahler, too.

CHRISTABEL. Well, I suppose you ought to know, Willy. You're such an expert on the trendy gay set. Willy's writing an article about the gay glitterati for *Vogue*, aren't you darling?

WILLY. Whatever you say, Christabel. My terrible reputation is entirely in your hands.

CHRISTABEL. Ugh! How disgusting! I must go to the bathroom straight away, and scrub them.

WILLY. And don't forget to use the nailbrush, dear!

CHRISTABEL. Bitch! I don't think that's very funny.

WILLY. Actually, I'm surprised you took my meaning at all. It's the first time I've known you to be listening when anyone else spoke.

CHRISTOPHER. What exactly are the gay glitterati, if you don't mind my asking?

CHRISTABEL. Oh, Willy doesn't mind, Chrissy. He loves attention, don't you, darling?

WILLY. It's awfully nice of you to do all my talking, Christabel, but Christopher was probably hoping for some stimulation as well as female company.

CHRISTABEL. I can be very stimulating, or have you forgotten after all the gay boys?

WILLY. Such a sweet girl! I can't answer your question, I'm afraid, because 'what' is rather like 'who' at the top end of the gay social scale. It's utterly different from all those tacky queens hanging out in pubs and lavatories. I mean, there's just no comparison. The glitterati have a different lifestyle. Very up-market, actually, and mostly with a continental or

161

transatlantic bent.

CHRISTABEL. Very funny, Willy. Isn't he witty? What he's trying to say is *he's* a jet-setting fag, which means the gay glitterati are.

CHRISTOPHER. I see.

WILLY. One of these days someone's going to break your nail-bitten fingers, dear, and that will be the end of your sensational career. But until then perhaps you can devote a little attention to your salmon, or shall we talk about you and Cressida that weekend at Wimberry?

CHRISTABEL. If you dare, Willy, I'll call Xavier and tell him all about your running sores. He won't be very pleased when he discovers what he's probably caught by now.

WILLY. Bitch!

CHRISTOPHER. Have you been often – to Wimberry?

WILLY. Only for tennis and weddings! The last one was shamelessly grand, and Lady Fitzherbert told me the whole thing had cost her a small Renaissance doodle by school of somebody.

CHRISTOPHER. Do you know her well, actually?

WILLY. Well, when she's in town we have tea at Fortnum's, and I always go to Hardy's with her.

CHRISTOPHER. Hardy's?

WILLY. Amies. You know – frocks and fripperies. Have you met her? Lady Fitzherbert, I mean.

CHRISTOPHER. Oh heavens, yes! She's probably my mother's oldest friend. I'll have to tell her we met.

WILLY. Oh, I shouldn't bother, really. Just send her love from a secret admirer. That will amuse her. Although I *do* know her frightfully well. She likes mysteries, though, and secret admirers.

RUPERT. Do go on about the gay glits, dear. Jasper's longing to know if we're going to be in it, and can you get Snowdon for the portrait?

WILLY. I'm feeling rather tired, I'm afraid.

DORA. Don't be a spoilsport, Willy. I didn't invite you to be tired! You're here to be sparkling, and cruel, and perspicacious and . . .

WILLY. Thank you, Dora dear. I wouldn't dream of spoiling your soirée with a premature collapse. It's just that I forget we're all invited to amuse and entertain. Perhaps it's something to do with the riveting conversation at Hugo's end of the table!

DORA. Now don't be cruel to little Hugo. Just because he won't give you a cuddle. He's just not like that, are you darling?

HUGO. Sorry?

DORA. See! He's such an *ingénu*, he doesn't even understand what we wicked sexual perverts are talking about.

RUPERT. Of course he does. Jasper's hand has been on his right knee since the artichoke, and he hasn't flinched an inch, so he must be 'bi', mustn't he?

WILLY. It's when they flinch more than a few inches that you know you're getting somewhere, darling. An inch isn't very much to hang on to. You're just a tart, aren't you Hugo?

HUGO. Sorry?

WILLY. See!

DORA. Hugo's a sort of token straight for the gay glits, Christopher. In fact, he's the *ideal* type; the sort they love to be seen with. You know: nice muscles, good teeth, and a touch of the Michael Yorks. He doesn't even shave yet, do you darling?

HUGO. Sorry?

DORA. Show us your hairy chest, Hugo, there's a dear. Isn't he sweet? He just does exactly what I ask. Not like raddled old Willy here.

WILLY. That's because some of us have minds, Dora, not programmes.

DORA. I never knew you had a mind, darling. What a surprise. Is it a clean one?

WILLY. Compared to yours I should think it's spotless.

DORA. Unlike your poor complexion, Willy. You really should find a tame dermatologist, lovey. It spoils your Byronic good looks. Now *look*! Hugo's hairy chest — smooth as a baby's bottom.

163

RUPERT. Put it away, Hugo, for God's sake! You don't want Jasper to die of heart-failure, do you?

HUGO. Sorry!

JASPER. It's broken anyway, so death, where is thy sting!

RUPERT. Jasper's problem is introspection, you know. He's such a poetic creature. It was all that breast-feeding. That's what did it.

CRESSIDA. Mummy says breast-feeding boys turns them into queers. It's Freud.

DORA. Well, there you are. What do you think, Christopher? You're not saying very much.

RUPERT. It was probably Hugo's tits that stunned him into silence.

CRESSIDA. There's no need to be vulgar, Rupert.

CHRISTOPHER. Actually, I did think they were rather impressive. Very Greek!

WILLY. Hear that, Hugo? Our author thought your pectorals were a touch Attic, thou still unravished bride of quietness!

DORA. What do you think, Johnny?

JOHNNY. I think queers are all right, as long as they keep their filthy hands off me!

WILLY. Oh, Johnny darling! I don't think you're butch enough for most fairies. Is he, Lucy?

LUCY. He's butch enough for me, Willikins, so there!

WILLY. He must have good tools, then, knowing what a do-it-yourself queen you are, Juicy.

CHRISTOPHER. Actually, I think breast-feeding is terribly important. I was, and my son was.

DORA. And there's nothing wrong with you, Christopher dear. Not like Willy here. He's my token queen, you know. Rupert and Jasper don't count, because they're lovers and dreadfully boring. But Willy's my moody, pouting poove, aren't you darling? We do absolutely everything together, you know. Fashion shows, openings, book parties, first nights and last — not a cultural stone left unturned. He even took me to *Querelle*, didn't you dear? He was reviewing it for *Vogue*, you know.

CHRISTABEL. I was in that issue!

WILLY. Christabel, darling! We thought you'd gone to sleep.

CHRISTABEL. Willy did a piece about mummy and me looking alike. It was awfully witty, and said I was my mother's daughter.

DORA. *Very* witty, dear. Now go back to sleep, before we do! You're not saying much, Tim. Dreaming about Florence, are we?

TIM. Leave it alone, can't you?!

DORA. Tim's very much the heart-throb of the moment, with sweet old Perry fawning at his feet and inviting him out to the Palazzo every weekend. Christopher knows Perry frightfully well.

CHRISTOPHER. Actually, I haven't seen him since your last exhibition. Remember? He came with some extraordinary-looking boy.

WILLY. I remember. I was in my pink linen suit, and the little queen he came with told me I looked like strawberry mousse. He got him from an agency, you know.

CHRISTOPHER. What kind of agency?

WILLY. An escort agency, somewhere in Bond Street. Two hundred pounds to wear a pretty boy on your lapel for the weekend. Some of my friends do it when times are bad. You have to be exceptionally attractive, though. Like so many of my friends.

CHRISTABEL. Well, you couldn't do it then, could you, Willy. Always boasting about his handsome friends. They're the gay glitterati, if you really want to know. Zooming about in BMWs, clean-cut and big-bottomed, trying to carry off the straight look with expensive butch shoes. They don't fool a girl, though. It's the eyes. You can always tell.

CHRISTOPHER. How can you tell?

CHRISTABEL. Well, it's obvious. Look at yours and compare them with theirs. I mean, you're obviously straight, aren't you? You look one straight in the eye. But Willy there, he's a shifty looker.

WILLY. Thank you, darling.

CHRISTABEL. You are! I've never known you look straightforward. It's because secretly you're ashamed of what you are. Either that, or you're always on the look-out for something to pick up.

DORA. That's what it is, Christabel. You couldn't accuse Willy of shame. He'd have to have feelings for that to be possible, wouldn't you, 'heartless'.

CRESSIDA. But he's passionately in love with Xavier, the Spanish bull-fighter.

WILLY. He's not a bull-fighter, he's a film-star, and it's not love, it's lust with a soundtrack by Bizet.

CHRISTABEL. No wonder you've gone all spotty again. The Spanish omelette look!

CRESSIDA. Film-star! I've never seen him in anything!

WILLY. In Spain he is! You're so parochial, dear.

CHRISTABEL. You're such a snob, Willy. Don't you know any common waiters with wiggly bottoms?

WILLY. Of course I do! They're very popular with the glitterati, actually.

CRESSIDA. I suppose that's because the gay glits always eat in restaurants, and never at home.

WILLY. Exactly!

CRESSIDA. How perfectly pretentious! I thought you were all *cordon bleu* cooks, and threw grand dinner parties for duchesses.

WILLY. Sometimes we do, depending on what vegetables are in season.

CHRISTABEL. Queen! I'm sick of gay boys, actually. You can't go anywhere these days without finding well-groomed boyfriends crowding out the cocktail bars. It's disgusting!

WILLY. You never complain when you're taken, darling.

CHRISTABEL. Just to give you a bit of credibility, Willy. That's all it is. And they're all such snobs, sneering at everybody in sight.

WILLY. I suppose you've got the common touch, Christabel. I'll remember that the next time I've got a freebie for the opera. If

166

you like, we could go to the wrestling. Maybe that's more your sort of thing.

CHRISTABEL. What! And sit there while you feast your eyes on some revolting men, grunting and groaning? You must be joking! It's all pornography to you. Just like *Films and Filming* and all those other magazines you used to buy for the train to Cambridge. All soft porn, the lot of them. Not to mention reading the lonely hearts columns in *Time Out*.

DORA. Willy! I didn't know you were so desperate, dear. I hope you send a charming photograph, lovey. Nothing too spotty, I think!

RUPERT. He's looking for a gay-libber, I bet. Someone with healthy left-wing tendencies, and a social conscience.

WILLY. Don't be pathetic. Gay-lib is the most tiresome thing since women got the vote!

CHRISTOPHER. Well, actually, I think it's rather important. I mean, it's rather sad if people have to advertise for love, isn't it? I'm sure you wouldn't be so relaxed about it if you didn't move in the circles you do.

DORA. Christopher, darling! I always knew you were sympathetic to the cause.

WILLY. What cause? And what is 'it', may I ask? If you are referring to my homosexuality, I can tell you that Narcissism has been a great comfort over the last twenty-five years. And as for the cause, if you think I've got a drawer full of pink triangles, you're wrong. Some of us prefer to be unobtrusive and discreet.

CHRISTOPHER. But that's a privilege of the 'gay glitterati', surely? What about the poor creatures who have to flaunt it in order to attract what they want?

WILLY. I can't help it if some queens are ugly and sad.

CHRISTOPHER. Nor can they. I'm sorry, but I don't think that a group of trendy young media boys and girls eating fresh salmon in Holland Park can possibly grasp the problems which some homosexuals must have to face every day of their lives.

JOHNNY. Give 'em page three of the *Sun*, that's what I say!

LUCY. Oh, shut up Johnny! This is a serious discussion.

CHRISTOPHER. What I mean is that the gay glitterati, whoever they are, are just a group of rather snobbish types who believe in the power of money, and beauty, and power itself. Frankly, the smugness of it makes me sick! If only they were unobtrusive. Instead, they run everything.

DORA. Christopher, dear. Whatever's got into you? Willy's just a trivial little columnist, trying to cut a figure and make a reputation. He's not worth taking seriously, darling.

WILLY. Thank you, Dora, for that epitaph, but I think I can defend myself.

CHRISTOPHER. Of course you can't. All you can defend is your particularly fashionable and superior kind of homosexuality. And one sees it, even in advertising and so on. Beautiful women seem to have been ousted in favour of sleek young men, who aren't really one sex or the other. You can't defend yourself, because you're nothing more than a style, and rather a superficial one at that.

WILLY. Charming! Perhaps you should write my article. You seem to have thought about it rather a lot. I really do think all this is rather rude.

CHRISTOPHER. It's by no means more objectionable than your writing some trashy little article praising the smart gay set, and ignoring the fact that there is still intolerance and prejudice. You're simply in a position to ignore it. That's all.

CHRISTABEL. He only goes to the Hippodrome, you know. Nowhere else. Up-market queen!

CHRISTOPHER. I'm sorry?

WILLY. Oh, shut up, Christabel! Let's change the subject.

JOHNNY. Hear, hear!

DORA. Let's move on to pudding. Raspberry sorbet should cool us all down. Willy, darling, perhaps you'd lend a hand.

Ben's Diary

¶ WEDNESDAY: One of the really good days in my life, which sounds pretentious, but it was. Listened to bits of Wagner very loud all day, and kept joining in with the cymbal crashes! Took all my black things to the laundry, thinking it was better to look the same as I did on Sunday, only cleaner! Didn't shave. I think I look better with stubble, although Ricky always says I don't. After a last-minute dither about wearing undies or not, I got a taxi to South Ken, where the film was. *Loulou*. A romantic story about low life in Paris, and a very modern version of how sad things can be funny. Sitting in the darkness made me feel really randy, and I kept thinking of how I could touch him, and all that! I made do with putting my arm round the back of his seat, and he gave me a sort of smile as I did it. A bit pathetic, I suppose, but I could hardly start nibbling ears! Afterwards we went to Khan's and ate too much – at least, I did. He's just broken up with some guy he'd been with for nearly two years – a singer with some band I've never heard of. So he's a bit wary of boys and things. I said I'd never really had a boyfriend, and how hard I thought it was. He was surprised, which was quite flattering, I suppose. I couldn't tell whether all this was encouraging or not, and felt myself sinking into a sulk. Then he said he thought I was very different, and he was fed up with dummies who just wanted sex and didn't understand anything else. I asked what the singer was like – very beautiful, he said, but selfish and always throwing fits about where Danny went and who he knew. He said he hated jealous people, because they were always neurotic and crazy in a bad way, and destroyed things which otherwise might have survived. This made me feel nervous and almost guilty for some reason. I already feel jealous of a singer I don't even know, who's supposed to be out of the picture. Suddenly I gave a little speech about how he was the most attractive and interesting guy I'd ever met, and how I fancied him, but also liked spending time just doing straightforward things. I felt that saying all this was a big mistake, and sat there wishing he'd say the same to me. He lit a cigarette, and stayed silent for a minute or two. Then he said it was hard, when you've only met someone twice, to start talking about big things like love and all that. He said things need time, and can't just be invented. I thought this was the brush-off coming up, and prepared myself to feel really bad. Then he said he wanted to see me again; he didn't want to sleep with me tonight because that was too easy and just what people do, and it always turns into one-night stands which are depressing and pointless. God! I really wanted him to come home, and was going to make the speech about how we could just sleep together and do nothing – how that would be bliss. But I didn't. Instead I agreed, and we had coffee and left, quite silent and full of thoughts. It was cold and clear, which was a good thing. We shared a taxi, which dropped me off first. I couldn't think of anything to say except 'Ring me, or I'll ring you – yes?' He said yes, and we squeezed hands very hard for the longest couple of seconds in my life. Then I got out and watched the taxi drive away. When I got into bed I felt incredibly sad and happy, and fell asleep remembering his dark staring eyes as he sat opposite, lighting a cigarette. And the hands in the taxi.

ANOTHER BAR: THE CREATIVE
QUEEN AND THE SKINHEAD

QUEEN. Very busy in here, isn't it?

SKINHEAD. Yeah.

QUEEN. I don't know where they all come from, sometimes. Have you been here before?

SKINHEAD. No. I 'aven't been anywhere, really.

QUEEN. Just on a visit, are you?

SKINHEAD. Yeah. From Birmingham.

QUEEN. Oh! Well that's a big place. I like cities, myself. Wild, exciting places, with the bright lights and the night-life. I've lived here for four years now, and I love it. I wouldn't go back again. Not if I was paid, whatever!

SKINHEAD. Where to?

QUEEN. Truro! In Cornwall. Beautiful but dull as ditchwater. Nowhere to go, no one to see. Nowhere like this, that's for certain.

SKINHEAD. There's nowhere in Birmingham either.

QUEEN. Really? I would have thought in such a large city there would be places to go for the gay crowd. Surely!

SKINHEAD. Well, there are, but they're no good!

QUEEN. Ah, well! That's it, isn't it. The problem is that people expect too much. Take these people here. It's Saturday night, so half of them at least are on their 'night out' – the only one a week. And of course their expectations are much higher when they only come out once a week.

SKINHEAD. Yeah, they would be, wouldn't they?

QUEEN. What! They expect stars to shoot from their spheres, a total eclipse of the moon, and mad fabulous passion with the man of their dreams. Instead of the usual crowd, and a few drinks.

SKINHEAD. Well, it can be a bit different.

QUEEN. Of course it can. I mean, that's why we're here, isn't it. All hoping for that someone a bit special. Let's take you, for example. You must be on the lookout for a particular thing, being a sort of skinhead.

SKINHEAD. Not really. I mean, I'm only down 'ere for a few days. *Capital Gay* said this was the friendliest place in central London, so I came.

QUEEN. Quite right too. You've met me, and who could be more friendly? I don't stand around afraid to speak, like so many of these people who come out and look miserable. I like talking to other people; I mean, they're interesting aren't they – people. I just leap in with both feet, and see what happens. Whatever!

SKINHEAD. Yeah!

QUEEN. What's the point of going out otherwise! What do you do?

SKINHEAD. Nothing!

QUEEN. Well, what do you want to do?

SKINHEAD. Nothing, really.

QUEEN. In this life you've just got to decide on something, and go for it. And don't let anything or anyone stop you. It's the only way.

SKINHEAD. Yeah?

QUEEN. Absolutely. I was lucky I suppose, because I knew what I wanted to be right from the start. So I just concentrated on that.

SKINHEAD. What do you do?

QUEEN. Design. I'm a designer.

SKINHEAD. A designer! Designing what?

QUEEN. Anything, really. Clothes, smashed mirrors, metal men – sculptural things, really. Hats – sculptural hats. I've done quite a few of them.

SKINHEAD. Oh!

QUEEN. It's style, you see. Take this jacket. Its period or era is about 1967 I suppose, and it's dated. It doesn't date from

then, actually. I bought it off a friend last year. She makes
Sixties clothes, you see. But some styles last. That's what I'm
into. Finding a style that lasts. Whatever!

SKINHEAD. Yeah! That's right. It's all style, isn't it?

QUEEN. Absolutely. Of course I have to be in London to sell the
things. There's a lot of money here, I mean people are prepared
to spend a lot for something they want. If it's unusual they'll
pay for it.

SKINHEAD. Yeah! It's money really. You've got to have money.

QUEEN. Actually I run a nut shop at the moment – bread-and-
butter money, if you like. I hate it, but it's more money. The
hats don't give me that much. I mean two nights out a week,
and the rent – and that's about it. Even then I spend twice as
much as I should. Tolerant bank managers are a Godsend!

SKINHEAD. Must be! I 'aven't got a bank manager.

QUEEN. So you've got to decide on something you want to be, and
go out there and get it. Be it! 'Don't dream it, be it', as Jordan
sang.

SKINHEAD. I'll do anything and anyone!

QUEEN. I beg your pardon?

SKINHEAD. I said I'll do anything and anyone. Know what I
mean?

QUEEN. I think I understand. Yes! But it's so important to
decide.

SKINHEAD. Yeah, it's all right for you. I mean, you run a shop,
and these other things. I mean, you've got money. You don't
know what it's like, working at a lousy job for lousy pay.

QUEEN. Well, I've had my problems. We all do.

SKINHEAD. Yeah! But it's going all right now, yeah?

QUEEN. I suppose you're right. But it's work, really. Hard work.

SKINHEAD. Yeah, I'm not saying it isn't.

QUEEN. It's the name. You've got to make a name for yourself.
Especially in design.

SKINHEAD. Yeah, well a name makes money these days, doesn't
it? I mean, it's the name that counts.

QUEEN. Absolutely. Mind you, some of the things I've done – I look back on them with horror. How could I have designed that, I think. I can't bear the thought of my name on them. It's funny, really, but I just can't stand some of the things — early work.

SKINHEAD. I don't think the skins would go for your sort, though.

QUEEN. What? The skins. Oh no, I don't think they would.

SKINHEAD. They'd probably kick you in, wouldn't they?

QUEEN. Well, I've only ever been mugged once. Not mugged, really. But hit — you know. I was in a chip shop with three ladies, and when I left there were three boys, and one of them I fancied — you know what I mean. Anyway, I've never been one for not looking at what turns me on, so to speak. So I turned round and looked in his direction. Suddenly they were all on top of me, screaming 'poof' and all that. But you should have seen the ladies. They just rushed out of the shop and floored them. They were so surprised.

SKINHEAD. Yeah. Women can be strong when they want to be.

QUEEN. And I just looked at him, thinking 'that's shattered your ego, dear'. Would you like a drink? Gin and tonic?

SKINHEAD. No. It's lemonade. I'll 'ave another lemonade.

QUEEN. A Pils and lemonade, please. Separately, thank you.

SKINHEAD. It all comes down to money. If you've got it, you can get on.

QUEEN. One pound ten? There we are. What? — oh, I'm so sorry, I thought it was a twenty. Voilà. Ten. Thank you so much. One lemonade!

SKINHEAD. Ta!

QUEEN. You've got to sit down somewhere quiet, on your own, and work it out. What you want to be.

SKINHEAD. I dunno.

QUEEN. I'm handing out words of wisdom again, aren't I? Must be the drink! Still, it's important. You've just got to get an act together.

174

BEHIND A PUB BAR

KATE. America? Well, that's nice. Whereabouts? Oh, Chicago. I always fancied being a gangster's Moll! Two pounds, please. Thanks.

BLANCHE. You're very friendly tonight, dear. What's going on!

KATE. They're foreigners, from America. Here to see the sights.

BLANCHE. Well, they haven't seen me yet, dear.

KATE. I said the sights, love. Not the ruins!

BLANCHE. Thank you very much. Keep your mouth shut, Blanche! Catty Kate's at it again.

KATE. Well, why shouldn't I socialize with the customers if I want to?

BLANCHE. It's such a surprise, dear. That's all. After last night's moodette, I thought we might be in for a week of bad weather.

KATE. Listen, Blanche. If you'd done the fuckin' ashtrays like you were supposed to, I wouldn't have been in a mood at all. Instead, you just cruised that queen in the tracksuit, while I served all and sundry, as well as having to go out and do the fuckin' ashtrays. It's not fair. And you're at it again.

BLANCHE. I'm not cruising anybody. I can't help it if she's got a fit of the stares, can I?

MILDRED. Come on you two. There's people waiting over there.

BLANCHE. Fuckin' 'ell. Slavemaster rides again.

MILDRED. Mistress, dear. Slavemistress – which is just what you girls need. Same again? And twenty Marlboro!

KATE. Excuse me. The guy at the other end of the bar, the one with the 'tache – he wants to buy you a drink. You don't want one? Sure? He seems very friendly to me. OK! It's up to you. You wouldn't catch this one turning drown a free drink, I'll tell you.

BLANCHE. What was all that about?

KATE. Oh, nothing! She's a bit stand-offish, that one. Sorry, love, but he declines your gracious offer. So 'up hers', that's what I say. One pound, thank you.

MILDRED. State of this misery, over here. She stands around, like Cinders looking for Buttons, and after three pints she's thrown caution to the winds and being chatted up by that old queen with the toupee. No standards, some of them.

KATE. And what did you get up to, last night? Miss Piggy said you and Patsy were off to a bathing beauties party in Maida Vale. Can't think why I wasn't asked?

BLANCHE. Well, Kate. It's a hard thing to have to say, but you're not exactly Miss World, dear.

MILDRED. Miss Cleethorpes, more like!

KATE. Right! That's it. If you think I'm doing the fuckin' ashtrays tonight, you can think again. It's been nothing but insults ever since I got here. I ask a simple question, and what do I get? Personal abuse!

BLANCHE. You should be so lucky! Anyway, it was a terrible party so you didn't miss anything.

KATE. Good! I suppose Miss Piggy went too, although she pretended to me she was going home to feed the cat.

BLANCHE. 'Course she did. She wore her ocelot bikini.

KATE. She never!

BLANCHE. I've got the Polaroids to prove it. Want to see while it's quiet?

MILDRED. What's going on? Mildred being left out again?

BLANCHE. You were serving, dear! Don't get all hoity-toity, there's a good girl. Want to see some pickies?

MILDRED. Love to!

BLANCHE. There's Patsy in her Fifties pink satin — a few spare tyres showing, but otherwise a star!

KATE. The state of her! She looks like Divine!

MILDRED. Let's have a look. Fuckin' Ada!

BLANCHE. And this is me in a low-cut number from Miss Selfridge, doing my Audrey Hepburn.

176

MILDRED. It's fabulous, Blanche. Why don't you wear it here?

BLANCHE. Couldn't cope with the offers, love! And I've never liked turning them away. Hello, Doreen. Want to see a picky of your sexy little self, all trussed up like a dog's dinner? I thought you weren't on tonight.

DOREEN. I'm not, but you just can't keep away, do you know what I mean? Let's have a look, then. Oh, the shock and strain of it all! It's worse than the one of me at Mabel's Bunny-Girl Ball, and that was bad enough!

BLANCHE. It's the Carmen Miranda head-dress that captures the Doreen we all know and love. Especially the bananas! Sorry, sir. Can I help you? Dubonnet and Coke. And a box of Hamlet. Of course! (The Duchess of Duke Street's arrived, girls: 'If you'd be so kind'. Talk about breeding! She's a prize cow, if ever there was one. I can't be doing with these old queens coming the airs and graces bit, as if we're waitresses in a Lyons Corner House.)

KATE. Well, *she's* got it together, hasn't she?

MILDRED. Who, love?

KATE. The peroxide witch, wearing the Olympic sweatshirt. She's got the hunk that was playing the machine, fuck it! The one with the Walkman.

BLANCHE. So that's who you were cruising! Bit on the big side for you, dear.

MILDRED. Nothing's too big for Katy, is it love?

KATE. I wish you two would do some bloody work, instead of getting at me all the time.

BLANCHE. Here we go. Tantrumette time! 'I am what I am, tra la la la la!'

MILDRED. Now that's nice, just coming in. Well, it would have been – without the girlfriend.

BLANCHE. Just look at her! 'We can't stay here, love. It's a gay bar!'

MILDRED. Stupid bitch! Well, he doesn't look too bothered, now does he? That's right, handsome. You tell her! Can I help you? Sweet white wine and a Pils? Sure.

BLANCHE. Don't fall over yourself will you, Mildred? Or have you seen something we haven't?

MILDRED. There's somebody waiting down there, girls, if you can drag yourself away from those photos!

BLANCHE. State of her! Marriage breaker! Come on, Kiss-me-Kate. Let's gather empties in the spring. Doreen! Get behind this bar, dear, and show 'em what you're made of.

DOREEN. Honestly! It's my night off, Blanche. Why should I?

BLANCHE. Don't be mean, dear. It makes your mouth go all rubbery. Ten minutes. That's all we ask. Ten minutes' freedom, while we have a little troll and look for the empties. 'I am what I am, tra la la.'

DOREEN. It's no work for a white girl, I can tell you. Whatever happened to my dreams of luxury, living in sin with a big butch cowboy and a stable full of ranch-hands?

BLANCHE. They were wet, love, like all your Bonanza fantasies. Now get behind this bar and do your stuff. And if that queen with the carnation tries the Lady of the Manor bit, give her short measure. Ugly cow! Come on, Katy. Let's see if we can't blow out the Olympic flame.

EDDY. Wot's that, then?

CHARLES. It's an ice-making contraption. A present from my mother, actually.

EDDY. 'Actually'.

CHARLES. I don't find it very funny, you know. In fact, it's rather irritating.

EDDY. Wot is, Charlie?

CHARLES. You know perfectly well — imitating my accent. It's jolly rude!

EDDY. 'Jolly rude!' Ah, cum on Charlie. Give us a break, will yer? It was just a larf, all right? Let's see it, then!

CHARLES. See what, dear boy? We're a little forward, aren't we?

EDDY. The fuckin' ice machine, sweetheart! I wanna see it make some ice, don't I?

CHARLES. It's already made some. Now what can I get you to drink? Scotch all right?

EDDY. You got any beer?

CHARLES. There's some light ale — is that all right?

EDDY. Or rum?

CHARLES. No rum, I'm afraid.

EDDY. Well then! I'll take the light ale, guvnor!

CHARLES. I do wish you could call me Charles. After all, you are my guest, and it's only polite.

EDDY. Sorry 'Chawles!'

CHARLES. That's better! I'll fix the drink, and put some music on.

EDDY. 'Ere! You got a video, then?

CHARLES. Yes, actually. Would you like to see something?

EDDY. Got any dirty films, 'ave we? Bet we 'ave, Charlie! C'mon, Charlie — where's the films, then?

CHARLES. It may surprise you to know that I don't have such things in the flat!

EDDY. Aw! An' I thought we could get a bit randy, like —
watchin' a bit of the old porn.

CHARLES. I'm afraid you'll have to 'get randy' without it. Does
that present difficulties? I'm not so repulsive, am I? I am
paying you, after all!

EDDY. Well, I dunno Charlie. I mean, if the flesh ain't willin' —
know wot I mean?

CHARLES. Well, I'm sure we can do something about that, dear
boy!

EDDY. Wot you playin', then? Bit 'ighbrow for me!

CHARLES. It's Monteverdi! Venetian. Seventeenth century.

EDDY. Wot?

CHARLES. The sixteen-hundreds — that's the seventeenth century,
you see. Just as we are the twentieth, but actually the
nineteen-hundreds!

EDDY. If you say so, Charlie! It's before my time — I know that
much.

CHARLES. There's your beer.

EDDY. Ta, mate! Where we goin' to do it, then? I ain't doin'
nuffin' funny, know wot I mean? You want a wrist job, or a bit
of a gobble. Blow-jobs is more, see?!

CHARLES. I thought we might just sit and talk for a while, before
doing anything else. I mean, you don't have to rush off
somewhere, do you?

EDDY. I ain't got all night, Charlie. I've got some more business,
down the dub. Know wot I mean?

CHARLES. I'm sorry. I only thought it would be rather
uncivilized, doing it straight away. After all, Eddy — I do like
you, you know. I thought we could talk about you.

EDDY. This the fuckin' inquisition? I mean, wot's there to talk
about?

CHARLES. Well — what you do; how you came to be . . .

EDDY. Rent? Well, it's wot I do, ain't it? I mean, I knew this guy
wot ran a shop, see? A cinema and shop. Well, like I worked
there for a bit, an' 'e said I'd earn more down the 'dilly. Well,
'e was gay, see, an' kept tryin' it on. An' I wouldn't let 'im,

180

see! Well, one night 'e just pulls it out and makes me give 'im a blow-job. All right? Then 'e gives me a tenner an' sez I could get by, 'cos like it made no difference, see?! I mean, it was money, right? Just for suckin' a bit of cock. So I thought, 'Well, it's fuckin' simple!' An' I started down the 'dilly, leanin' on the railin's till some geezer comes up an' asks if I want a drink or somefin'. I mean, there's a lot of posh geezers – City types, like you – an' they just come up, an' that's it!

CHARLES. Yes – I suppose it is. People like me!

EDDY. Well now! We've 'ad our little talk, an' I gotta make a move soon, Charlie. So wot's it goin' to be? I ain't got no time for the works, 'cos like I said, I've got some business matters to see to.

CHARLES. Well, whatever you have time for, I suppose. I must say, I do think it's a bit much – setting the next one up when you were with me!

EDDY. It's work, Charlie. Know wot I mean. I mean, right now it's you, all right? An' in an hour, it's another geezer, see!

CHARLES. All right, all right. I'll just go to the bathroom. Perhaps you'd like a wash?

EDDY. Clean, sweetheart! Eddy's always clean, see. Now you go an' get rid of them thermal undies, an' I'll get ready, yeah? Where's the bedroom, then?

CHARLES. Just down the hall, on the left. What are you doing?

EDDY. Gettin' a hard-on, Charlie. I gotta rub 'im up, see!? Otherwise, 'e won't do 'is stuff. Gets a bit tired sometimes.

CHARLES. Yes – I imagine 'he' does.

EDDY. Don't be long, then. Like I said . . .

CHARLES. You have some business matters to attend to 'down the dub' – no, I won't be long.

EDDY. Lot of pictures, 'aven't yer? Old-fashioned like. Lot of books, too! You must earn a packet – smart place like this! A fuckin' packet!

CHARLES. Well – I'd better go to the bathroom. We're losing time, really.

EDDY. That's right, Charlie. An' Eddy's time costs money, see?!

Ben's Diary

¶ THURSDAY: He didn't ring and I thought it was probably better not to call him — just let things ride for a while. Sam rang to see if I was going to the Asylum, and I said yes so he came here first. It was the first time I've been there sober, and it felt really weird. Everybody looked pissed, and people I used to think were really attractive suddenly looked naff. Sam spent a lot of time talking to that guy called Adrian who makes films. I think he was angling for a job, and reeled off a list of parts he'd like to play, including Salome and Scheherazade — just to be provocative! The guy's an old trendy who knows everyone. He kept playing with himself as he was giving Sam the name-dropper's guide to London artistic life! It always sounds like bullshit to me, but little Sam swallowed it all, and kept making clever remarks about Buñuel, and how the best acting was in films and videos — not on the stage any more. I said that film was lifeless in the end, and too much a finished product. At least plays went on and might change from night to night. Well, it sounded good, and Adrian banged on about posterity and time. All heavy stuff! They left together, so maybe Sam will become a star. The pretty blond was there again, and I hung around a bit, without really intending to do anything about it. After a bit he asked me to dance, so we freaked around on the dance-floor, me showing off and feeling I looked sexy and exciting! We left together, which I didn't mind, considering how pretty he was, especially with a few of my cast-offs standing around looking lonely and envious. We looked really good together, me in my young Heathcliff gear with a frown and scruffy hair (filthy!), and him the classic pretty blond with a ripped

182

white T-shirt and tight faded blue jeans, frayed open round his bum and at the knees! It's a bit like a competition, going out to that place. If you win you can keep the prize for a night! At home we got down to it straight away, with my Dinah Washington tape crooning in the background. It was really good, energetic sex — lots of struggling and biting, etc. . . . When I woke up he'd gone, which was probably just as well. I thought about Danny, and felt odd and guilty, because I'd intended to save myself for some crazy reason. But it was good fun. I think his name was Michael, but I could be wrong!

THE LEATHER QUEEN IN THE
BACK ROOM

It's not very good tonight. Too many gropers doing their own thing, and not getting into the fuck. If they don't want to screw, they should jerk off in the corner and fuck off home. That guy with the beard — last week he was fucking like there was no tomorrow, and tonight he's picking and choosing, and doesn't even remember me. After the best fuck he's ever had! But that's it about this place. Sometimes it's hard, heavy sex, and other times just tossing each other off, then out to the loo and washing the hands, like suburban cottage-queens! Take that pretty boy in the shorts. Once he'd come that was it. Too friggin' selfish, some of them. And the skinhead I screwed last week. All over me while I'm doing the fucking, but offer him a drink and he doesn't want to know. I mean, it's all a fucking game, isn't it? Nobody pretends it's a tea party, but there is a kind of keeping an open mind thing, like when there's somebody you want to take back. Watching it now, though, there's just the pushing and shoving, and everybody getting off on some totally physical fantasy. And that's what's best about it. Just the atmosphere, with bodies everywhere, and seeing enough of somebody to be turned on. Especially in the dark, when all you can make out is a pounding arse, or someone's cock being sucked. That tall guy looks pleased with himself. Maybe I'll get in there for a while, unless — hello! That was very friendly. I wonder what this one wants. Hands and knees! Wanting a mouthful, are we? There you go, then. Try that for size! Yeah!! Things are looking up a bit. Ooops! Careful, love. The floor's slippery enough, without mine going every-where. Wouldn't mind that one in the string vest. Looks the well-hung type. Wonder what he's into when he's not here?

Something heavy, if looks are anything to go by. Must be quite old, too. Balding! I like that. This place needs a few more Colt types, instead of kids like this. I'll be bruised black and blue if he takes much longer. Come on mate, I'm dying to get in that corner and see who's getting all the attention. Anybody'd think you were dying of starvation, the way you're going at it. Talk about 'Gentlemen's Relish' – I think I'll start charging if he doesn't get a move on!! Nearly there, dear. Come on, will you?! Yeah! Yeah! Oh shit! Almost there, and he starts to choke. Honestly, some queens don't know what they're doing half the time. Fuck this one! I've had enough. Get away will you! Climb up somebody else, love, and take some vitamins before the next time – I haven't got all night, not just for you. Some people have no energy at all! Get back in, will you! Bloody jeans! Hopeless with a hard-on. Just let me squeeze through here. Get off, you hideous little Nip. Can't go anywhere without those prickless dwarfs groping about. It's worse than the cinema. Get off!! What's that behind? Feels quite nice. Mmm! Feels familiar too! Last week, I think – a Scottish copper, if that was the truth. Unforgettable! Don't run away, fuck you?! I haven't finished. Shit! It's like Paddington Station in this place. Some of us are trying to get it together, for fuck's sake. It's all these little queens. I don't see why they can't stay in Heaven, instead of poking around here, getting in a man's way. All they do is peer about, always watching and never screwing. Last week there must have been five of them at least, all huddled around me and that bearded guy, just squinting and jerking. Like a bloody sex show! Can't see a thing at this end. Not a thing! And these stupid chaps are such a pain. Next week it's just jeans and T-shirt. Where's baldie gone, for God's sake?! Now that looks good, over there – tall, anyway, which makes a change tonight. If I can squeeze through – for God's sake, what is going on here? Might as well have some of this – everyone else seems to be. Jesus! How could I have missed that? Next week I'll wear the miner's helmet – that'll sort out the men from the boys. It's fantastic – just too much. Come on, big boy! Let's take a bit of time over this. Fuck off, will you! It's mine, now. Wow! I wouldn't mind seeing more of this one! Nice! Fuck these bloody kids! Get away, can't you? That's better. Shit! Some wanker's dropped his poppers. This cess-pit's going to smell like one in a couple of minutes! Occupational hazard, I suppose!

THE OLD QUEEN
GOES TO THE CINEMA

BOY. Want the cinema, mate? We got some really hard films on downstairs!

OLD QUEEN. Different from last week's?

BOY. Get new ones every Monday, mate. American. The hard stuff. Five pounds to you!

OLD QUEEN. Thank you.

BOY. Just through the curtain, then.

OLD QUEEN. I know where to go, thank you!

BOY. 'Course you do, mate. 'Course you do.

OLD QUEEN. (They're so familiar here. That's what I hate. He's laughing at me, and thinks I don't know. Well, here we go again. Always smells of disinfectant, and other things. Makes me feel quite sick sometimes. Oh dear! Hardly anyone here yet. Perhaps they're all downstairs. I don't like this little room. It's too light, somehow, and nobody does anything because everyone can see. Especially when they're leaning on the stairs. I don't like it when they do that – not at all. It's rather embarrassing. Dear, dear! Not those two, again. Same old faces – older than me! I don't know what's become of us, really I don't. Better not to think about it, I suppose. This place! Broken seats, and goodness knows how many germs. Just imagining the filth is enough. As for the rickety projector breaking down every five minutes! Then the light switched on all of a sudden! And it always seems so bright, as people do up their trousers and try to look as if nothing's happening at all. Nothing happening! Well, for some of us nothing ever happens – hardly ever. Last week! When that boy practically punched me in the chest! What are they here for if you can't have a bit of fun? That's all I want – just a little feel. It's not too much to ask. One day he'll know what it's like, pottering around Soho in spite of yourself, and having to come here because there's no other way of doing it. Oh! It's so dark. You could twist an ankle on that step. Got to be careful, Leslie! Now then. Where shall I sit? It's quite full, really! Tut! Someone's sitting in my favourite place, damn them! It's quite dark, but more seems to happen in that corner, because of the little room I suppose. And I can always see *something*, if I look hard enough. Oh well! Let's see if there's – 'Sorry!' – stupid place to put a briefcase! If it isn't those or noisy executive ones which make everybody look round, you're tripping over plastic bags. Still, I've no room to talk, with this shoulder-bag! Those two seem to be getting on quite well! And there's a seat on the other side of the blond boy. Oh dear! I don't really like interrupting, but after all, it's something to watch, isn't it?) Excuse me, please!

STRANGER. Fucking hell! Nosy old queen!

OLD QUEEN. Excuse me! I'm so sorry. Thank you! (So rude, some people! I've paid just as much as they have! Now then, if I keep my bag here, I can stop them seeing, like that. That's it. He's got a nice one, I must say. Very excited, isn't he? Oh yes! I do like to see boys do that. Mmm! That's right. Make yourself more comfortable. It'll be easier for him. Now, if I just put my foot next to – that's it. Now watch the film for a bit, Leslie! Don't put them off. I knew he was lying. I must have seen this at least half-a-dozen times! Honestly! Five pounds. It's not a very good one, either. Except for the bit set in an army bunk-room, with three young soldiers. They get up to all sorts of things, and the biggest one is such a he-man! There's a while to go before that, though! More people! Can't really see them, that's the trouble. Ah! Oriental boys! They're usually a safe bet. I might as well stay here for the moment. They are going at it a bit strong, aren't they? I wonder if I might just lend a hand to this while he's doing that. Move this bag an inch or two. There! Now I can reach – oh! It's lovely.)

STRANGER. Get away, will you. Filthy old queen. Fuck off!
OLD QUEEN. (Come on, Leslie. Don't want any trouble, dear. They shouldn't come here if they aren't going to let you have some fun. This bloody bag!) Excuse me. Excuse me. (So rude! Honestly! Now then, where are those two Oriental laddies? There they are! I'll have to stand for a bit, until somebody moves. Over by the little room. Heavens! There's a lot going on in there! Good Lord! They're all taking turns with that scruffy young lad. He doesn't look very involved, I must say. In fact, he looks positively 'couldn't-care-less'. What a performance! Perhaps if I press up against this little Chinese boy, he'll do something. There! Nice little boy, aren't we? Tut! You didn't have to move away like that. I wouldn't have done anything horrible. Ah! There's a seat. Funny how they make a sort of noise! You can always tell when someone's changing place, because the seat goes 'clunk!' Just like the cinema. Well, they are cinema seats, aren't they? Old ones. This *is* a cinema, after all! Calling me a filthy old queen! What a thing to say to anyone! Still there, aren't they? Ah! The blond one's doing it now. I like that one's, even though he was so rude! Oh, look, Leslie. It's the army bunk-room. Now is it the boy in the bottom one who starts, or the one in the top? The big one comes in soon. I remember that. Ah yes, it's the one on top. Mmm! He's so well built. Not as good as the big one though! Let me just put my bag here — that's it — then no one can see. Are we comfortable? Yes!)

189

Ben's Diary

¶ FRIDAY: Stayed in bed for hours. Raining outside and no point in feeling worse. When I did get up it was almost dark again. Rang Danny, but no reply. I really wanted to go out again tonight, but knew it was a bad idea. Started a French book, *Against Nature*, which Kitty raved about, but couldn't get into it, although it is very *fin de siècle* and my kind of thing. Staying in is so hard! After about an hour I was nervy and restless, and rang him again. A boy answered the phone, and said Danny was out and was there a message. I said no, and wished I hadn't phoned. Sat around wondering who the boy was, and got gloomy. Slept badly, and had funny dreams about acting in a play and not knowing my lines at all — just standing on the stage with everybody looking at me, waiting for some key line which affected the whole story. No prompt either! Woke up very early and lay there having a vague sense of crisis.

THE PLATES

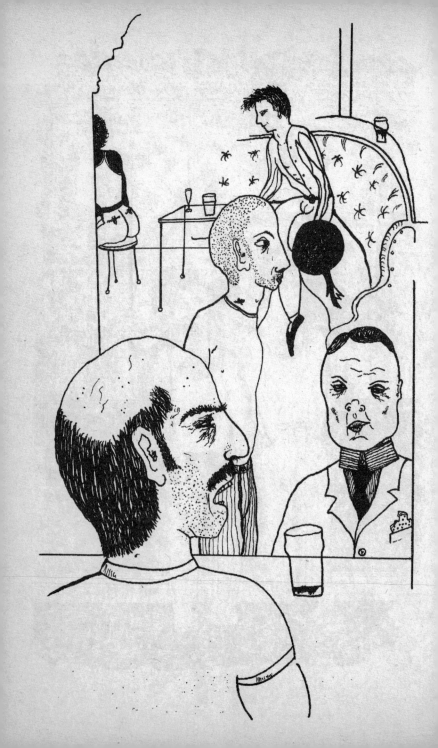

AFTER ALL, TOMORROW IS ALWAYS ANOTHER DAY

I'm sick of it! Sick to the back teeth! Another night on the bloody tiles, and for what? Some naff queen from Beaconsfield — Beaconsfield of all God-forsaken places! — and she can't even get it up. After what she'd drunk, it's not surprising. I don't know! And she never bought a round, either! Anybody'd think I was rolling in it, the way she was knocking them back! As for those bloody late buses! They're a dead loss, they are. Standing around for nearly an hour in the freezing bloody cold. And her, throwing up outside the café! I could have forgiven that, but not the carry-on back here. I mean, what's the point if you can't get it up? Might as well give up altogether. I should have known, when she said she felt a bit funny! Funny! She shouldn't have had those bloody chips. I said so, but she wouldn't listen. The times I've thrown up after those chips. I should bloody know. But do they listen? Do they hell-as-like! Oh, Gloria! There must be more to life than this. It's about time somebody sensational walked into your life, and swept you off your feet. There must be somebody, somewhere. And as for the body! If there's one thing I can't stand it's a pimply bum. Terrible! And all that business with the bloody KY! She must have used half the fucking tube, and still couldn't get it together! It felt like I'd done it in my pants. I should have stuck with that Italian. At least he'd have got it up! I can't stand tourists, though! Not when they can't talk English. It's really gone downhill, that place. I used to get butch men when it first started, but now all the bloody trendies have started going it's full of clever-dicks poncing around in naff little caps. Makes you sick, it does! One of these days I'm going to smash one of them in the face. They're so bleeding stuck-up, anybody'd think they owned the place! I should have done something about that skinhead, though! He was butch. And I think he fancied me, too. It's always the same, though. It's always me who has to make the first move. I was looking really fabulous last night as well. Fabulous! Miss Beaconsfield! She probably had the clap, knowing my luck! Oh! And those spots. Spotty bums are the pits. They really are. Can't think why I dragged her back. It's always the same in the last half-hour. Just standing around, half-pissed, making do with anything that looks passable. I'm sick of making do. It's not fair, Gloria. You deserve more than a few hopeless one-night stands. 'All you need is love.' Too fucking right! Better phone Mavis. I'm not telling her, though. She'll crow all night if I do. And she's bound to pretend she had something fab. I know her backwards . . .

Hello! Is that you, Mavis? You sound terrible – just like I feel, love. The state of last night! What happened to you, dear? The last I saw, you were staggering about with Doris in tow, going on about some film-star in the loo! You what? Paul Newman?! Don't be daft, Mavis. It can't have been! – So it looked like him, dear, but that's not the same thing at all. – Well, you should have made a move, instead of getting weak at the knees, dear. It's no bloody use just batting your eyelashes every ten seconds, hoping he'd notice. He probably thought you were with Doris. – Well, I've told you before – you'll never drag anything home with her in tow. She's always after my trade, let alone yours. Can't trust her an inch, that one! An evil queen – that's what she is. Always has been – You what? Me? – Well, I had the most fucking awful time. Oh, Mavis, I was so pissed I could hardly see straight, let alone get my act together. I was just leaning at the bottom of the stairs, feeling like an abortion but looking fabulous, when this guy starts coming up the steps. Well, dear, you've never seen anything like it in your life! You remember that film about the gods and stuff, and the guy on that horse with wings . . . No! The hero, dear. Well, it was just like him, only fifty million times better. Blond, blond hair, and a tan, Mavis! A real one! Well, I lifted my skirts and tottered upstairs like Joan Crawford on a bad night. I'm not exaggerating, Mavis, but there

216

wasn't one queen who wasn't giving him the once-over. Talk about meat market, dear! You'd think fucking Christ had walked in, the way they were all carrying on. And he just stood, looking hunky, and knowing it! Well, I had to have it, Mavis. I just had to! So I went up to the bar, and stood next to it. It nearly killed me, the effort, dear! And all the queens watching what was going on, like they do! Anyway, I was just standing there, trying to work out what to do next, when he turns round and asks me if I want a drink! Well, you could have knocked me over with a feather! Talk about laid-back! He was laid back so far he was already in fucking bed! Anyway, I said I'd have a vodka, and we got the drinks and went to sit on the steps. Well! We'd hardly been there ten seconds before he starts necking and groping and all! – What do you mean, 'What a surprise?' – What else do you expect with a fabulous girl like me in the picture?! He couldn't resist, dear. Who could? So we sat there, necking and all, and then I said did he want to come back to my place, and he said yes. So we left, and he had this really fabulous car, Mavis. A sports car – you know. One of those Porsche jobs. And when we got in, he said we should go back to his place, because it was easier. Well, I was quite relieved to tell you the truth, because I haven't done the sheets for a couple of weeks and the bed's beginning to look like an ashtray! So we went to his place . . . Hampstead! Really posh, Mavis. Fitted carpets, and a telephone in every room. He's an architect or something. Educated! You know the type. But nice with it. And he had a video, Mavis! And a sauna, too! Well, I was in my element, dear! I just laid back and let it all happen! All of it – and that's saying a lot. Dick of death! Just incredible. And you'd never have known. I was sitting on this settee, and he comes back from the bathroom stark naked! With the dick of death! I couldn't believe it. You know the sort you really have to think twice about, Mavis? . . . Well, I thought a few times about that one, I can tell you. But what the hell! If it hurts you don't forget it, do you? And I don't think I'll be forgetting that one in a hurry. – Well, I took his phone number. He didn't give it to me, but I saw it on the phone, so that was all right. – I don't know, dear. Probably down the pub at about eight, I suppose! — Well, you never know your luck, do you? Who knows what might happen tonight? All I know is I'm just in the mood for another fuck, dear! It's always the same. When you've had something like that, you just can't get enough, can you? — OK. See you down there, Mavis. Tata!

¶ SATURDAY: Cold, clear and sunny — thank God! Wrote a couple of letters, another one to Christian, in which I moaned about loneliness and how I felt there was no point in going out, and hated staying in. A classic for the problem pages, to which there can only be Christian's usual advice about getting down to something worth doing, and ignoring the scene — which he hates. I wonder what it's like if you're not 'on the scene'. Presumably there are perfectly happy guys out there, wandering around parks on Sunday afternoons, kicking damp rotten leaves, getting on with things. Hard to imagine, though. Ricky rang and we arranged to meet, so he could show me a shirt he wants and can't make up his mind about. He must buy something new every week! Anyway, it was unusual and expensive (£49.95!), so he bought it! Purple and emerald green, which he'll look fabulous in — so he said! I'd love some new things, trousers especially, but they're hard to find. Sick of jeans, but somehow trousers never fit properly (although they look good on everybody else!) When you're in love, or at least wanting to be, there's always a crisis about appearance. I remember the last time, when I wandered around in tracksuit bottoms because the guy I liked was always on his way to the gym, or coming back. A complete waste of time. After days of standing around looking sporty, I finally spoke, only to discover he was a classic prissy queen. And now when I see him, it's impossible to understand how I could ever have thought otherwise. So now it's black PVC! Ricky was full of raunchy advice about how I should just pounce and get it over with, which is one way of looking at things. The point is that doing that solves the easy part of it all. Would it ever happen again? Probably not. Anyway, my new big idea is falling in love, not just into bed! So we dragged around, trying things on and irritating shop assistants by not buying anything. Then Ricky had to go to a class, and I wandered into the Portrait Gallery for something to do. There were lots of foreign couples there, hugging or hand in hand, archetypal love affairs! I suddenly wished I was with Danny, and made a resolution to get it together! When I rang he was there, and said he'd just been trying to call me, which made me feel incredibly happy. I said we should meet, and he said it would have to be tomorrow because he had to go to a dinner party. Damn! So he's coming round tomorrow, after lunch. I intended to stay in and not drink, so I'd look good and not raddled. As it was, Sam rang and we went to the leather bar for a change. I threw on the *Waterfront* gear, and frowned all night, while he was chatted up by a middle-aged leather queen wearing every conceivable bauble. They are all the same, those guys — ugly, and into anything that looks like they do. It turned out that he was really interested in me, and had asked Sam if we wanted to go to an orgy at Vauxhall. Sam had floored him by saying that orgies were really boring, which is probably untrue! Anyway, we didn't go, although Sam kept asking me what I thought it would have been like. I think he might quite like all that groping and throbbing in the darkness, but turned him off the idea by mentioning VD, which terrifies him. Come to think of it, I haven't had a check-up for a couple of months. We hung around after time, and watched a couple of geriatric monsters, draped in chains and keys, cruising each other. Then we left, Sam down to Heaven (again?!) and me home, although I was in the mood for dancing. Still, I need a lot of beauty sleep. My fingers were really yellow with so many cigarettes, and smelled disgusting. I always smoke more in that place than anywhere else, which proves how much time gets wasted in keeping an image intact. When I'm not wearing leather, I'm sure I smoke less. Anyway, one last cigarette, and then bed.

ALEX AT HOME WITH THE
FRENCH BOY

ALEX. Well, we're here. I'll put some light on.

Silence.

   (Better get to the bathroom, and make sure I'm looking OK.)
   Would you like some coffee?
GÉRARD. It's real, yes?
ALEX. Of course. You don't think I'd have instant, do you?
GÉRARD. All the English drink instant, I think.
ALEX. Well, I don't.

Pause.

   Black all right?
GÉRARD. Pardon?
ALEX. Black coffee! There's no milk.
GÉRARD. It's OK.

Pause.

   You live alone, here?
ALEX. Yes.

Pause.

   I don't have a boyfriend, if that's what you're wondering. Do
   you?
GÉRARD. In Paris, yes.

Pause.

ALEX. I see.

Silence.

Is he beautiful? Your boyfriend, I mean.
GÉRARD. I believe it.
ALEX. Why didn't he come with you, then?
GÉRARD. He working all the time.
ALEX. I see. Maybe you take your coat off, or something.
GÉRARD. OK!

Pause.

ALEX. Would you like some music? (Talk! It's always a mistake
   with foreigners.)
GÉRARD. You have many of Tchaikovsky's. You like him?
ALEX. Well, I quite like loud music.
GÉRARD. Is very loud, I think!

Pause.

The disco was very loud, yes?
ALEX. Yes. Very. It's a bit much after a while. There's some jazz
   there. Or maybe you'd like some piano — Chopin or
   something?
GÉRARD. *Oui!* Chopin — is good for now.
ALEX. (Well, at least that's the music settled. Get the coffee, and
   then work out a seating plan!)
GÉRARD. You have many books!
ALEX. I suppose so.

Pause.

GÉRARD. Ah! Genet! You like?

222

ALEX. He's all right.

GÉRARD. I love Genet! You have see *Flowers* — the Lindsay Kemp ballet?

ALEX. No, actually. I haven't.

GÉRARD. Oh! He's fantastic. In Paris we saw him — Bertrand *et moi*. So crazy! Is very popular in Paris. The spectacle, and the boys. In Paris the boys go crazy for it. You would like, I think. In the saunas they were speaking of it!

ALEX. Yes, I'm sure I would.

GÉRARD. Is so decadent. You know decadence?

ALEX. Of course. It's the same word in English.

GÉRARD. Ah!

Silence.

You like Andy Warhol?

ALEX. What? Oh, that poster! Yeah, I do. I think the poster's better than the film was. I got it in Paris, actually. That's where I saw the film.

GÉRARD. We also saw in Paris, *Querelle*. I think is no good, but my friend — Bertrand — he like it very much. The sailor boys!

ALEX. I thought it was crap.

Silence.

There's your coffee.

GÉRARD. *Merci.*

ALEX. (God! It's such a drag bringing people back! Pathetic attempts at conversation, when all you want to do is roll around. And it's worse when they're foreign. One word here and there. A few questions! As if either of us was interested!)

GÉRARD. You have lived here long?

ALEX. Three years. Not that long, really.

GÉRARD. Nice place. You like?

ALEX. It's all right. (Good legs! Just quite boring. And hands — good hands! Maybe some different music! I can't just pounce,

223

can I? He looks so incredibly bored. Maybe he doesn't fancy me any more. I look so tired, too. The French are so bloody moody and arrogant. That's what I hate about them.)

GÉRARD. Where is the toilet, please?

ALEX. Just through there, on the left.

GÉRARD. Thank you.

ALEX. (When he comes back I'll do it. I can sit so he has to get close, and then it can just happen. All this fucking planning! Why do some queens always make you feel as if they're doing you a favour? He said he wanted to come back – well, not exactly, but he said he would if I wanted. I should have stayed with the Italian. At least he couldn't speak, so there wouldn't have been all this sitting round and coffee lark. I hate coffee at this time of night, anyway. Wish there was something to drink – I'll buy some Scotch tomorrow. That'll solve these little chit-chats. What the fuck's he doing in there? I suppose I could just throw him out and go to bed. I haven't had a good night's sleep for weeks. I haven't had a good fuck, either. Not since – not since that other French boy. And he didn't sit around playing 'I spy'.)

GÉRARD. Hello!

ALEX. All right?

GÉRARD. I was just washing.

ALEX. (Washing what?) Why don't you sit here – Gérard?

GÉRARD. If you would like.

ALEX. (So fucking polite! Sit down, and let's get on with it, for God's sake! It's already three o'clock.)

GÉRARD. Cigarette?

ALEX. Thanks!

Silence.

GÉRARD. You are very strange!

ALEX. I don't think so. What's so strange about me?

GÉRARD. You are not like the other English queens. Strange!

ALEX. Well, some of us are quite normal, really.

224

GÉRARD. You are normal?

ALEX. Well – not exactly normal. What I mean is, we're not all poncy little queens. I mean, you can be gay without being a queen. Do you understand?

GÉRARD. *Pédé sans etre folle.* Is 'queen' so bad, you think?

ALEX. Well, it depends, doesn't it? There are different types of queen, so it's hard to say. English queens are so boring, usually.

GÉRARD. And French? You think we are boring too?

ALEX. (Boring me stupid!) Well, you aren't. Anyway, I like the French. French boys, I mean. At least they're different. They have a sort of style I like. I quite like arrogance, you see. And French boys can be friendly as well as arrogant.

GÉRARD. The English are very serious, yes? And they look very unhappy, I think. In the disco they look like so.

ALEX. Yeah! Well, most of them have nothing to be happy about.

GÉRARD. You look different, yes? You were angry at them.

ALEX. Well, not angry. I just don't think it's worth it, wandering around smiling like an idiot, when the place is full of jerks and giggling queens. Not my style.

Pause.

Come here.

GÉRARD. Sorry?

ALEX. Come closer. That's better.

Pause.

You have very beautiful hands! Very!

GÉRARD. Is this where we are sleeping?

ALEX. No. Why? You want to go to bed?

GÉRARD. Is very late. You are tired, yes?

ALEX. Come on, then. Let's go to bed. It's a good idea.

GÉRARD. Very strange, Alex! Very strange boy!

VERA HEARS ABOUT MABEL'S
NIGHT OF HORROR IN EARL'S
COURT

VERA. Hello, Mabel. I just had to had to ring, dear, to find out how you got on with the incredible hulk. I'm dying to know.

MABEL. Oh, Vera. I'm half dead. Really I am. The incredible hulk was about as incredible as you can get. Fuckin' Ada! I thought I was going to pass out.

VERA. Start from the beginning, dear, like a good girl. Aunty Vera wants every last sordid detail!

MABEL. Well, after I saw you with that black guy – remember – the one with the big bum –

VERA. It wasn't that big, dear! Quite petite, if you want to know – but that's another story. Carry on, then.

MABEL. I will, if you'll let me, Vera! Where was I? Oh, yes – well after that we left, and got a taxi down to Earl's Court –

VERA. Earl's Court! Is that where he lives? I can't think why I haven't seen him around before –

MABEL. Vera! Will you let me carry on. Either you want to know, or you don't!

VERA. Oh, stop moaning and carry on!

MABEL. Well, we got to his place. Just off the Earl's Court Road. A tiny basement flat, dear. More like a bed-sit than a flat, actually. When I say it was filthy, Vera, I do not exaggerate. Talk about sleaze, dear. The stink was something else again. Stale poppers, cum, gum on the carpet – the filthiest carpet I've ever seen. The pavements are cleaner – even in Earl's Court!

VERA. And?

MABEL. Well, I did my 'What a nice place to live' line, which

226

went down like a bucket of cold sick. Sick! That's what the place smelled of. Puke! Well, I felt a bit uneasy-like. Nervous. I mean, anything could have happened, and my imagination was running away with me. Bodies under the bed – that sort of thing. You can never be too careful, can you? Not since that head-hunter from Muswell Hill. A girl's got to keep her wits about her when she finds herself in darkest Earl's Court, trapped in a room the size of a closet with what might turn out to be a madman!

VERA. Don't get carried away, dear. Just tell us what happened. I think I can picture his palace!

MABEL. I am telling you, if you'll let me. So there I was, sitting on the edge of this disgusting mattress on the floor. He found a bottle of vodka, Polish, and rolled a joint.

VERA. A what?

MABEL. A joint, Vera. Are you listening or aren't you?

VERA. Oh! A joint! How nice and polite! So you got stoned, then?

MABEL. Stoned! I was out of my box, dear. Right out of it. I was so pissed anyway, and what with the drink and dope – I actually knocked my glass over – on purpose – I just couldn't face any more. Well – we sat there for about twenty minutes, not saying much – he's not very talkative, and anyway, he was as pissed as I was. Then he put this tape on, Vera! Well – it was dreadful! Dreadful!

VERA. What was it? Vera Lynn?!

MABEL. I wish it had been, Vera! But it wasn't.

VERA. Well, what was it?

MABEL. Sounds, Vera. Just sounds – like sound-effects. But horrible. From a horror film or something. Groans, and screams and stuff!

VERA. Fuckin' 'ell, dear! I bet you gathered your skirts in a hurry. I'd have been out of the place like a shot! Like a shot! Kinky bugger!

MABEL. Well, how could I leave? I sat there trying to work out how I could say – you know – say I had to get back, or something. But at that time of night what could I be doing?

Whatever I'd have said he'd have known was a lie. So! I treated it all like a joke. I laughed a bit, and said it was very amusing, and where did he get it? And you know what he said, Vera?

VERA. I can't imagine! What did he say?

MABEL. He said he'd made it himself. It was guys he's dragged back there, Vera, just groaning and screaming and all that. With funny sounds, like being beaten up and things. Worse than that, even!

VERA. Worse! What do you mean — 'Worse than that!'?

MABEL. Whips, Vera. Whips!

VERA. My God! Are you all right, Mabel? Shall I phone for an ambulance? What's he done to you, dear? I feel terrible. It's all my fault for pushing you into it. Oh, if only I'd known. I thought there was something funny about him, though. I did. All that chewing-gum and big hands. Definitely something peculiar, I thought.

MABEL. Well, why the fuck didn't you say so? There was I getting all randy and into him, when all the time he's a fuckin' maniac. And now you say you could tell.

VERA. Well, how was I to know? It was just a passing moment of feminine intuition. That's all.

MABEL. Anyway, there we were, getting stoned, listening to this — this torture tape. That's what he called it. He said — 'It's my torture tape!' Imagine! I was nearly sick, then and there. What was he going to do? I didn't dare think about it. But I had to, Vera. I thought the best thing to do was just act normal, have the drink, and then say I was feeling ill, and had to go home.

VERA. Wise girl. So you got out of it, then?

MABEL. Out of it, dear. This was just the beginning. When it was over — the tape — he got up and took all his clothes off. Every last stitch.

VERA. Took his clothes off! Well, there's nothing wrong with that, dear. Was it fabulous? I bet it was out of this world, yes?

MABEL. Oh, it *was*. Nobody could have complained about that. Magnificent. Everything in place, big and hard, like a porn-star — you know the sort of thing. Huge!

228

VERA. So you fucked all night to the flip side of his Torture Tape!

MABEL. No, Vera. I wish we had. But that pleasure was not to be Mabel's!

VERA. Well, what happened, then?

MABEL. He tied me up, Vera. Imagine! Tied me up with black leather thongs.

VERA. Tied you to what? I thought there was no furniture.

MABEL. Not to anything, dear. Just tied up. Like ankles, and all that, so I just wriggled on the floor.

VERA. Didn't you scream? I'd have woken the whole fucking street!

MABEL. How could I? He gagged me.

VERA. Gagged you? Oh, Mabel. What a performance. I bet you thought you'd never get out of there alive.

MABEL. Oh, I did. I did. I thought – 'This is it, Mabel.' I just lay there, trying to think of something nice – like chocolate, and Philip. God, how I wanted Philip to break down that door and rescue me from this weirdo. But they're never there when you need them most, are they?

VERA. Well, it's a bit much to expect Philip to know you were being molested by a bondage queen in a cess-pit in Earl's Court!

MABEL. Well, you know what I mean, anyway. I needed him, Vera. And he wasn't there.

VERA. But what happened, Mabel? How did you escape, love?

MABEL. Well, I lay there while he messed about. What else could I do?

VERA. What do you mean, 'messed about'?

MABEL. You know – messed about. I just can't tell you what it was like, Vera. First one thing, and then the other. And me all tied up and covered in it. He certainly wasn't a Kleen Kween. And I wasn't Miss Super-M, either!

VERA. You don't mean – ?

MABEL. I do, Vera. I fuckin' do! And all the time recording it on his tape-recorder. Me making funny little grunting noises, and him doing the same, and saying 'Shit, man' and things like

229

that. It was absolutely dreadful. I thought I was going to faint, but I didn't let myself. All I kept thinking was 'It's bound to end soon. Just keep thinking of Philip and home, and don't let him see you're terrified.'

VERA. Oh, Mabel. Poor love, I'm coming straight over to see you're all right. And it's all my fault. I'll never forgive myself. I won't! So what happened next?

MABEL. I can't remember exactly, but after all the dirty stuff, he seemed to go a bit funny, and just sat in the corner, playing the tape back to himself. Imagine! And it was so cold, lying there.

VERA. I thought you'd got your clothes on, at least!

MABEL. God, no! I took them off after he'd taken his off. I mean, I thought we were going to fuck, didn't I? So! – after he'd played with the tape-recorder, he got up and stood over me, and played with himself. And then he came – all over me – hair, face, everything! What I must have looked like by this time doesn't bear thinking about. And the smell, Vera!

VERA. Oh, Mabel! The humiliation!

MABEL. After that, he untied me and gave me a filthy shirt which I used to clean everything up! Disgusting, it was! There was a disgusting little sink, which was something. And all the time he just sat there, smoking – watching me. Talk about terrified. I put my clothes back on, and tried to be really laid-back. I lit a fag, and acted a bit breezy. Then when I'd finished it, I just said I'd better be going. And that was that.

VERA. You mean he let you?

MABEL. He just sat there, Vera, looking really pleased with himself. Oh, it was very odd – he looked weird, smiling to himself, all smug and satisfied. And so I left.

VERA. Thank God you got out! However did you get home in that state, dear?

MABEL. State! What a state I was in! I stank to high heaven, so I couldn't get a cab. So what could I do but ring Philip? I prayed he'd be in, Vera – prayed, I did! And he was. So he came and picked me up, and here I am.

VERA. Mabel! You'll never forgive me, I know you won't. What a monster. I suppose some queens are into all that, but not yours truly, I can tell you. I mean, it's just insane, isn't it? And what could anyone do? You might have been found in the river or anywhere. They should be locked up, dear! I must say, I thought I was having a wild time with the queen of spades, but after what you've told me it was like Babes in the Wood in comparison. I'm coming straight over, though. I've never felt so guilty in all my life! See you soon, love. Tata!

MABEL. By bye, Vera! Bye bye!

Ben's Diary

¶ SUNDAY: Got up feeling like an unemptied ashtray, and had a shower to wash last night down the drain. Spent a long time fiddling with my wet hair, trying to make sure it would look wonderful – and it did when it had dried. Washed up, which took about an hour! Then tidied the place, leaving the most interesting books and things lying around! Found twenty pounds in my grey jacket, which seemed a good omen, then had a bowl of Batchelor's Tomato Soup, and felt ready for the big scene! It was about one-thirty, and I kept looking out of the window, and looking in the mirror! The phone rang, and I imagined some excuse and 'See you around', but it was Sam going on about some incredible guy he'd picked up last night. Blah, blah, blah! I said maybe I'd go to the Bell, but didn't know, and that was that. Then I accidentally split a nail as I was having a nervous nibble, which pissed me off, and looked really ugly after I'd rescued what was left with the clippers! I was beginning to crumple after another half-hour passed, and wondered whether I'd given him good enough directions, when the doorbell went. I nearly collapsed with nerves, and had a last look in the mirror before letting him in. God! He looked wonderful, really, incredibly good. We both seemed a bit shy, and I opened the bottle of wine he'd brought, which left him looking around for a bit. It is impossible to write about the bizarre way in which I felt happier than I have ever felt before, even allowing for exaggeration. I wish I could describe it as it actually happened – walking back into the room, seeing him sitting down, looking through the Bruce Weber book, absolutely there, silent and relaxed, as if he belonged here. Well! Somehow it seemed like that, although it sounds over-the-top. He looked round, smiled, and I felt completely moved. I showed him my favourite photograph in the book – the twins with cupid-bow lips – and he sat on the sofa while I sat on a chair. He looked through some tapes, and wanted to listen to Kurt Weill. And so we drank and talked about how boring it was, going out all the time, and how it was better to stay in and do things – but hard to get it together. Too right! And after the music finished, I went to the loo, and thought I looked really good! As I came out, he was just standing there in the corridor, looking strong and hunky in a grey Arran sweater and baggy Fifties trousers. 'Hi', he said. I said the same, and we just stood, looking at each other incredibly hard and boiling inside (like characters in Lawrence!) I stepped forward to go back into the room, and he reached out, taking my shoulders in his hands, and brought us close together. Then we kissed. Ah!! I know this all sounds naff, smouldering tat, but even so, it is a poor description of what happened and how it felt. I mean, it felt more general, like a sort of revelation of something vast and timeless, something that's always there but only vaguely sensed, until it's unleashed by a simple physical act, which gives you a feeling of existing somewhere else, in some other way, as well as being here at a particular moment in time. It was the sheer unselfishness of it, that finally it was possible to give, and receive rather than take, and somehow become natural. Whatever it was, it was a kiss which made me feel completely and without any doubt thrilled to be alive, and gay, and with this particular guy. So there!! The next few hours were like being new, and full of simple big feelings and bizarre complicated ones, all zonking around like atoms in a bomb. We went for a walk in the park, and the cold blue sky, beginning to darken, seemed like something we ourselves had stretched across the long horizon. Maybe I should get a job writing romantic novels! Except I think that romantic novelists never *do*, but only imagine. We went into the second-hand bookshop, where I bought a photo-essay about Lubitsch, and Danny bought short stories by Joyce. And we both felt pleased with ourselves, talked about whether we should go to the cinema, or stay in and watch TV. Whatever we did, I was content, and when we got back we sprawled on the sofa in each other's arms, nibbling ears and occasionally holding each other very hard. It seemed as if Sodom and Gomorrah were inevitable, and it was very dark outside after we finally parted, each lighting a cigarette, feeling that private sadness which makes everything still and quiet after sex. It is very hard to say what it was like, and I feel as if I don't want to write about it like I have about other times. There's always something hysterical about fucking, especially when you're half drunk and don't even know the guy apart from a few pick-up lines you can't even remember. This was utterly different. Unlike the others, it was not an end but hopefully a beginning. It had happened, rather than been done. Its time-scheme was mysterious, and not like the usual desperate humping about, with breaks for a pee because you're pissed. And so it felt different — less simply physical; passionate and incredibly strong, but also full of care. It was the sort of thing that could be remembered, unlike so much sex. Even as I write about it, I can recall the feeling that it was like speaking a language I'd always spoken, but now understood for the first time. And now it was dark, and he had gone to the bathroom after ruffling my hair, and there was the loo flushing and ordinary sound again. I didn't want to speak, but there was the rest of the evening to get together, and it was important to get beyond the feeling that something was over. So I made tea, and we looked at the Lubitsch book, before deciding to go to the Bell. His first words had been 'Thank you', which seemed rather American, and made me feel weird, like every time somebody says it after sex. I don't really understand why, except it's a bit formal. Still, I just smiled (I could hardly say 'Thank you' back!) and we did all the bathroom stuff, after which I dithered about what to wear, and decided on brown and grey, which he said looked beautiful. Ricky was at the Bell, and Sam too, so we stood with them for a bit, me feeling self-conscious and pleased with myself for being with a guy as stunning as Danny. Sam gave me a look like a pat on the back, and I got a bit worried when he started talking to Danny about this and that. Also Danny seemed to be looking around quite a lot, which made me feel neurotic and jealous, although I was looking around as well! It was the first time I've ever felt OK in that place, and I suppose we looked really good together. At least, a lot of guys kept staring and looked interested. I wondered what would happen next, and whether he would come back, or just go home. We drank quite a lot, and Kitty was there in a lurex jumpsuit, all Sixties finery, which Danny really went for. They got on well, and had a dance together while I purred to Ricky and Sam, who kept saying 'He's fabulous!' It was closing time, and we were just leaving when a guy with dyed-blond hair, very good-looking, came up to Danny and started talking. I sort of melted into the background, and watched them. The guy was dressed in a steely-blue suit, like slubbed silk or mohair, and looked like a success. He was a bit character-less, although beautiful. And he looked completely cool and heartless. They seemed to get on well enough, but then something was said, and the guy seemed pissed-off, and started to go back to his friends, but suddenly stopped and turned back to say something. I saw Danny say 'No' and the guy turned away really furious. Then we were on the street. 'Was that him?' I asked. Danny was walking ahead looking angry. 'Yes!' I asked him if he wanted to come back, and he said no, then he was sorry, then yes – he didn't know what he wanted to do. So I said we could go back and sleep, and he smiled as if a light had been turned on somewhere, and we took a taxi home. We were silent, and after tooth-brushes, etc. went to bed and sleep.

NARCISSUS ROWS WITH THE
BOYFRIEND

NARCISSUS. For Christ's sake, David! What are you sulking about now?

DAVID. Nothing!

NARCISSUS. Come on! What am I supposed to have done wrong? Eh?

DAVID. It's always the same these days. Not like it was.

NARCISSUS. What is?

DAVID. Us. That's what! Us!

NARCISSUS. What about us? Fucking hell!

DAVID. You never stand and talk to me!

NARCISSUS. You expect me to stand at the fucking bar all night? Fine! I'll just go to Heaven and stand at the bar while you serve all your bloody admirers. Can't think why I didn't think of it before. I mean, what a wonderful way to spend time and money!

DAVID. You don't spend money. I give you free drinks, for God's sake!

NARCISSUS. I spend money to get in, David! Jesus! Always in a mood, whether I stand there or not! You'll become a bitter old queen if you carry on like this.

DAVID. Queen? Me? You've got a fucking nerve!

NARCISSUS. Try listening to yourself, sometime. It's pathetic. You don't talk any more. It's just a kind of whining — on and on. Never stops.

DAVID. Don't talk any more! How can I talk to you when you're tarting around Heaven, getting your rocks off with every cute boy who gives a second look? I'm not stupid. I've watched you.

NARCISSUS. Oh, I see. Watching me now, is it? It'll be private detectives next. The gay divorcee! Ah well! I suppose I'll get used to it. The loneliness, I mean. And the guilt! I suppose I'm the only guilty one. Yes? I mean, you never look at another boy, do you? Of course you don't. It's just me who looks at boys, while you stand around serving all the little pretties who hang on every word and little glance! I've been watching you too, David!

DAVID. I can't help it! I'm a bartender, for fuck's sake. What am I supposed to do? Tell them all to fuck off? Don't be stupid! I can't stop queens fancying me.

NARCISSUS. It's always been the same. Flirting's always been your game. It's how we met. And it's how you'll always be. I've tried to get used to it, but it's a pain. Why the fuck do you think I don't stand there all night? Why? Because I can't stand watching you playing little games with Steve, and Tim, and all those other little trendy queens, with their shaved heads and arty talk!

DAVID. Come off it! They're not my type. You know that! Just kids!

NARCISSUS. How do I know what you get up to when I'm not there? You've probably had them all, if the truth's known.

DAVID. You're just jealous!

NARCISSUS. Jealous? What, me?

DAVID. Yes! Jealous! Take Jeremy. You fancy him rotten. I can tell. He's told me, anyway. You look at him, he says.

NARCISSUS. I look at lots of bloody people. It doesn't mean to say I want to drag them all into bed. You're stupid. Really fucking stupid. I'm going to bed.

DAVID. No you're not. You're staying here till we've sorted this thing out.

NARCISSUS. What thing?

DAVID. Us!

NARCISSUS. Oh shit! It's in-depth conversation time, is it? Just don't expect me to stay awake, that's all.

DAVID. Well, for a start, you've stolen all my friends. I never see

237

anybody any more. I used to see Mark, but now he's always at the gym, watching you do your work-out. And when I'm there, he ignores me. It's not that I care, really. Except I introduced him to you, and now I never see him.

NARCISSUS. Mark! But you never liked him that much, for God's sake! Stole your friends! I've never heard anything so pathetic. You're like a schoolkid. Shall we draw up a list, so I know who I can talk to? If it makes you feel better, let's make a fucking list. Sometimes I think you're getting paranoid. A paranoid jealous queen!

DAVID. It's not me who's the fucking queen round here.

NARCISSUS. Who are you kidding? It's pouts and flounces every five minutes, like the other night when I brought Jim back. We'd hardly got in before you were having a bath, and going to bed. You could have stayed up and watched the movie. But no! It was 'make a little point' time. Pathetic! As if he didn't notice. Do I have to ask sir's permission to bring a friend back? I'm sorry for not asking, sir!

DAVID. Fuck off! I just wanted a bath, that's all. I was going to have a bath before you'd even got here. The fact that I don't like Jim was nothing to do with it. You know I can't stand him, anyway. So I can't see what difference it made.

NARCISSUS. You've never liked any of my friends, have you? You've never tried. When we started living together, you just couldn't be bothered! I didn't care at the time. I mean, we were together, so who needed friends. But since you started all this fucking jealous scene, it all fits into place. You didn't want me to have friends. You wanted me all to yourself, didn't you. Well, I'm not a fucking possession, David! I'm alive — you know — flesh and blood. I can't stand on a bloody pedestal in a glass case, while you pull lagers behind a boring fucking bar!

DAVID. I don't pull lagers. They're electronic pumps, thank you!

NARCISSUS. Jesus! What a queen! You know what I mean. What's got into you, David? Are you having a breakdown or something? You need some fucking help.

238

DAVID. I don't need help. I need you.

NARCISSUS. I see. Now you're getting all sentimental and trying the 'nothing's really happened' line. Well, it has. You want me to sit around while you make me feel bad. You want me to say I love you, and behave as if none of this tacky little scene had ever happened! Jesus! Come on, David. You can't have it both ways. I'm sick of boring rows about fuck all. What are you trying to say?

DAVID. Nothing!

NARCISSUS. What do you mean, 'nothing'?

DAVID. I said 'nothing'!

NARCISSUS. OK! Nothing! Fine! Can I go to bed now? Or do you want to stay up all night?

DAVID. I don't know what I want. I've no idea. Everything I thought I wanted I've got, but somehow it's not the same. It's just not. Can't you see that? We're not the same any more. When we go out together – when! When we're out, you're just not there. It's a waiter, or a guy on the street, or anything other than me! I suppose I should have known it would happen, but even so – I never thought it would. I've tried hard not to think about it. I don't want a life of looking around for someone else, for God's sake! I couldn't bear it. Going to Heaven, the Embassy, pubs and all that, just looking. No one ever finds anything there – it might be for a night or two, but nothing else!

NARCISSUS. David! We met in a bar – we did! Come on. It can happen, like it did to us. You talk about 'us'. Great! Well – we've got something together – we have. And you're fucking it up with all this paranoia and crap about other people. It's natural to fancy other guys, isn't it? You do, don't you? You do! I've seen you. It doesn't mean you don't love me, or I'll stop loving you. It's what we are. Queens! We cruise, for Christ's sake. What else is there to do when you're on your own? You can't just stand there, not looking. Let me tell you something. Come on, David – don't get all moody. I want to tell you something.

DAVID. OK! Tell me something. I know what you're going to say. You've found someone else! You have. I know you have.

NARCISSUS. OK! Who is it? Come on, David. Who *is* it? You know so fucking much – tell me.

DAVID. I don't know who it is. I just know, that's all. I do.

NARCISSUS. Well, I'll tell you. Yesterday I met this guy in the Y. I've seen him before, and he fancied me, and I fancied him. So we did it. That's all. We fucking did it. It was nothing, really, except a good fuck and forget it!

DAVID. He was a good fuck!?!

NARCISSUS. Yeah! He was.

DAVID. As good as me? I mean – was he as good a fuck as me? – Well?

NARCISSUS. He was a good fuck – all right? Really good! But not like you.

DAVID. What do you mean, 'not like me'? You did it, didn't you? You wanted to, and you did. I've wanted to do it with lots of guys. But I didn't. I couldn't . . . because of you. Because of us.

NARCISSUS. Well, you should have. It means fuck all, David.

DAVID. Fuck all! Jesus, you make me really pissed-off. If you thought I was OK – I mean, if it was like when we first met . . .

NARCISSUS. It is. Exactly the same, apart from all this winding-up. Exactly!

DAVID. It's not any more. If it was, you wouldn't have to fuck some guy in the Y for kicks. Would you? Why did you do it? Am I so boring?

NARCISSUS. No! You're not boring. You're crazy – yes! But there's nothing boring about you. You're just in love.

DAVID. With myself, I suppose! I hate myself, if you really want to know. Hate myself!

NARCISSUS. I don't hate you, though. After the guy last night – and one tonight, in Heaven . . .

DAVID. Another? Jesus, it's too much!

NARCISSUS. Yeah! Another! Straight! Nice! Never see him again –

so what! It was just sex, David. Not like us! It was just like pissing or having another drink! Easy! No —

DAVID. Complications! That's it, isn't it? You want to be on your own again. I understand! Why not? If you want to, then let's agree.

NARCISSUS. Agree about what?

DAVID. Let's just say it's over!

NARCISSUS. I said you were in love — yeah?

DAVID. Yes.

NARCISSUS. And you're in love with me?

DAVID. Yes. I am.

NARCISSUS. And I'm in love with you, David. I love you, for fuck's sake!!

DAVID. You fuck two different guys in the last twenty-four hours, and you're in love with me. Great!

NARCISSUS. Other guys do it all the time, and stay together. It doesn't mean anything. I'm here, aren't I? Trust counts more than faithfulness.

DAVID. I don't know. Maybe you're thinking about last night's — or tonight's. How do I know? How can I ever know after this whether it's me, or some queen from Heaven or the Y, wherever?

NARCISSUS. Trust me! It's you.

DAVID. How do I know? How? You talk crap. Faithfulness is just as important as trust. It makes for trust.

NARCISSUS. I'm telling you, David. If I said I've felt shitty ever since the guy at the gym, and tonight as well, would you believe me?

DAVID. Why do it then? You didn't have to. You could have stopped yourself — like I have.

NARCISSUS. I did it because I wanted to.

DAVID. Well, I think you should have starved!

NARCISSUS. Yeah! I suppose you're going to starve me tonight now.

DAVID. Jesus! You've had enough for a fucking army! It's dessert now, is it?

241

NARCISSUS. OK! I'm *sorry*! I'm sorry. I shouldn't have done it.

DAVID. Them!

NARCISSUS. *Them*, then! So I did. So let's forget it – them!

DAVID. Yeah! OK! Let's forget it – them! I'll try. But it won't be easy.

NARCISSUS. Well – bed?

DAVID. Yeah! Bed! Why not! And have a good wash, yeah?

NARCISSUS. An acid bath if you like!

DAVID. No! Just a good wash. Then sleep! You must be exhausted! Maybe I'll kiss you good night! Not that you deserve it. Still, it's too late to carry on like this. I might feel different tomorrow. Come on!

Ben's Diary

¶ MONDAY: Up early because Danny had a modelling job to get to. We didn't talk about the guy last night, and I made a resolution not to let it freak me out. It's just the idea of two years with the same guy. He probably dreamt about him last night, and there's nothing I can do about that — until he starts dreaming about me! On the other hand, here I am moaning and worrying when at least I've had him. But that's the point. So what! So I've had maybe fifty, or even more. And how many of them mattered beyond a fuck? Even the few I liked and thought it would be more than that — I get bored too easily. How long before this one goes the same way? After two years with the same person, I should think he's pretty bored with the idea of even a week with someone, especially after something so beautiful. I haven't even got a job, just a few brilliant ideas — and I hate my body!! And so I sat around, thinking of everything that could go wrong, getting neurotic and attacking my nails. After going to get some more cigarettes and seeing an amazing boy with superb thighs and a long thick neck, I decided I was obsessed with sex, so that what people were like was irrelevant anyway! Called into the Pollo, where Jon and Kitty were having coffee, discussing the alternative fashion show. Felt cheered up to be with friends, and wandered through Soho with them, watching the punters duck into nude encounters and peep shows. Then home and sorted through pockets to find spare cash — I'd forgotten to go to the bank. The bell went at about six — it was Danny, complete with bags of fresh fruit and veg from the market, announcing a plan for the evening — him and me, a meal and TV! Which is exactly what it was. I thought of the winter, and how good it is to have someone to cuddle when it's cold! We went to bed, and messed about for a bit, then fell asleep after talking about how much cheaper it is staying in!

KEVIN WRITES TO CAMP SHEILA

Dear Sheila,

Well, here I am in sunny London. Actually it's been cold and miserable and really gets you down. Eric's still got his job at the pizza place, but I haven't got anything yet. I've been trying to start as a model, but it's very hard, even though Dennis said it was easy. When are you coming down? I really miss you all and wish you'd hurry up. There's some right funny fellas down here, I can tell you. I've met a few as well, but they're not like they are back home. Not as friendly – do you know what I mean? I met this one last night. They called him Adrian. He was old like – about forty I'd say. Not bad-looking for forty – if you like that kind of thing. But he was famous, Sheila! He knows Sting, and all sorts of pop stars and things. We met in this thing called the Asylum – it's a club. Quite good really. At least there was a lot of younger types. Everywhere you go in London is just old men and ugly clone types. It's terrible, Sheila. You've no idea! I've practically got to fight them off. Anyway, this Adrian who knows Sting and all these famous sophisticated people – imagine! – well, he says he's going to help me. I went back to his place last night, you see. He's a painter, Sheila. A bit of a weirdo if you ask me. There was all these pictures – proper paintings – you know what I mean. And it was just boys in the nude, all done in silver and blue. Quite good really. Well, I know what you're thinking, and let me tell you, it's just what I thought when I saw them. Nude boys! It's like that fella from Batley who took me back to his place and showed me all those mucky photos. I suppose paintings is not the same, but nude boys says the same thing, doesn't it? So there we were, in his place. It were a funny place, as well. Bits of bone and God knows how many books and stuff like

245

that. He was a bit too clever for my liking. Who wants to know about bloody art and stuff? I mean, it was quite interesting really, but at three in the morning you want to get to bed, don't you. Well that was right out! We sat there while he rolled a joint and kept giggling to himself. A bit weird! And then he got out all these photo albums and showed me all the boys he's had. There must have been hundreds, Sheila. At least they weren't in the nude though. Well — one or two were, and right good-looking too! There weren't any of Sting, though, which was a shame. I'd have loved to see one of him starkers! I really would. And after that we had some tea and watched a really peculiar film on his video. He does stuff like that as well. In fact, there's nothing he doesn't do as far as I could make out. Anyway, I was beginning to feel really stoned, and proper tired. Clubs in London tire you out, Sheila. They really do. They're so big, you see. You have to walk a fucking mile to the toilet. And it's always full of little queens just hanging around for trade. Anyway, there's never anybody having a pee — hardly ever. Just standing around, really obvious. There's some bona clothes, though. A lot of them have sugar-daddies, I think. Although there's a lot that's rich too. Makes you sick, doesn't it? I've bought a few new things — a fabulous pair of trousers, all black and red blotches! But the dole goes nowhere, and Eric's a bit fed up of lending me a fiver every other day! I think he's getting a bit pissed-off with me, Sheila. His room's so small, and until I get a job we can't start to look for somewhere bigger. What can you do? Anyway, I was with this Adrian fella, wasn't I? And it was really late by now. So I said I thought I'd better be off, and I'd give him a ring about getting some contacts for the modelling. And do you know what he said, Sheila? He said he wanted me to stay and let him cuddle me. Cuddle me! The state of it! So I said I knew bloody well what he meant by cuddling, and I had Eric to get back to. So he looked really put out, and pissed-off. Well, I felt a bit of a prick, really. After all, he'd offered to help me, hadn't he? So I said I'd stay — but only for a cuddle. So we took us clothes off and I was going to get into bed, when he suddenly said he wanted to have a bit of

246

fun. Bloody hell, I thought – I bet I know what that means. But it wasn't what you're thinking, Sheila. Do you know what he did? Baby oil! He covered me with baby oil. Imagine me swimming in fucking baby oil. It felt really sexy though. I mean, when he was putting it on and rubbing it in – really sexy!! I said it would make a right mess of the sheets, but he didn't care, he said. And then he took some photos of me. I tried to stop him, but he wasn't having any of it. Well, what's the harm of a few photos, I thought. So I posed a bit with a towel, and he took his photos. It was really camp, Sheila. Just the sort of thing you'd have loved! What would my mam have thought! She'd have died laughing, I bet. Anyway, after that we went to bed and he did a bit of cuddling and wanted a bit of the other. But I wouldn't let him, Sheila! I've got my pride, you know!! And what with Eric and everything, it wouldn't be right. You would have, I know. But I just couldn't have done it! So we got up quite early, because he had to do some work, and went out for breakfast to a cafe in Soho. I must say I don't like them cwasson things. French rubbish. There's nowt like jam on toast, is there?!! It was full of trendy types, right stuck up. I can live without all that at nine in the morning! There was a dishy boy though. I think he must have been a model or something, with blond hair all ruffled about at the front. I think I might dye mine. I'm sick of it now. It's ages since I was blond, isn't it? When are you coming down, Sheila? I'm dying to take you places, and have a laugh! You'd have a ball. You really would. Are you still with the butcher, or is it all over? I never know with you. I'd better be finishing now because I've got to go and meet Eric at the pizza place. Do you think that painter will make me into a star? When you come down, I'll introduce you – he's bound to want to take some photos of you in all your suspenders and stuff! You'd like that, wouldn't you. Come down soon. There's not much room but you won't mind our floor, will you? Knowing you, there'll be no shortage of beds in London! Look after yourself. I'm signing off now,
lots of love, Kevin. XXXXX

P.S. They can't dance down here at all. They just stand in the same place, and hardly move at all. And then they get all stroppy if you bump into them. When you get here, we'll show them, Sheila, won't we love?!

Ben's Diary

¶ TUESDAY: Sex in the morning seems to start in sleep and happen with both of you only half awake, in a sort of warm limbo. Beautiful! After that, we lay there, and murmured sweet nothings to each other. And then he mentioned the singer. 'Don't worry about him,' he said. I said I wasn't (!) and he said of course I was, and it was all over. I asked what he'd said on Sunday. 'He wanted me to go home and fuck him!' For some crazy reason I said 'Well, why didn't you?' Suddenly he got really pissed-off – what a stupid question; why did it matter? He'd come with me, hadn't he? I said it mattered because it affected him and me, and I wanted to know. That's all. 'Is he a good fuck?' I imagined he was, and wanted to know. Anyway, he was good-looking, and it interested me to know what I was being compared with. It terrified me too. And all of this was the most pathetic kind of jealousy, worrying about old boyfriends, things that you can do nothing about. 'Fantastic!' I wished I hadn't asked, when suddenly he pulled me towards him and said, 'But not as good as you. OK?' Why is it hard to believe what you want to? I lay there getting all moody and untouchable. 'We lived together for two years, right? So I must have liked something about him. He was good in bed, and in the end I realized that was all he was. And after a while he wasn't even that. I suppose I loved him – at first – but not any more.' I said I was sorry for asking, and as we kissed he broke off and said 'I came home with you, because I wanted to be with you, which is why I'm here now. I can go away, if you like, or I can stick around.' 'Stick around!' And we rolled around in a sort of fighting embrace, each proving his point. And then we slept some more, and after that got up and had a bath together. He groaned about wanting a clean T-shirt so I lent him one, and he said he'd have to bring some clothes round because going to work wearing the same things was bad for the image, as well as filthy. And so he left, and I rang Ricky and gave him a blow-by-blow account. Ricky said it was *Love Story* time, and thinks I'm going to start staying in, having dinner parties, and showing everybody my scrapbook of 'Danny photos'. Actually, he sounded envious and bitchy, but maybe I imagine that. I went to the library and borrowed a biography of Cocteau. Danny rang later to say he was staying at home tonight to develop some pictures, so I stayed in and read, going to bed early with a face covered in Oil of Ulay, and a dollop of Panoxyl on a bloody spot!!

AN OPERA QUEEN AT HOME

OPERA QUEEN. This pasta is not exactly *al dente*, dear! I'm sorry, but the oven clock must be slow!

GEOFFREY. Tastes fine to me. Mind you, I'm hopeless at cooking. Always have been. If I didn't live with Susan, I think I'd starve.

OPERA QUEEN. How is she? I haven't seen her in months.

GEOFFREY. Just the same. A fifty-five-year-old fag-hag, with a half-bottle of gin in every handbag. I feel sorry for her, but there's nothing you can do! She comes to the pub every now and then, and sits in a stupor watching all the goings-on. Can't see what she gets out of it!

OPERA QUEEN. It's obvious. She hates men and feels threatened unless they're queens. It's a common syndrome, dear. She lives for you and the boys!

GEOFFREY. Well, I think it's tragic!

OPERA QUEEN. 'Course it is! What isn't these days? I've told you before, Geoffrey – this gay little existence takes a lot of patience and suffering. I've suffered all my life.

GEOFFREY. What you need is another boy. I can't understand why you got rid of that theatrical one – Glyn, wasn't it? At least she got freebies!

OPERA QUEEN. Yes. Glyn – or Glenda to his Glyndebourne chums. She was so stuck-up, though. Always had to be the queen bee. There was no one she didn't know, dear – from the House of Lords down. It was always shishy little DPs with Lady Muck and some famous continental actor or something. Hated it! But could she cook! And if you set foot in the kitchen, it was screaming fits and 'don't touch the truffles!' I've never known a queen so tidy. It was like an obsession.

During a five-course meal, she'd make sure the kitchen was spotless. Always cleaned up as she went along. Talk about domesticated. Always washing her hands, too. It's unnatural if you ask me, to wash so much. I like a clean queen, but she was too much. It was the same in bed. Always wiping things with a pink towel, as if you were defiling her or something!

GEOFFREY. She never went to the pub, though! I must say I thought that was odd!

OPERA QUEEN. Couldn't stand cigarette smoke, dear. Or beer. Well, you remember what she smelled like. I used to call her Coco Chanel. She only had to be in a room for ten seconds and it smelled like a ladies' loo for weeks!

GEOFFREY. But didn't she make it big? I thought she'd started her own opera company or something!

OPERA QUEEN. Well, dear. She had a lot of backing – if you know what I mean. Even when I was having it, there were long-distance calls to Italy and all over the place. Some middle-aged rich-bitch queen took her up, and gave her whatever she wanted. We were there, anyway. The first time she did something. You can't have forgotten it!

GEOFFREY. Oh! That fairy thing – *Undine*, wasn't it?

OPERA QUEEN. 'Undone', more like. Appalling! All those old bags rolling about on Bakofoil, with bits of tinsel in their wigs, trying to be water-nymphs! I've never seen anything like it in my life!

GEOFFREY. Wasn't the hero called Hildebrand, or something? I can remember the bit where she goes to the wedding.

OPERA QUEEN. It was a few tatty banners and shields, wasn't it?

GEOFFREY. And he turns into ice – do you remember? That heap of see-through plastic was thrown over him when the lights went out, and when they came on we were supposed to know he'd turned into ice! Talk about tat!

OPERA QUEEN. Oh, she's dreadful! And the people there. It was like the Royal Command, dear! All for that! And Coco Chanel, swanning about as if it were *The Ring*, or something. As for all those opera queens, I could never bear them. All standing in little gaggles, pursing their lips and bitching like mad behind poor little Coco's back. Until she swanned over. Then it was all smiles, and hugs and kisses! 'Darling! What a fabulous production! You must be very proud. Fabulous! Truly!' Horrors, the lot of them.

GEOFFREY. Well, she was quite pretty, I always thought.

OPERA QUEEN. Like a china doll, dear! I thought it would make a change, but the rough ones are best! They might not always be clean, but they're definitely better in bed. And there's none of that snotty competition scene. Do you know – she once told me I was too common for her friends! Me! Too common! That was the night I smacked her one. And that's when it ended.

GEOFFREY. You never told me you'd smacked her one!

OPERA QUEEN. I could have killed her, Geoffrey. Killed her! What's she but a jumped-up little fag! She's a nobody – but she thinks because she's got her rich friends in high places that she's something to write home about! Well, there's one consolation, dear. She's talentless!

GEOFFREY. Still – after what we suffered tonight, it makes you wonder whether anybody's talented at all!

OPERA QUEEN. Shall we listen to some music, dear? What would you like? I've got a very camp Offenbach – *Robinson Crusoe*!

GEOFFREY. I'm not really in the mood for twiddles. Do you know what I mean? I fancy something soothing. *Lieder*, do you think? A touch of Schumann? Something a bit languid, anyway. What have you got?

OPERA QUEEN. What haven't I got!? How about Lotte in the Thirties? *Frauenliebe und Leben*. It's one of my little rarities.

GEOFFREY. Oh, heavenly! The divine Lotte! Throw her on the turntable, dear. I'm going to flop!

OPERA QUEEN. I didn't see you at the Pogorelich concert. Did you go?

GEOFFREY. I'm furious about it, dear. I forgot! Imagine forgetting that!

OPERA QUEEN. They were all there, Geoffrey! Everybody. It was like a bloody convention. Never seen so many queens outside of the Embassy. All sighing and saying how beautiful he is. It was like going to *Death in Venice* when it first came out! He was divine, though! Absolutely sensational!

GEOFFREY. I knew he would be. I can't tell you how cross I am.

OPERA QUEEN. I haven't shown you the garden, have I?

GEOFFREY. Is it finished?

OPERA QUEEN. Well, I'm still waiting for a little bronze nymph to go by the pond, and I've not really made my mind up about the grotto. Come and have a look at it. See what you think. I got them to put concealed lighting everywhere, so that in the summer you can sit out on a balmy night, and look at all the flowers.

GEOFFREY. Oh! It's fabulous!

OPERA QUEEN. Not bad, is it? Who'd have thought that such a tiny space could be turned into such a refined jungle? It's not very pretty in the winter, apart from the evergreens, but in the summer it will be a dream. Over there are four different Clematis, and they'll cascade down that wall like nobody's business. And that's Wistaria. I've had a bit of trouble with it, but she's settled down now.

GEOFFREY. I just love the smell of Wistaria!

OPERA QUEEN. Can't beat it, can you? That's why I put a mauve bulb in the light that hits that corner. To pick out the blossom — when she flowers!

GEOFFREY. The pond's very sweet, isn't it?

OPERA QUEEN. The trouble I've had with that pond, Geoffrey. You wouldn't believe it! After they'd finished it, I bought some goldfish, and water-lilies. Well, what do you think happened?

GEOFFREY. They all died!

OPERA QUEEN. Well, yes. But before that. The water disappeared! There must have been a crack or something, because the next day I went to feed the fish, and they were just lying there, in half an inch of water. I was so livid! What I didn't say to my landscape gardener and pond-maker!

GEOFFREY. And where is the nymph going?

254

OPERA QUEEN. Well, I thought just there, next to that Victorian sink. I got that for a song in Camden Lock. It's got snowdrops in it, but they won't be up for another month or so. So – there it is!

GEOFFREY. Well, I think it's fabulous, dear!

OPERA QUEEN. And that's my new *objet d'art*.

GEOFFREY. What is it?

OPERA QUEEN. It's a Georgian wig-stand! Something I've always wanted.

GEOFFREY. Oh! Very nice!

OPERA QUEEN. Well, now I've finished restoring that bit of moulding in the corner where it needs painting, I thought I'd treat myself to a little prezzy! You can't tell, though, can you? It took me hours of fiddling to get the acanthus right. But I did it! The next thing is painting, and then the gilding. And next month they're coming to instal one of those fake gas fires with coal and flames. They're terribly convincing, actually. After that, this room's done. And do you know – I've done it all! Every last little brush-stroke. Howard's done nothing at all. Nothing!

GEOFFREY. How is Howard? I haven't seen him in months.

OPERA QUEEN. Never marry a travelling salesman, Geoffrey. It's a life of total misery. He's never here, dear. Last week it was Birmingham, and this week it's Slough. Still, we've learned to live our own lives after all this time. He has his boys and I have mine. And ne'er the twain shall meet. We did once share a Malaysian, but it didn't really work. We just squabbled and rowed. So she got the boot and we decided to go back to one each. He finds them in cottages, mostly. I suppose in the provinces there's nothing else, is there? Still, they'll do it for a packet of fags and two pints of beer, so it doesn't break the joint account! By the way – we've got new neighbours!

GEOFFREY. Really? Nice?

OPERA QUEEN. Queens, dear. Antique dealers. You should have seen the furniture when they moved in. I was green, bright green. It was like 'Going for a Song'. And then they invited us round for a drink! You've never seen anything like it. Grand piano, *two* harps dear — and a fabulous musical box, with those big round discs. You know the sort. They've even got a fucking chandelier in the 'drawing-room'. Imagine! It's like Buckingham Palace. She's Jewish, the butch one. All airs and graces, and Egyptian fags. They stink something rotten, but she likes the posh boxes. You can imagine the type. I was very cool. Howard did all the talking, and I drank all the gin! He's always been too friendly, has Howard. No discretion at all. There they were, talking down their noses, and Howard doesn't even notice. But I did! Stuck-up queens!

GEOFFREY. They sound hideous.

OPERA QUEEN. Horrendous, dear! Still, I suppose we'll have to have them to dinner. I mean, they might get me some cheap rugs for the bedrooms, and I've already blagged a sweet little coffee service they had in one of the display cabinets. Twenty quid — a bargain! They have a shop in the West End, but keep a lot of stuff at home. So it's a bit like a shop, really. At the weekends they toddle off to their country cottage — well, not cottage, but converted church or something. Very *House and Garden*, dear!

GEOFFREY. I've never liked antique dealers. There's something vulgar about them, isn't there? And they always think they're a cut above everybody else. They're only shopkeepers, when all's said and done!

OPERA QUEEN. Oh, listen to that! She sings that as if her heart was breaking! Sometimes, Geoffrey, I just put this record on and pour a G and T, and sit here in tears. Let's put it back, shall we? I've just got to listen to it again. There'll be no grooves left on this one soon! And it's deleted now!

Ben's Diary

¶ WEDNESDAY: Today I decided to grab my life by the balls, and do something. The Panoxyl had done its stuff, and I put on a shirt and tie as if to celebrate. Rang Kitty, who's got a job for the Beeb, doing Roman extras' cozzies for Ant. and Cleo. I asked if she needed any help, and could I get some work there too, and she said I was to go straight over and pick up some brass curtain-rings on the way. Rang Danny and arranged to meet later, then off to Kitty's new studio, which has to be seen to be believed. It's up in Islington, overlooking a graveyard, and stinks of cow-gum and cat-pee. Her cat's just had kittens, and Kitty couldn't drown a fly, so there are five little bundles, groping about, mewing in that sad way kittens do. Of course the curtain-rings were the wrong size, and she threw a wobbly and told me I had no hope whatever of being a designer if I couldn't realize which the best curtain-rings were for this job. She could have told me herself, except that she always presumes you know. After that we ripped into the muslin, and set about creating. She played Strauss all day — *Fledermaus* — and when it ended, she started it again. I fed the cat, and started a hard job, painting some authentic design round the purple bit on a toga. It was gold, and the paint not very good, so it just soaked through and looked really naff. She blew a fuse, and I had to go out and get some different paint. Kitty had about fifty more kittens than the cat, and said I was absolutely hopeless. After a poisonous Wimpy I left and said I'd come back tomorrow. She gave me fifteen quid and said I wasn't Erté, to which I said I wasn't ninety either. I felt quite pleased that I'd done something close to what I want, and wondered how much the Beeb was paying her . . . Danny wasn't at the Cap when I got there, so I had a pint on my own and tried to fend off a couple of marauding skins by glaring a lot! Any other time and I might have gone for one of them, but not now. They all seem so territorial up there, as if you're standing where a regular stands, and shouldn't be. Danny was quite late, and I'd had a couple while waiting. The guy behind the bar clearly knew Danny, because they had a little chat while he was getting served. And Danny? He looked like a pearl before swine, all wind and rain-swept. Then suddenly the place was full. It's crazy how a bar can be empty at eight, and minutes later crammed with half North London. He didn't want to stay, and there was no reason to, so we went back to his place for coffee. I'd often tried to imagine what it would be like, and wasn't disappointed. The top floor of a Victorian house, knocked through into one huge room, except for the bathroom. There was no carpet, only black floorboards, and a black futon at the back, open as a bed. On the white walls were lots of photographs, either taken of him or by him. One of them was a faked-up classical pose à la Victorians, with Danny bursting out from a split tree-trunk, and wearing only a pearly-coloured drape, diaphanous and almost transparent. Apart from these photos, and a small black and gold painting, there was nothing else. Maybe one or two books — a Warhol magazine — and some white silk draped across the windows for a curtain. There was one photo of the singer, in which he looked icy and incredibly beautiful. Danny made some coffee, and I put some music on — all jazz, apart from some New Wave, and a few Sixties albums — so I settled for Oscar Peterson Live somewhere, and lay on the futon very tired but unrelaxed. It was weird, because the place was set up as an uncluttered space, which he obviously found relaxing and attractive. I suppose rooms are like vital clues if you want to understand someone. This one said a lot about style, as well as suggesting controlled emotions and a kind of Spartan dedication to work. There was a strong impression of ego, too – straightforward and untheatrical. The classical photo had been taken for a French magazine doing a feature on look-alikes in life and art!! Danny sat next to me, and lit a cigarette, obviously wondering what I thought about it all. I think he's quite proud of how he lives, and I said I thought the pictures were brilliant. He likes street life, and many of them were of wrinkled bag-people, tottering through Charing Cross with rusty old prams laden with rubbish. I said I thought it was sad, and he disagreed, saying they were much happier than people like us because they'd escaped money and boredom. I was amazed by this, and felt that we had never really spoken like friends do – arguing about the problems of life and art and all that! I suddenly felt deeply relaxed, almost as if I wanted to go to sleep, and lay back gazing at the ceiling, silent. He asked me what I was thinking about. 'Struggle,' I said. It had occurred to me that love must always be a struggle, and can't last unless there's masses of effort and anger, as well as the afternoon walks, and cuddles in the cinema. In fact, being in love is completely exhausting. It creates new feelings and energy, and immediately uses them up and has to create more. And the hard thing is that they always have to be different, so that love doesn't get bored. That's why so many queens sleep around – because their emotional imagination is too naff to develop a set of endless variations on the same theme, or person. I said this last thing to Danny, who agreed. That was obviously the story with the singer, and I felt sad and sorry that something had stopped which Danny had probably needed. It's a pain that miserable experiences produce bitterness and suspicion. And they make it very hard for anyone who comes after. It was quite cold, and I mentioned the heater. But he said it was a waste of money, and found a duvet which he laid on top of us. So there we were, fully clothed, dozing away, until soon we were asleep. We woke late in the night, took our clothes off, put out the light, and went back to bed.

THE STRAIGHT QUEEN REPLIES
TO A LONELY HEART

'Blond boy (22). Athletic build. Student. Sick of scene. Seeks handsome older man for cultural evenings, dinner, concerts, etc. . . . Must be straight-acting. Discretion assured. Photo/Phone please. a.l.a. Box T352.'

Dear Blond Boy,

This is the first time I have ever answered a lonely-hearts advertisement, and I'm not sure that I'll post this when I've finished. I read all the advertisements after a particularly gruelling evening in a gay pub, where everyone seemed so worn out and unhappy that I felt there must be some other way of meeting someone. I ought to begin by being honest with you. I am a happily married man with three small children. You may wonder why I am replying to your advertisement, then. I think part of the reason is that I have felt for some time now the need for the love of someone of my own sex. It is hard to explain how this has come about. It simply has. It is, of course, imperative that my family do not get to know about it. If we were to meet, therefore, it would be necessary to behave with great discretion. I am telling you this because it does mean that I am what you would probably consider to be very inexperienced in these matters. Indeed, apart from one brief experience at Cambridge, I have never slept with another man nor had sexual relations with one. I hope that this will not discourage you from replying to this letter, however.

I have never had to describe myself to a stranger before, and don't really know where or how to begin. I am thirty-six, and five feet and eleven inches tall. I have a slim build, and I suppose I am what women call handsome. I am not sure whether you would think so, but there it is. I have dark brown hair, am clean-shaven, and dress conventionally. I think you would find me rather old-fashioned in appearance, rather like a character out of *Brideshead Revisited*! In fact, I do go to church quite regularly, although I would not describe myself as a religious fanatic. I like the music a great deal, and am also very fond of ecclesiastical architecture. Actually, it was the reference to cultural outings in your advertisement which interested me, as well as your description! I am very keen on going to the theatre and concerts. Since my children are very young, there has not been much opportunity for me to do those things with my wife. Perhaps we could do them together? Unfortunately, I do have a certain number of friends and colleagues who are fond of the same things. So we would have to invent a reason for you being with me. That could be quite good fun, couldn't it? Since I am a teacher, I suppose you could be one of my students or something. After all, you are a student aren't you? I am very interested to know what you study. Is it on the arts side, or are you frightfully clever and scientific or mathematical? I'm afraid I ought to confess to being rather bored by scientists, but I'm sure if you are interested in cultural pursuits, we will have enough in common. I'm terribly fond of painting, too. Especially Constable's landscapes. I do hope that you have some interest in all that.

I must say it is awfully difficult writing this letter. I've no idea what to say next! Does that sound ridiculous? I wonder if there's anything else you would want to know. I don't really have any peculiar characteristics, like some people. I don't drink an awful lot! And I don't like ham, for some reason. Pigs, I think, disgust me. I am very fond of Dickens, actually. (In fact, I think that *Bleak House* is the greatest of English novels.) Apart from Jane Austen, that is. She remains the loftiest of them all, don't you think? Or perhaps you aren't familiar with her novels. I feel sure that you are, even though I only know that you have an athletic build, and are 'sick of the scene'. Have you been on the 'scene' for long? It is rather dreadful, isn't it? I don't think I could bear becoming a 'regular', like so many of the people one sees in those places. Have you had a lot of experience? From your description, I imagine that many men must have been interested in you! The trouble is, a lot of those types are only interested in one thing, which must be very depressing. Is that why you feel the need for an older man? I ought to say that I don't actually look my age — younger, if anything. Anyway, there's a very fine play on at the moment — *Another Country*. I'm not sure when you will receive this letter, but I thought we could meet in order to do something, rather than an embarrassing encounter over a cup of coffee. Don't you think that would be a good idea? And then, after the theatre, we could have dinner and get to know each other. As a plan, it satisfies your advertisement's requirements, although I'm not sure whether I do! I look forward to hearing from you, and do hope that you will reply to my letter. I feel sure that we would get on.

Yours,

Christopher.

P.S. I don't have a good photograph, I'm afraid. If you really want one, then I could have something done in time for your reply.

Ben's Diary

¶ THURSDAY: Danny to work and me to Kitty's for another
Roman session. I got the gold paint right, which was
something, and she let me loose on some head-dresses,
which were very fiddly and complicated, but more fun than
doing decorative borders. Looked forward to the time when
I might be doing something of my own, not that I'd call
myself ambitious. Called in Flip on the way home and tried
about twenty things on, none of which fitted. One
three-quarter-length coat, all speckled black and yellow and
red, which I loved but which must have belonged to the
Incredible Hulk. I did find a lovely grey shirt, cotton and
voluminous, for only three pounds. Meeting Danny in the
pub at ten-thirty to go to the Asylum. Dithered about what
to wear, as usual, and settled on the tatty DJ, with a thin
black sweater and no shirt. I looked like a ballet dancer, as
though clothes were an encumbrance and had to be
super-casual! And I gelled my hair back, which looked very
Italian. Early to the pub where I saw Jeremy with a cute
American, very YMCA and clean. The American is from
New York, doing a grand tour, and about to go to
Germany, which he says is a very sexy place. He seems to
know the Gay Guide backwards, and doesn't think much of
London, although Heaven was better than he thought it
would be. Jeremy sat there looking like a proud dog-owner,
so after a while I thought I'd leave them to it. Danny came,
though, so we all stood together. He's so good with
strangers, leaping in with both feet and appearing to know
things about whatever is said. I bullshitted about the state
of gay sex in America, while Danny talked about the
architecture of skyscrapers like Alistair Cooke! People who

263

know what they are talking about can be a real pleasure —
they can also be very boring. The American was sweet, but
boring. At the Asylum we danced a lot, then hung about in
the upstairs bar, where a crazy gang of Fifties bike-boys
were getting very pissed on cans of beer. They were all
about thirty-five or more, covered in grease and brass and
silver studs, with Norton and Vincent beautifully lettered
in white paint on their battered jackets. They looked like a
tribe of hunters who had come to terrorize the pretty blond
hairdressers and teddy-bear clones. Not at all like leather
queens who've never been on a bike in their lives and
wouldn't know one end of an exhaust from another.
Actually, there are far too many queens wandering about
looking uncomfortable and anxious. It's one of the
problems of trying to create an effect. And the Asylum is
pretty full of guys trying their hardest to look something,
even when as people they are real dross. Clothes are such a
bizarre necessity, when it comes to sex. I'm sure Jeremy's
right when he says that the Y is fabulous because you can
make up your mind in the showers, and save all that time of
picking them up, getting them home, and discovering the
hideous truth. The American kept hanging around,
laughing and joking with Danny and trying, as I thought,
to make a date. Why do people always get the wrong idea?
The problem is that Dan is a born flirt. Effortlessly sexy and
dark gleaming eyes which provoke a kind of pornographic
fantasy. Sam waltzed up with a French boy he was having a
few language problems with. Apparently they'd met in the
loo, where Sam had done him a favour only to realize that
the guy spoke almost no English. Not that it's possible to
talk doing that! He was a classic Parisian, all chic modern
clothes and arrogant look. Better than most of the English
boys, though, and probably sexier because he couldn't
really speak without stopping to say 'trop difficile'! Danny
had said he liked French boys, so I was a bit wary. And of
course he speaks French, so they banged on about this club

264

and that, which pissed Sam off and made me feel rather boring, although he wasn't as pretty as all that! So we ended up staying until the bitter end, with Adrian hanging around, burbling '*enchanté*' every ten seconds, and trying to persuade them both to go back to his place! It all looks so bleak when the lights go up, and everybody ages about twenty years! We left them to it, and got home knackered and too tired to talk. Bed was a place to sleep – for once!

RENT BOYS IN A SOHO DIVE

PETE. 'Ow yer doin', Eddy?

EDDY. All right, Pete! You?

PETE. All right! This place is a dead loss, tonight. Where's all the fuckin' punters, eh? Makes yer sick, it does. Wot you been up to, then?

EDDY. I 'ad a bit o' luck down St Martin's Lane. Lawyer! I rolled it for twenty-five, an' nicked a neat pair o' cuff-links into the bargain!

PETE. Well, that's all right then!

EDDY. Fuckin' closet queen, 'e was! Rollin' in it! You shoulda seen 'is place, Pete! Fuckin' rich bastard!

PETE. See that Indian geezer, sittin' by the bar? Can't fuckin' stand 'im!

EDDY. Yeah! 'E was down the pub, earlier, chattin' up some little queen!

PETE. Yeah! Well, if 'e keeps lookin' at me like that, I'll smack 'im one!

EDDY. Come on, Pete! Not worth the effort, mate!

PETE. I'd love to really smack 'im one.

EDDY. Wot you been up to, then?

PETE. Pissed! Gettin' pissed. I was right out of it last night. There was these three snotty-nosed wankers down the pub. I was leanin' at the bar, like. So this geezer – real old queen, 'e was – 'e comes up an' asks me if I wanna drink. Like an old lady, 'e was, talkin' posh and smilin' like a fuckin' loony! So we 'ad a drink, an' I was gettin' a bit pissed, when 'e says 'e wants to take me down 'ere. So I says I'm not interested. You shoulda seen her face fall. Well! I'm sick of old queens, Eddy. I mean, maybe it's money but it gets yer down. Wot I need's a

266

fuckin' 'oliday. That's wot! Not all these ancient clapped-out wankers! I was down the 'dilly last Friday, seein' wot was wot, an' this mousy little queen was jerkin' away there. An' there's these two geezers just parked near the dryer. Coppers! 'Course I gives it a miss, an' combs me 'air like I was passin' through. An' the fuckers nabbed 'im. Poor sod! Shakin' like a leaf, 'e was. They was givin' 'im all the strong-arm stuff — bastards! I'm not kiddin', Eddy — 'e can't 'ave been a day under sixty!

EDDY. 'E probably died in the dock — 'eart-attack case!

PETE. Poor old fucker! Seen Tommy about?

EDDY. Nah! Got a job down some new Gay Theatre, 'an 'e? Last I 'eard 'e was prancin' about like a fuckin' Tiller girl, with some black stud playin' with 'is cock. They's not allowed to touch, see! So it's solo numbers, an' a bit of dancin' an' stuff. Bleedin' naff! Ron says they get all these punters 'angin' around for intros, like! 'E's new — pretty boy! Where's he sprung up from, then?

PETE. Scotland. About a month ago. Ron found 'im 'angin' round King's Cross. Stony-broke. One o' them Adidas bags, an' that was it. So 'e takes 'im down Mickey's place, an' they come to some financial arrangement like. Then Mickey fucks 'im, an' tells 'im to fuck Ron, an' 'e says e's never fucked arse before. So they show 'im the ropes, an' e's doin' all right. Bit like "And-job', 'e is. Sits on a stool an' waits for the punters. Then straight down the lock-up with some toffee-nosed geezer; tosses 'im off, an' 'e's back on 'is stool in ten minutes, ten quid richer. 'E's not on tonight, see, 'cos 'e's wearin' blue.

EDDY. Must be 'is night off.

PETE. Nice bit of sailor, that! Where's 'e from, then?

EDDY. Looks like Spanish to me. 'Ere, remember that geezer from the Foreign Legion? Wot a lark, eh? Was 'e fuckin' pissed! I think they'd all 'ad 'im by closin' time, one way an' another. Even fuckin' Cora! Talkin' of the devil . . .

CORA. Hello boys! How are we this evening?

EDDY. All right, Cora? Wot's this then — a dead tom-cat?

CORA. Sable, dear. But we wouldn't expect a man of your means

267

and refinement to know that, would we?

EDDY. 10p down the Oxfam, was it?

CORA. Fuck off, darlink! Cora's not in the mood for abuse this evening.

EDDY. Only self-abuse, eh? It's all you get these days, wot?

CORA. I used to be class, darling. When you were in nappies, Cora was a star, and don't you forget it! A fucking star!

EDDY. All right, all right! I'm not fuckin' deaf.

CORA. And how's Peterkins? We have become a big boy, haven't we? With your tits and my looks and personality, we could run at the Palladium for months.

PETE. You couldn't give the fuckin' tickets away, darlin'! Don't kid yourself.

CORA. OK, muscles! Cora knows when she's not welcome, so she's just going to sweep that gorgeous old man off his feet, and have a cosy little supper at the Hilton.

PETE. Oh yeah?

CORA. Just watch me move, dear. Like a tornado!! Au revoir!

PETE. The state of 'er. She's got a bit rough, wot?

EDDY. Fuckin' scrubber, mate. Not like she used to be. Mickey says she 'ad it all, once upon a time. Started down Park Lane, trollin' the Dorchester lobby. Looked like a cover girl, she did. Stilettos, paste, the lot. 'Ad some MP for years, Mickey says. 'Ere. Who's that, then, standin' with Colin?

PETE. Dunno! Reckons 'e's American, or somefin'! Fuckin' joker! Tasty though! Pricey too. Thirty-five for the works. Last night this punter starts tryin' it on, an' gets no joy, see! So 'e calls the pretty boy a cunt. Know wot the pretty says? – 'It's cunts like me that makes pricks like you stand to attention!' I like that! That's a good one!

EDDY. On tonight, is 'e?

PETE. Looks like it. Dunno whether 'e's met 'ilda yet. She'll sort 'im out, won't she! 'Er an' Mickey!

EDDY. Yeah! 'ilda won't stand on no ceremony with that one. 'E could make a bomb, 'andled right.

PETE. Jesus! I 'ad a randy number down the pub, last Wednesday!

Starts chattin' me up at the bar, like. I was with Colin, an' 'e's gettin' all worked up about me talkin' to this young geezer. So there's me with this fuckin' black eye wot Colin 'ad laid on last weekend, an' I pretends I'm in the army, see! An' this guy gets really turned on by all that paratrooper lark. Anyway, 'e's got 'is knee nudging my cock, see, an' Colin's got 'is back to us, in a bad mood. So I say I'm goin' down for a piss, an' tells 'im to follow. So I gets down there, an' 'e walks in, an' there's these two piss-artists jerkin' away there. So I pulls 'im into the lock-up for a quickie! Well, there's no fuckin' lock, is there? So I'm givin' 'im a blow-job, with one 'and pullin' the fuckin' door shut, an' the other pullin' 'is balls, right. Then 'e starts on me, right! An' suddenly, the fuckin' door's pulled open, an' it's Colin lookin' like 'e's ready to tear the fuckin' place apart. 'We're gonna miss the fuckin' bus!', 'e says, an' fucks off. So I zips up fast, like, an' the fuckin' cock's still stickin' out like a fuckin' banana! Jesus! Wot a song an' dance that was! We shoulda been down the Gay Revue with that lot! Caused a bleedin' sensation, we would!

EDDY. Wot about the geezer in the lock-up, then?

PETE. Dunno, Eddy. Last I saw, he was standin' there, jeans round 'is ankles, finishing 'imself off. I didn't fancy another bruiser, see! 'Ere comes that fuckin' Indian bastard! Wot you lookin' at, eh?

INSIDIOUS QUEEN. I was not looking at anything, please. Very sorry!

PETE. You fuckin' was, weren't 'e Eddy?

EDDY. Come on, Pete! It's not worth the trouble, mate!

PETE. I said I want to know wot you was lookin' at! I can 'andle this, Eddy, all right!

INSIDIOUS QUEEN. I am very sorry, sir, if you think I am causing offence, very sorry!

PETE. Slimy little bastard! I'd be makin' a move if I was you. Know wot I mean? Understand the lingo, eh?

INSIDIOUS QUEEN. I was just getting a drink, you see. That is all. If you would like, I can get you a drink also. Then we can be friends, yes?

PETE. Dunno about that, do we Eddy? Mine's a double rum an' Coke, all right! and the same for my mate.

INSIDIOUS QUEEN. Then we are becoming friends, please?

PETE. You must be fuckin' jokin', wanker! What are you?

INSIDIOUS QUEEN. I am sorry?

PETE. You're a wanker, mate. What are you?

EDDY. Leave 'im alone, Pete. For Christ's sake!

INSIDIOUS QUEEN. If you are being made happy, I am saying I am wanker. You are happy now?

PETE. I'll be 'appy with a rum an' Coke, wanker. Double!

INSIDIOUS QUEEN. I am going to the bar for the drinks, if you will kindly let me pass.

PETE. An' don't forget Eddy's!

INSIDIOUS QUEEN. I will not forget Mr Eddy's rum and Coke – oh no! It is a double also.

PETE. Right then! Two doubles, on the double – 'Meester Wanker!'

Ben's Diary

¶ FRIDAY: Today was a disaster. Up so late that Danny had missed some modelling job, and sank into a really foul mood. I couldn't be bothered going to Kitty's, and felt half-pissed anyway. But she rang up twice I think, although I ignored the phone. Panadeine and bacon sandwiches! Danny left, still in a bad mood, and said he'd ring later. I sat around making resolutions to go on the wagon, and never go out again. I must have spent twenty pounds, at least! I don't know why, but I kept thinking about the French boy, and wondering whether Danny had fancied him. That wasted about an hour, and then it was about three o'clock, so I went for a wander before the sun disappeared and breathed very deeply to try and clean out the lungs. Saw a boy standing outside the café with a take-away tea. About twenty, built like a sex-machine, he just stood with his legs apart looking as if he'd fuck anything at all! He spat just after I walked past, which can't have been a compliment! Another little fantasy had, I came back and watched TV, children's programmes through to the news. Felt exhausted and all my muscles ached as if I'd been screwing all night. Danny rang to say he was staying in and going to bed early. Why not! So I read a bit of the Cocteau book, and after another dose of TV went to bed at about ten.

BUTCH THE LEATHER QUEEN
PLAYS BACK THE ANSAPHONE

'Hi! Yeah, it's me — Butch. I'm sorry I'm not in to talk to you, but I'm probably out screwing some well-hung stud on the back of his bike. If you want an appointment for the same service, leave your vital statistics after I've come. Aaaah!!!'

What a night! I feel terrible after all those poppers, I really do! As for the man of my wildest dreams! If only he'd wanted to come back! He wouldn't even come out to the bar — just wanted to fuck all night, and fuck everybody, not just me! Maybe he'll be there next week. I just wish I'd packed this morning, instead of making small-talk with that American. Apart from anything else, I was late at the theatre, and all my wigs had perms instead of ringlets. What Madame is going to say when she sees them will probably cause a mass resignation scene. And after the heat, the frost. Ah well! All in a day's cock-ups. At least I wasn't there when the pyramids were flown in upside-down. And thank God I missed her doing the La Stupenda number, frock and all, while the diva went into labour. I should think the dress rehearsal was nothing but everybody having babies — deformed ones! Still — at least it's finally here: the gay away-weekend for one in raunchy Amsterdam! My God! I deserve it! Now off with the leather and into the vanity case with it. Where's that list.
Passport.
Money.
Poppers.
Jockstraps.
Yeast tablets.
Protein build-up.

All coloured handkerchiefs. Esp. black-and-white, and red.
Gum.
Cock-ring.
Leather undies.
Ripped T-shirt.
All the leather. *Not* the harness.
501s — oldest pair.
Joan Crawford's biography.
Valium.
Shades.
Peaked cap?
Trim 'tache.
Make appointment at clinic for Monday fortnight.
I must have forgotten something, but never mind. It's only three nights, so that lot should see me through. Oil of Ulay! That's what's missing. I can improvise if there's a sudden need for heavy metal! There are quite a lot of calls on the machine, aren't there? Let's see who's been wanting Butch! Could be a paratroop regiment from the number of flashes!

Aaaah!

'Hi! It's Trevor here. Neville wants to know if, while you're in Amsterdam, you'll get him some hardcore. Ever since the fuzz moved into Soho, he says there's nothing worth buying. Can't think why he wants it, except he's started this new thing of pasting ladies' corsets and bras on top of the beefcake. Anyway, Butch, if it keeps her busy, what's the harm? We'll settle up when you get back. Suck one for Trevor, there's a dear! And don't forget your rubber gloves!'

Rubber gloves! Thank God he reminded me. As for the porn — I'm not risking that, just so Neville can play Bunty with her nail-scissors! The cheek! I'd never get the money back, that's for sure!

Aaaah!

'You filthy old leather queen! How are you? I was just wondering
if you wanted to go to the movies next week. There's this thing
called *Rumble Fish*, which looks like a take-off of *The Wild Ones* —
leather-and-bikes sort of thing. Give us a ring when you get back
from the wicked city. And don't catch anything I wouldn't
catch!'

Why is everybody going on about this 'fish-film'? The cinema
must be full of queens every night, the number I've heard
banging on about it. If it isn't Burt Reynolds it's some other idol
impossible to have, apart from in wet dreams! They only depress
me, those dreamy butch numbers with unbuttoned shirts and
satin pecs! They're always straight. It's the fucking producers
who turn them into fodder for the gay soft-porn audience. All
straight! It makes me sick!

Aaaah!

'Aaaah!'

I wonder who that was! There's always some queen who doesn't
leave a message!

Aaaah!

'Darling! It's Trevor again. Neville says can you try and find
something really hirsute — mags, I mean — because that's what
there's a shortage of in Soho. Thanks again dear. Bye! Oh, wait a
minute! Neville wants a word.' 'Hello, dear. I just had to tell you
what arrived this morning. A letter. From George! He's
throwing me out, dear, after twelve years of happily married life!
Well? What do you think about that, dear? Talk about *De
Profundis*! "Out of the depths, O Lord!" — out of the pits, more
like. Anyway, I just thought you might be interested to know. It

274

means I'll be moving in here, you see. And we're going to throw a fabulous party, fancy-dress I thought, to celebrate the divorce and the second marriage. "Love is lovelier the second time around," as the divine Miss Bassey sings so fabulously! Don't forget to come, will you. It's next Saturday, same day as Patsy's orgy. Silly old cow. As if anyone wants to go to one of her tacky orgies. Corsets, dear. That's the theme, so see you in John Lewis's! And don't forget the porn, there's a dear! Byee!'

The state of her! After all those years. I'd kill her! Poor George. I'd better give him a ring, I suppose. Treacherous queen. Always two-timed him, poor sod! I wonder how long it will last with the divine Trevor. It'll be Bassey and Eartha Kitt at the party, with a touch of Tamla for the nostalgic! As for the hairy porn mags! Hirsute! If I find anything answering that description he'll be real and mine. Why can't Neville join a mail-order club or something? There's no way I'm dragging round shops when there's all the bars to do!

Aaaah!

'Hi! You probably don't remember me. I'm Jim. The guy from the Copacabana the other night! Remember the guy in the khaki dungarees – that's me. I'm just ringing to say I went to the clap clinic on Wednesday for the results, and I've got a bad dose of the brain-rotter. So you've probably got it too. Sorry about that. But I thought I'd better ring. See you around sometime! I enjoyed it, by the way. I suppose that's no consolation, though. Anyway, I'm sorry!'

Fucking hell! Sorry! Just my luck! Well, I'm going to Amsterdam come hell or high water. Maybe I haven't got it anyway. Some people don't! I can't go and not do anything, can I? Fuck the bloody Copacabana! I didn't want to go in the first place. I only dropped in for a quick one. And now this! He was cute, though, poor thing. Jabs in the bum for two weeks is not

275

much fun. God! I hope I'm OK! If I'm not, half London probably has it after tonight! Ah, well! 'I am what I am . . . tra la la la . . . I am what I am!' Better drop a couple of tetracyclone, and have a bath. Might as well be clean on the outside, and hope that the gate to paradise hasn't let in any nasty germs. I'll give it a good scrub with the carbolic. That ought to do the trick! Thank God tonight's an empty bed. I don't think I could bear somebody taking up all the room. Not tonight. Sweet dreams! That's what I need — and beauty sleep!

NEVILLE'S LETTER FROM
GEORGE: DE PROFUNDIS

Dear Neville,

This is a very difficult letter to write, and one I never thought I'd have to — but something has changed between us, and it's since you came back from that weekend in Amsterdam with Trevor. I've never liked Trevor. I've tried — God knows — but he's never liked me. He never visited me when I had hepatitis (it was a different story when he had it — *you* were there all the time!) and Patsy said he'd said that I deserved it for sleeping around. I don't want to bitch, but if anybody sleeps around it's Trevor. I could never understand why you liked him so much, but I think I know why — now.

It's funny how somebody you meet in the shower at the YMCA can ruin your life like Trevor has ours. You probably didn't even see it happening. You were always a bit naive, Neville — or pretended to be. But I can see right through you now, and it's not a pretty sight.

Why do you act like the little boy who never grew up? You're no spring chicken — you're forty-two Neville, forty-three in February, a typical Aquarian, down to your purple underpants and pink nylon socks. Don't get me wrong. I'm not criticizing. They're little things, I know, but I've loved you for them. Don't ever change them, Neville — they're a part of you I'd like to think was still there, even though we're through. It's funny, I'm beginning to sound like Marilyn. I've even wondered what she'd do in my place. Does that surprise you? After all, she brought us together in a way (remember *Gentlemen Prefer Blondes* at the Biograph, and that loo door we couldn't lock?) Poor cow! She suffered all her life. I suppose I should be grateful for the last

277

twelve years — they're more than she ever had. Twelve years! We've had some camp times, Neville — camp times! I suppose they mean nothing to you now, those weekends in your mother's caravan at Margate, the time I won second prize at the Drag Ball in Fulham Town Hall — I went as Dusty Springfield, remember, in a shocking pink frock. 1970! It seems like yesterday, and now it's all over. Did it really happen? All I know is you're walking out of my life as if it was a tacky B movie or something — and I'm supposed to take it — just say 'Tata' and lose everything.

The gay world is very cruel, Neville. There's a lot of sadness and pain. Nobody really cares about you. They pretend to, but all the time they're thinking 'Just look at the state of her, silly queen!' That's how Trevor is, and he enjoys it. I just wonder how long it will be before he starts slagging you off to Barry and your body-building friends. Don't worry — I won't say I told you so — I'm not that bitter. I feel sorry for you, actually.

You'll go off to Earl's Court and live in Trevor's lovely garden flat with his Siamese cats (you never liked cat smell, but then I suppose love conquers all), and I'll stay in Islington, trying to forget. It won't be easy, but at least you'll be on the other side of town. I'll try not to go where you might be (I never liked the Coleherne anyway), at least for a while. You probably think I'm being a drama queen, but the hurt's too deep. I'd rather not see anybody we know. I don't want their pity, or their poisonous prying. It's all right for you — you'll be the good guy whatever happens. It's always been the same — just smile and flash those big blue eyes — they'll all be there, like moths around a flame. And I have to begin all over again. It's all so unfair!

I never thought that at forty-five I'd have to start playing the game again, tarting up and trolling from pub to club in search of Mr Right. For twelve years I thought you were Mr Right, Neville, but it seems you were Mr Wrong. What a fool I've been! Were there many before Trevor? Those weekends in Brighton — were you really visiting your mother? — and that hairstyling course in Leeds — did you ever go? I trusted you, Neville, but now I don't know what to believe. I suppose everybody's been laughing at me, knowing all along, and trying to spare my feelings. Barry's been really kind, actually. He's even offered to stay with me for a bit after you've gone — just to keep me company until I get used to being on my own. Sweet, isn't it? But I don't want sympathy — not even Barry's. As far as I'm concerned, it's a new life, and although nobody loves a fairy when she's forty, I'm quite looking forward to it, actually. Don't worry about me, Neville, I shall be brave — in my situation you have to be, don't you?

We've built a nice home here, and enjoyed it for twelve years — at least I have. I don't know about you any more, but I'd like to think you have. Now you're going to destroy it I'd rather not be around to watch. Is that silly? I don't think so. Anyway, I shall go to mother's for a week so you can move your stuff out. You can take anything you like — I don't care. But leave the video, will you? I've a lot of lonely evenings to look forward to, and there's always *Gentlemen Prefer Blondes* to keep me company.

Goodbye Neville,
all love, George. X X X

P.S. Your smalls are in the airing cupboard. Don't forget them, will you? You'll need them to keep up appearances.

Ben's Diary

¶ SATURDAY: Woke up feeling convinced that Danny had gone out last night and screwed the French boy. I suddenly realized that I had dreamt the same thing – Heaven was all red and green glass, and they were doing it in front of everyone, not realizing that I was watching. Hideous! One of the problems of not seeing someone every night is wondering what they were up to. But it's impossible to be together all the time without getting bored or neurotic. I'm not even sure whether I could live with someone without going crazy, and domestic queens are such a boring parody of the well-adjusted straight couple. But how do you keep a thing going and lead a separate life as well? I decided that it would be a good idea to talk to Danny about what we are doing, and whether we should make some sort of decision about being together – or just let it float on, regardless. And as I was thinking all this, I suddenly felt that I did love him, without knowing why, but sure that it was more than sex. After a bath and disastrous hair-wash, which left me looking like Worzel Gummidge, I rang Sam to see what had happened with his French boy. Apparently he had banged on about Danny, which is exactly what I thought, but he stayed at Sam's the last two nights and goes back on Monday. So that's all right then! I would have thought Sam would be more pissed-off, but he said he was bored with trying to talk French, and thought it was odd that French boys were always a bit dirty underneath the expensive leather jackets and Yves St Laurent undies! So much for the *entente cordiale*! It was a very cold, clear day, and made me want to do something different – maybe a walk in the City or something constructive. I rang Danny, who was in a

280

good mood – thank God! – and we decided to go to the Hockney exhibition. He'd been before, but wanted to go again, so I said I'd be on the steps of St Martin's at two o'clock, and started the search for a clean shirt I could wear. Everything filthy, so I went to the launderette, which was cutting it fine. Made it by ten past two, though, and Danny was just arriving as I got there. Some people look good all the time. They can get up after a night on the tiles and everything is still in place, glowing. Danny's like that. It would be impossible not to notice him – anywhere. He was wearing a black overcoat which gave him a sort of classic sexy look, especially with a black scarf blowing around in the wind. He has style in a bath-towel! We smiled at each other as if we were sharing a secret, and wandered down to the river and over the footbridge. London can be quite thrilling on days like this, and I made some remark about it which he laughed at, saying that Paris was much more spectacular as a place of shifting moods. It's all very well idolizing Paris, but when you're in London it's a bit boring to be told there's this other place which is better. I said anywhere depended on what you were like yourself – some people hate Paris, after all! But he just said that anybody who hated Paris was a soulless wanker! I'm not sure whether you are supposed to be calm and tactful when the boyfriend's feeling argumentative, but it's not in my nature to make a simple remark and stand around while it's shot down in flames! 'I'd no idea I was a soulless wanker,' I said with casual sarcasm. 'Nor had I,' he replied. So there we were, standing on Hungerford Bridge, tight-lipped and together, staring towards the City with different opinions about it all. As if it mattered. I lit a cigarette and felt incredibly angry. Little things always gnaw at your efforts to rise above them, and bloody Paris was a stupid thing to get wound up about. He suddenly moved off and started walking towards the South Bank. I followed, slowly, and we didn't speak or walk together.

When he got to the other side, he stopped at the bottom of the steps and leaned against the wall, watching some roller-skaters. Then he turned round. 'This is stupid,' he said. 'What is?' I was all prickly and unhelpful. He went on: 'You think one thing, and I think another. So what?! Let's forget it. OK?' I had that funny stomach feeling of regret, knowing I had said the wrong thing, and as if on purpose too. 'It's very hard,' I said. 'What is?' And without really thinking, I launched us into a crisis. 'Us,' I said. 'What are we doing? I don't know where we're going, and we haven't thought about it. You might be gone tomorrow, for all I know. You bang on about Paris, and going to live there, and how the boys are cute. Then you spend hours talking to one at the Asylum, as if I didn't exist!' Why the hell I was saying all this I can't imagine. Maybe it was wanting to make him declare undying love and all that! 'This is the most incredibly complicated and bizarre way of saying something completely different. Why don't you say what you mean?' he said. I felt twitchy and nervous, and couldn't think what to say at all. And all around us was a beautiful day, suggesting other feelings and remarks. 'I spoke to the French guy because he didn't speak English, and I thought he must be bored and felt sorry for him, being there and not being able to talk. That's all. Why are you so jealous? Why do you think I should just keep quiet about something – Paris, or whatever – just because you won't agree with it? It's crazy. You want us to get something together, but it's like part of you wants to smash it before it's got anywhere. I don't understand you!' I actually felt like I'd blown it completely. Then I turned away, and said, 'I just don't want it to end, that's all' – very self-consciously. 'Well, if we're quarrelling like this about fuck all, at least we know it's begun,' he said. I smiled. 'And the best way to do it is to not to become mindless yes-men, cooing in each other's pockets. If you want us to be together, then we've got to be separate as well. I spent

282

two years being expected to change my ideas to suit someone else, and in the end you get eaten up by the feelings that were supposed to be good but turn out to be rotten. Hasn't it struck you that I might have wondered whether you were just another bullshitter, and not what I hope you are and want you to be?' 'What's that?' I said, fishing like mad! 'Just someone who loves me, and who I love back.' He stared at me, and the day seemed to define some vast and significant feeling, the edges on things getting sharper and light bouncing off things, like all the thoughts zonking through my head. 'I'm sorry,' I said. 'We don't have to be sorry,' he said, 'as long as we know what we feel – and how could we forget that?' And so this little crisis, which I had created out of nothing, produced a sort of declaration of independence – so that being together could work. We hugged like someone might prize us apart, then went to Hockney and got headaches looking at the Polaroid mosaics. Then tea in Valerie's and a long talk about how clever but over-exposed Hockney is. I was still unsure exactly what we had agreed on, but felt that to start again would just be boring and achieve nothing. If you're in love, then all you can do is be in love – two of you, that is. When it's only one-sided, there's a whole world of moping about, and theatrical depression to fill the time. Maybe that's why people prefer the pursuit so much. Once you've got something, the demands really pile on, and a different kind of hard work begins. And the hardest thing is keeping the thing fresh, and not getting bored and taking the easy way out. It all ought to be incredibly natural and take care of itself, like plant life. But plants don't think and feel! And for all the desire to be in love and have one person, queens are so instinctively and circumstantially prom- iscuous that there's always the feeling of 'Why not?', and a meaningless grope in a bar becomes that little act of betrayal and destruction. I know that a lot of queens live together and have flings, but keep everything going. I just

283

don't think I want to live with that sort of bizarre hypocrisy. Better not to do it at all – be in love – than do that! We went for a drink, and decided to go to the cinema and see some new longer version of *The Leopard*. It was utterly moving and wonderful – the ball scene an endless and almost erotically charged image of a doomed lifestyle and world. Nothing could have been better. It's really good doing things with someone you love. As we stood waiting for a taxi, I said so, and told him I loved him, and that everything I did and thought about was affected by that. He just put his hand into my coat pocket, and squeezed my hand very hard . . . it felt so good, standing there knowing that in this little world of bars and clubs and nameless, numberless fucks, we had found something. Home to an epic session!

OLD QUEENS AND QUEEN
MOTHERS: A STREET SCENE

LESLIE. Well, well, well! It's Maurice Watson. I haven't seen you for years.

MAURICE. Hello, Leslie. How are you keeping?

LESLIE. Very well, Maurice. But I thought you'd gone to live in Bournemouth.

MAURICE. I was going to, after Frank died. But something told me not to. Is your mother still with us?

LESLIE. Heavens, yes! Ninety-three, and sprightly as a sparrow.

MAURICE. It makes you wonder, doesn't it? Ninety-three! Well, Leslie, we're not that far away ourselves, are we?

LESLIE. I've stopped feeling my age, you know. After a certain point, it doesn't make any difference, really.

MAURICE. And she still doesn't know, after all these years?

LESLIE. Not a dicky-bird! Extraordinary, isn't it? She's finally stopped talking about me getting married, which is something I suppose. But I couldn't tell her, you know. It would kill her, I'm sure.

MAURICE. I don't think she'd understand, would she? It's a different generation, after all.

LESLIE. I wouldn't want her to blame herself, you see. And she would. I know she would. Especially after trying so hard to give me what she never had. And it was difficult, what with father being a failure, and all. She never forgave him for not being successful, you know.

MAURICE. Isn't it funny? It was just the same in our family. And your mother — she always wanted something better, didn't she? Just like mine.

LESLIE. Oh heavens, yes! It was always important to be getting on, and seen to be. Class! That's what it was. I suppose she had ideas above her station, as they say. Always had to be the best china for visitors, and flowers in the front room. I appreciated it, of course. But father never noticed. Never!

MAURICE. She pushed you, didn't she? Mine was always pushing me, wanting me to be something better than father was. In the end it made me hate him, her always going on about what a failure he was.

LESLIE. Exactly! Mother never left my father alone. Moan, moan, moan. Well, it drove him to an early grave, you know. And he knew that I was on her side.

MAURICE. I sometimes wonder if we might have been different — you know — if our mothers hadn't been so strong. Dominant, they call it.

LESLIE. Well, that's it, isn't it? When a mother's wearing the trousers there's nothing left for the father to do. Especially if he's always being told what a disappointment he is. All father did was sit there, deaf to it all, watching her mollycoddle me as if *I* was the only man in the family.

MAURICE. And it all turned out wrong, didn't it? I don't think they'd understand if we told them. Mothers are very powerful women, Leslie, when they love too much.

LESLIE. Well, I always said I'd never tell her, and I haven't. I think *he* suspected, though.

MAURICE. You've just been for a drink, have you?

LESLIE. Just a drink, yes! You have to get out, don't you? I like my little drink. Get out and see people! That's what they say.

MAURICE. I suppose so. But everywhere's so young, these days. Noisy bars, and kids everywhere! It's not the same any more, Leslie. We've been left behind, dear. Since Frank died, I've felt very lonely, you know. After thirty years with the same person, it's a bitter blow when they're taken away.

LESLIE. It must be. I often wonder what it will be like when mother goes. There's Smoky, I suppose — the cat! But she'll miss her a lot, will Smoky.

MAURICE. Will you stay in the house, after she's gone?

LESLIE. Oh, yes! It's a cosy little place. And it's home, isn't it?

MAURICE. That's what I said after Frank went. I thought of getting a bungalow in Bournemouth — selling up, and starting a new life. But we're too old for that. Where can you go? Even these local groups and meetings — well, it's all young people, isn't it? Somebody should start something up for the older end. That's what I say.

LESLIE. No one will come along, now. I know that. It's hard to admit to yourself that there's never been any love in your life. Very hard.

MAURICE. Oh, Leslie! There's been your mother. That's something, after all.

LESLIE. Oh, there's always been mother. Don't misunderstand me! I'm not being ungrateful or anything. It's just that I get a little depressed, sometimes, if I think about things too much. Soul-destroying!

MAURICE. Well, you mustn't think about the bad things, Leslie. Think about the good. Remember after the war, when all the boys came out of the Forces. That's when I met Frank. Oh, what a good time we had in those days! And very discreet, if you know what I mean. Not like they are now, rubbing everyone's nose in it, cavorting in public places and so on. No! We were a straightforward pair, always like old good friends. Trust! That's what's missing these days. Nobody trusts anybody. It's like in those bars — there's only lust and wickedness. They don't have feelings like we do. One day it will dawn on them — that their lives have been spoiled by all this liberation and so on. Frank and me had something that was very special, Leslie. I was very lucky to meet him.

LESLIE. You were — very lucky.

MAURICE. Getting a bit nostalgic, aren't we? And what's wrong with that!? Shall we stroll through Fitzrovia, Leslie? I always liked a late-night stroll through Fitzrovia. Fresh air, and not much traffic. The walk will do us good. The important thing is not to let yourself go. Keep up appearances!

LESLIE. Just what mother always says.

MAURICE. Exactly! Well, Fitzrovia here we come! Not as we did thirty years ago, painting the town red! But here we come, nevertheless!

Ben's Diary

¶ SUNDAY: Up late, and feeling very happy. Another exquisite day. Danny slept longer while I pottered about making tea and doing the washing-up. He had a bath, and stayed there for hours!! When he got out we started all over again, him wet and me trying to blow him dry! All very silly and carried away! Then up to Camden Lock, where we bumped into Ricky and Sam, each boasting some fabulous purchase – Ricky, a black cashmere coat for twenty quid; Sam, a red and gold drummer boy's jacket, which will turn him into a multi-rape victim the moment he puts it on – so he hopes! I tried on a tweedy jacket, but it looked dowdier on than off. Danny found a cream silk evening scarf for only two quid – with a very grand-looking monogrammed 'D' at one end, in black and cream. I said it made him look like a mad European aristocrat, living in a time-warp. I wondered how many Sundays we would come here together, and thought it was best to think of this Sunday and not worry about the things I knew nothing about. Time is a thing which if you think about it starts to make you feel frightened and helpless. The only thing to do is live from day to day, and be pleased to be you and not anybody else. It takes a lot of imagination to be with the same person for any length of time – and lovers are not the same as friends. Something can always go wrong, and things be changed for ever. But walking through Camden Lock with Danny, I felt that at least I knew that there could be nothing better than two people feeling the same for each other – however long it was fated to last. In the evening we went to the Bell, which was very crowded. And I realized how good it was, not having to look around and see if there was anyone worth cruising, knowing I was with the thing most of them fancied, and that he was with me. Bliss!

READ MORE IN PENGUIN

In every corner of the world, on every subject under the sun, Penguin represents quality and variety – the very best in publishing today.

For complete information about books available from Penguin – including Puffins, Penguin Classics and Arkana – and how to order them, write to us at the appropriate address below. Please note that for copyright reasons the selection of books varies from country to country.

In the United Kingdom: Please write to *Dept. JC, Penguin Books Ltd, FREEPOST, West Drayton, Middlesex UB7 OBR.*

If you have any difficulty in obtaining a title, please send your order with the correct money, plus ten per cent for postage and packaging, to *PO Box No. 11, West Drayton, Middlesex UB7 OBR*

In the United States: Please write to *Consumer Sales, Penguin USA, P.O. Box 999, Dept. 17109, Bergenfield, New Jersey 07621-0120.* VISA and MasterCard holders call 1-800-253-6476 to order all Penguin titles

In Canada: Please write to *Penguin Books Canada Ltd, 10 Alcorn Avenue, Suite 300, Toronto, Ontario M4V 3B2*

In Australia: Please write to *Penguin Books Australia Ltd, P.O. Box 257, Ringwood, Victoria 3134*

In New Zealand: Please write to *Penguin Books (NZ) Ltd, Private Bag 102902, North Shore Mail Centre, Auckland 10*

In India: Please write to *Penguin Books India Pvt Ltd, 706 Eros Apartments, 56 Nehru Place, New Delhi 110 019*

In the Netherlands: Please write to *Penguin Books Netherlands bv, Postbus 3507, NL-1001 AH Amsterdam*

In Germany: Please write to *Penguin Books Deutschland GmbH, Metzlerstrasse 26, 60594 Frankfurt am Main*

In Spain: Please write to *Penguin Books S. A., Bravo Murillo 19, 1° B, 28015 Madrid*

In Italy: Please write to *Penguin Italia s.r.l., Via Felice Casati 20, I–20124 Milano*

In France: Please write to *Penguin France S. A., 17 rue Lejeune, F–31000 Toulouse*

In Japan: Please write to *Penguin Books Japan, Ishikiribashi Building, 2–5–4, Suido, Bunkyo-ku, Tokyo 112*

In Greece: Please write to *Penguin Hellas Ltd, Dimocritou 3, GR–106 71 Athens*

In South Africa: Please write to *Longman Penguin Southern Africa (Pty) Ltd, Private Bag X08, Bertsham 2013*